The Wilderness

Morgan Bates

The Wilderness

Olympia Publishers
London

www.olympiapublishers.com
OLYMPIA PAPERBACK EDITION

A CIP catalogue record for this title is
available from the British Library.

ISBN: 978-1-80439-000-9

This is a work of fiction.
Names, characters, places and incidents originate from the writer's
imagination. Any resemblance to actual persons, living or dead, is
purely coincidental.

First Published in 2023

Olympia Publishers
Tallis House
2 Tallis Street
London
EC4Y 0AB

Printed in Great Britain

Dedication

For everyone who supported me.

Acknowledgments

Biggest thanks to my sister, Jillian. Thank you for always being my rock and my biggest believer, and for pushing me to keep going when I felt like giving up. I wouldn't be here without you. I love you.

PART I

1

I

Alan was nearly jogging to the time clock. His expectation and excitement for what was waiting for him after his shift ended was nearly palpable. Not only would he get to have time away from the back breaking work he endured five days a week, but he would get to spend it in what he considered to be the most beautiful place on earth. He would be lying if he told himself (or anyone else) the thing that excited him most was the landscape, and not getting to share this trip with his daughter.

Although he was not estranged from Jeanie, they had grown apart over the years. Not by choice on either person's part but by the way of full-time jobs and the general business of adult life. When she was young, they often spent time together on the golf course and at home on weekends. They bonded through their mutual love of art, reading, and the outdoors. It had been five years since they had gone on a camping trip together. Living in Colorado made it easy for them to frequently take trips to the mountains when Jeanie was growing up and the refreshing embrace of the alpine air was long overdue.

Lost in nostalgic thought, he made his way across the sawdust and fiberglass covered floors of the door manufacturing warehouse where he worked. Alan walked along, his eyes on his boots and his mind wandering in a daydream of the past. Suddenly, there was another shadow in view beside his boots, and when Alan snapped his head up, it was already too late. He slammed headfirst into the other man. His boots slipped haphazardly across the particles of debris. His right leg slipped from underneath him, and he hit the cool, dusty concrete with a surprised yelp.

"You all right man?"

A lean but muscular man in his early forties stood above Alan, extending his hand to aid him back to his feet. His hair was worn tightly cropped and, although it was just showing signs of graying at his temples, his goatee was fully white.

"Yeah, I'm fine. I'm fine," Alan replied.

Alan met the man's firm grip with his own and was promptly hoisted back to the upright position. As he brushed the dust and dirt from the back side of his jeans, he shook his head.

"I'm really sorry about that, Gary. I guess my head's just in another place right now."

"No worries at all. If I were on my way out the door for a weeklong vacation, my head would be in the clouds too." The man flashed a friendly smile, showing straight but slightly yellowed teeth, stained from years of cigarette smoke.

Alan and Gary worked in this shop with one another going on twenty years. Although they were not best friends, they knew each other well. They frequently took their smoke breaks at the same time and spent lunch in the dimly lit break room, sharing the day's frustrations with one another. It was not uncommon for them to mosey over to the closest sports bar after a long shift and during these times they spoke of their lives outside of work.

Gary gave a faint chuckle and placed a friendly pat on Alan's shoulder with a heavy hand.

"How are you feeling about seeing Jeanie? How's she doing? Is she flying in from Washington or are you meeting her up there?"

"I'm feeling good about seeing her." Alan glanced downward with a furrowed brow. He rubbed the back of his neck with a work calloused hand. "If I'm being honest, Gare, I'm not real sure how she's doing. We don't talk as much as I would like and when we do, she seems to keep things strictly business. Only mentions her work and then focuses the conversation on me, mostly. It's been that way since her mom died. Always concerned with how I'm holding up. I'm flying out to Washington tonight. Be pointless for her to come here, just for us to go back that direction again."

Alan let his mind wander a bit as he answered the questions his friend had tossed in his direction. He got almost an entire week to spend with his daughter, and most of that time would be spent in the remote wilderness off the coast of British Columbia. He could almost feel the crisp, mountain air filling his lungs. A backpacking trip on one of the islands off the coast was a dream they had both spoken about for as long as Alan could remember. Now that dream was becoming a reality.

They reached the time clock perched on the wall of the dingy dispatch office. Alan used a rough finger to punch in his five-digit clock code and ended his one-day work week. Gary mirrored Alan's actions. They walked together through the nearby side door and let it slam behind them. The sound of the metal door meeting the frame filled the air with a resounding *bang*. The brightness of the late summer sun made them both squint.

"I guess this means you're out of here, buddy!" Gary gave his friend a light slap on the back. "You make sure you stay safe and try to relax. You're wound too tight all the time. Tell Jeanie I say hi."

Alan placed a hand over his defined brow, shading the sun from his eyes to better see Gary's face.

"Will do. I couldn't be happier for the break. You take care too, Gary."

He gave a smile with the corner of his mouth and made his way across the faded asphalt lot, throwing a wave over his head as he went.

As he approached his worn-in (which is the term he preferred over old or beat-up) pickup truck, he tossed his lunch box into the bed, unlocked the driver's side door, and slid into the torn fabric seat. He put the key in the ignition, placed both hands on the wheel at ten and two, and let out a heavy sigh, his lips blowing a small raspberry as he let the air escape them. Alan let his shoulders slump. He was excited for his trip, but this was a long day. Every second that ticked past on the clock seemed to last at least a minute. He was feeling thankful he packed his suitcases last night.

He turned the key and the aging engine roared to life, squealed for a few seconds, and then settled into its normal rhythmic rumble. Without looking down he felt around in the compartment of the driver side door with his left hand. He retrieved a pack of Marlboro Reds, flipped the top open, and shook a cigarette into his mouth. As he lit his cigarette with a faded blue lighter, he backed out of his parking space. His stomach filled with the fluttering butterflies of anticipation. It took all the effort left in him to keep himself from accelerating excessively over the speed limit on his way home.

Twenty minutes later his truck swung into the driveway of his house, bumping over the curb. He parked in the middle of the two-car garage. Its walls were lined with shelves holding miscellaneous tools and supplies for yard work. As he opened the door the familiar smell of stale cigarette smoke and gasoline for the lawn mower greeted him.

Alan didn't waste any time. His suitcases were waiting for him directly inside the door. He grabbed them and loaded them into the bed of his truck. He made a quick trip around his humble home to ensure all lights were off and the windows and doors were securely locked. He made a pit stop in the half bathroom near the garage to use the toilet before the first leg of his journey began. As he washed his hands he looked up and caught a glance of himself in the mirror.

There were times he barely recognized himself any more. His light brown hair was now graying at the temples. Years of laughter and hard work left him with deep wrinkles around his eyes and weathered tan skin. Deep set, blue eyes still shone as brightly as they did when he was young. A tiny hint of that spark left them when his wife passed away, but the life was still in them.

Alan turned around to dry his hands, but the towel was absent from its usual spot on the holder behind him. He made an irritated grunt before wiping his hands on his dirty work t-shirt. His hand drying method made him double think his outfit choice and he thought, for the sake of the passenger seated next to him on the plane, he'd better throw on some fresh clothes. He looked rough, and he was sure he didn't smell like daisies, either.

He dashed into the attached laundry room, yanked the dryer door open and stooped down to gaze into the mouth of the machine. The surprisingly bright yellow glow of the internal light created a spotlight effect on his face. Jackpot. The treasure he retrieved was wrinkled but smelled fresh, at least. He ripped his dirty clothes from his body, wiggled into a fresh pair of blue jeans, and slid a clean t-shirt over his head. As an extra measure he brushed the top of his head to loosen any remaining sawdust and dirt that might be trapped in his hair.

His small hint of obsessive-compulsive tendencies wouldn't allow him to leave the house without one more look around. After he felt confident his house was secure, he made his way back into the garage. Before climbing back into the truck, he checked his bags were all there and secured properly.

He started his old Ford up again and as he backed out of the garage, he pushed the button of the remote attached to the visor to close the door. He couldn't remember the last time he felt so many strong emotions at once. Excitement prevailed over nervousness as he headed toward the Denver airport. After too many long years, he was finally going to see his little girl.

2

I

Jeanie was excited to see her father. Although they had drifted apart after her mother died five years ago, she was ready to spend some quality time doing something they mutually loved. Grief had changed them both, but time had a way of healing wounds. She hoped they could reignite their once close bond on this isolated backpacking trip. There would be no calls, texts, or social media to distract either of them once they reached the trail head.

The trip had been her idea and when her father agreed, she was nothing less than shocked. She spent as much time as she could at work in the last five years. The ache in her heart seemed to only be eased by an occupied brain. The stress of a continuous, heavy workload over the years made it hard for her to take any relaxing time away to herself. Her patient load had recently decreased and the few she had currently were only in need of bi-weekly or monthly sessions. In case of an emergency, she left them the phone number of a trusted colleague.

The backpacking excursion she planned was only four days and three nights, but she took two weeks off. She needed time to prepare before departing into the wilderness. Recovery time after the rough expedition was also built into her plan. She was fit for her age but had also accepted that she was no longer what people would consider a 'spring chicken.'

Her father would be flying in late tonight. She was excited to see him, but she couldn't ignore the twinge of nervousness she was also feeling. Why in the hell should she be nervous? It was still her dad. The man who wiped away many tears and who bandaged even more cuts and scrapes throughout her childhood. The man whose deep, crystal blue eyes she inherited.

The thoughts she would normally suppress, she let flood into her brain as she sipped her glass of pinot grigio. Perched in a large, heavily cushioned chair on her back deck, she looked out over the water. As a cool sea breeze wafted in around her, she brought her sweatpants-clad legs into her chest and wrapped her cardigan more tightly around herself. The dirty blonde, messy bun perched on top of her head swayed slightly at the command of the wind. Small goose bumps rose on the nape of her neck. Her nostalgic concentration remained unbroken. Another sip of her wine allowed her to drift further away.

When cancer took her mother, Jeanie was only twenty-five years old. Guilt held tightly on her heart. She should have spent more time with her mother while she could have. She was so busy building her career in Washington that she rarely called back home. Visits were even more of a rarity. Her therapist recommended she work on releasing herself from those feelings. After all, nobody had expected the sudden death and she was just doing what she thought was best for herself at the time. And that's what her mother would have wanted, right?

The stage four pancreatic cancer diagnosis took her mother in only one short month. Her mother didn't tell her until two weeks after the diagnosis. Jeanie thought she would have more time. She had requested time off and booked a flight to Colorado. Her mother passed one week before she was scheduled to fly out. She never got to say goodbye. She used the trip for a funeral instead of a visit.

She was forced back to reality by the ping of a text message arriving on her cell phone. She gently shook her head and took another sip from the large wine glass in her right hand. She gently placed her glass on the white-washed oak side table and picked up her phone. The message was from her father.

Boarding the plane now. See you soon.

She read the message twice, her head feeling a bit fuzzy from the wine. Was it already eight o'clock? The digital clock on her cell phone read 8:09 p.m. She wasn't sure why she was so anxious. She had arranged for a car to pick her father up at the Seattle airport when he arrived. A hired fishing boat would bring him across the sound. She had paid one of the locals she had befriended from the community to bring her dad to her home once the boat delivered him to the island.

Her father knew she made a good living for herself, but he had never seen her home or the other luxuries her job as a well-established psychiatrist afforded her. Compared to her parents, who both chose to live a modest lifestyle and worked middle class jobs, she lived lavishly. She thought her anxiety must be stemming from the fear that her father would judge her.

Really, Jeanie? Now you're going to analyze yourself, too?

She shook her head and her bun bobbed from side to side. She was annoyed with her tendency to make every feeling anyone felt into a clinical study.

Her home was nestled on an island about four miles off the coast of Washington and was only accessible by ferry or boat. The island had a private golf course, along with other luxurious amenities, and many of the residents cared about that sort of thing. Jeanie just loved the seclusion and the views the location provided. The quietness helped calm her soul in a way the city never could. She kept to herself and saw her home as a sanctuary rather than something to flaunt.

She decided she shouldn't overthink. She picked up her glass and made her way through the French doors into her kitchen. She placed the wine glass and her cell phone onto the granite countertop and opened the refrigerator. She retrieved the bottle of wine she opened earlier in the evening. She removed the cork and was greeted by a gentle *pop*. She poured until the liquid reached the brim of the glass. She didn't see the need to follow the rules of wine pouring tonight.

She let out a heavy sigh and gingerly lifted the glass to her lips, sipping slowly to avoid spilling. Her father would surely love her and view her in the same light, no matter her financial status. She made her way around the kitchen island to one of the three bar stools on the other side. She slid onto the first stool, swiveled to face the counter, and opened her laptop.

II

As she looked over the itinerary for her upcoming trip, her anxiety began to abate. She was truly excited. It was a feeling she hadn't felt in years. She let it wash over her as she closed her eyes and inhaled deeply. Her father wouldn't arrive until around one a.m. but she was glad to know he was en route to her. She took another large gulp of her wine and closed the screen of her laptop.

Their trip would eventually take them to a remote island off the coast of British Columbia, Canada. They would first make the drive from her home near Seattle to Vancouver, Canada. From there they would take a small plane (what people frequently referred to as a 'puddle jumper') to the remote island.

Jeanie arranged for a local fisherman to take them on a short boat ride to the beach where their desired trail head was located. He would also retrieve them on the evening of their third day to take them back to the village to catch their flight back to the mainland. There was access to the trail head without taking a boat but not only was the boat a time saver, it was safer. The fisherman she hired, Kai, told her the locals had blocked the access road that stretched across the island off long ago and nobody dared use it since. Something about legends of monsters or hauntings (she couldn't remember which).

Although Jeanie and her father were experienced in outdoor activities and had some primitive survival skills, neither had been keeping up with it in the recent years and they were both getting older. Jeanie was only comfortable going into the untouched, remote wilderness of the island with certain checks and balances. The fishing boat and its captain were the most important. If anything were to go wrong and they missed their pick-up, Kai would be able to send help.

While she waited for her father to arrive, she decided to check the packs she had put together for them earlier in the day. Alan had insisted on packing his own and bringing it with him, but she had convinced him it would be easier to have her pack for both of them, rather than have him check the bag on the flight. She wanted this trip to go as smoothly as possible and the last thing she wanted was for his bag to get lost. There would be no time to attempt to recover it.

In the middle of her living room floor, she sat cross-legged and slid the closest pack toward her. She popped the buckle and unzipped the main compartment of the pack. Leaning forward, using her left arm as a stabilizer, she stretched her right to its maximum length and grabbed the piece of paper lying on the coffee table with the tips of her fingers. As she settled back into position on her backside, she looked over the carefully compiled checklist.

There were already six check marks next to each item. Three were marked in black pen and three were marked in green, indicating that both packs had been obsessively checked. She let out a heavy sigh and rubbed her temples with the forefinger and thumb of her right hand.

"Why are you being like this, Jeanie?"

The sound of her own voice brought her back to the present. She dropped the checklist on the floor in front of her and glanced at the clock on her cell phone.

12:54 a.m.

Her father would be arriving at any moment. A wave of butterflies and excitement struck her stomach. She stretched her legs out in front of her, each knee greeting the movement with a pop, and dragged her tired body to the nearest couch.

Just as her body hit the soft microsuede of the cushion, the doorbell rang. Jeanie's heart raced. Her palms immediately went clammy. She knew she shouldn't be so nervous, but she had never gone such a long stretch of time without seeing her father. And, given the tragic circumstance that helped them grow apart, she wasn't sure exactly who the man standing on the other side of the door would be any more.

She wondered if he was feeling the same way about her.

She took a deep breath and clicked the deadbolt into the unlocked position. As she swung the door open, her father stood there on the porch wringing his hands, confirming that he was nervous too. He was the same as she always remembered, only with a few more wrinkles and gray hairs.

As their eyes locked, his began to well with tears. To her shock, she already had a steady stream of tears falling from her own eyes. They embraced in a bear hug and squeezed as tightly as either of them could stand. She couldn't tell if he was laughing or crying but his back heaved up and down and she held him. He smelled exactly the same as she remembered. Irish Spring soap, laundry detergent, and a hint of cigarette smoke. She inhaled deeply and felt the memory of her home envelop her.

3

I

Alan woke abruptly to the sound of the pilot announcing their arrival to Seattle and their soon approaching landing. He did not plan on falling asleep but was grateful for the rest he was gifted.

I wonder how long I was out for?

His inner dialogue was broken by the loud rumble that emitted from his stomach. In his anxious hurry to get out of town, he had forgotten to eat dinner. He likely had time to grab something to eat in the airport but didn't want to waste any time getting to Jeanie. He didn't know the state of Washington very well, but he was sure the journey to his daughter's home would be at least an hour drive from the airport.

The airplane landed with an unusual smoothness. Another thing Alan was extremely grateful for. Once they were safely on the ground and taxiing to the gate, Alan powered on his cell phone. In big white numbers the clock showed 11:29 p.m. Alan couldn't remember the last time he was up this late. He felt a bit like a teenager breaking curfew, not a fifty-three-year-old man who was just up way past his self-proclaimed bedtime. The plane came to a gentle stop, the doors were opened, and the passengers were informed they may begin deboarding.

His knees, hips, and back quickly reminded him of his age as he stood stooped over waiting for the line of passengers to exit the aircraft. He expected to feel exhausted, even with his in-flight nap, but he was pleasantly surprised with a burst of excited energy. The trip seemed like a dream until now. As the joy of his reality and the thought of seeing his daughter in less than two hours soaked in, he couldn't hold back the smile the broke across his aging face. Body be damned, he did feel like a teenage boy in this moment.

II

After immediately running for the nearest restroom, Alan made his way to baggage claim. He moved with purpose but didn't push his aching body too hard. He knew from experience that even if he arrived at the carousel with haste, he would still be waiting there for quite some time until the siren signaling approaching luggage wailed.

To his surprise, the light at the assigned baggage claim carousel was flashing as he arrived. The silver belt moved around slowly as tired passengers crowded around anxiously awaiting the moment their luggage would be spat from the gaping hole in the center of the revolving island. Alan spotted his black suitcase, marked with a neon orange piece of yarn tied around the handle, already present on the belt. He muscled his way through the crowd, excusing himself as he went, to the spot just in front of where his bag would be passing by. As it passed in front of him, Alan snagged the handle with both hands and swung the luggage to the ground in front of him.

Jeanie told him to pack light because she would be supplying and packing everything in his bag for the trip. He greatly appreciated the gesture made by his daughter but packed all the necessary items anyway. It wasn't that he didn't trust her. He did. He just wanted to be fully prepared. What if she had forgotten something vital? At the thought of his daughter forgetting anything, he chuckled. Jeanie was notorious for her obsessive preparation.

He was instructed that someone would be waiting to pick him up at the airport. He was a bit disappointed that she wasn't going to be there in person to retrieve him. She did lead a very fancy life these days and a busy one, so he understood. He was sure she had important matters to attend to before leaving, and picking her father up from the airport wasn't a top priority on that list.

Near the array of sliding glass doors leading outside he found a man holding a sign bearing the name Alan Risley in all capital letters. As he approached, the man greeted him with a warm smile.

"Are you Alan?" the man asked.

The man was tall, muscular, and had a deep caramel complexion. His teeth were unnaturally perfect, and their whiteness almost hurt to look at for too long. The man's large stature was initially intimidating but his voice was smooth, pleasant, and professional. Alan gave a polite smile and nodded. As he did so, the man he assumed would be his driver extended his right hand in an invitation to shake. Alan returned the gesture, and the driver's large hand engulfed his own. He gave one gentle shake before releasing. Alan had never been a very social man and the exchange was a bit awkward.

The man sensed Alan's insecurity and immediately went to work to ease his discomfort.

"My name is Terrance and I'll be driving you to your next destination tonight. You can rest assured that I will get you there safely. How was your flight this evening?"

"It was all right." Alan's voice broke slightly on the last

syllable, and he cleared his throat before continuing, "I slept for a good chunk of it, I think."

Terrance led him outside the automatic sliding glass doors to a large black SUV parked in the pick-up lane. He opened the back passenger door and gestured for Alan to enter. Alan started to head to the rear of the vehicle and Terrance stopped him.

"I've got your bag, Mr. Risley. Please, have a seat and relax."

"Thank you," Alan replied, a bit sheepishly.

Alan clambered into the rear passenger seat of the SUV. Once he was sure Alan was in the vehicle safely, Terrance closed the door behind him. Alan pulled his cell phone from the front pocket of his blue jeans and swiped the screen to unlock it. He composed a short text and shipped it off to Jeanie. *Leaving airport now* was all it read.

III

Just under an hour and a half after departing the airport, Terrance and Alan arrived at a small marina with a well-kept boat house. As they pulled up along the side of the building, a young man in his early twenties appeared from the interior and gave a friendly smile and a small wave. Before Terrance had the opportunity to open the door for him, Alan let himself out of the SUV and stretched his tired, aching body.

The young man met Terrance at the back of the SUV and grabbed Alan's bag. Alan wasn't used to other people doing things for him (and he wasn't sure he ever could get used to it). It made him very uncomfortable, which only increased his awkward demeanor. He stood near the front passenger side of the car and waited for instructions on what to do and where to go next. Terrance climbed into the driver's seat of the SUV, flashed

Alan his thousand-watt smile, a quick wave, and put the SUV in gear.

As Alan watched the taillights of the SUV grow smaller, the young man appeared at his side.

"My name is Cameron."

He was lost in his own inner dialogue and the sudden sound of an outside voice made him jump a bit. Now that he had his senses about him again, he looked toward the sound of the voice and saw the young man anticipating his response. His hand hung in limbo between them.

"Oh, sorry. I'm Alan. It's been a long day. I must be a bit foggy." Alan quickly returned the young man's handshake.

The truth was, he was out of his element and that made him uncomfortable. Today, everything seemed to be making him uncomfortable. He just wanted to get to his daughter and for this day to be done.

Cameron gave a small chuckle.

"It's no problem at all. I bet you're wiped out from traveling all day. Let's jump on the boat and get moving so you can go crash. It's only about twenty minutes to the island from here. Come on, this way."

Cameron waved his hand in a *follow me* gesture.

Alan followed Cameron to an older boat docked at the marina. It was small and tidy and was clearly well taken care of. This boat was loved. Alan looked around and, as if Cameron read his mind, he piped up.

"I already loaded your bag up, safe and sound. Don't worry. This was originally my dad's boat, but he handed it down to me. It's not much but it's mine." Cameron let out a small sigh. "I sometimes will run charters for people to make some extra money for school. That's how I met Jeanie. She was a guest lecturer in one of my psych classes."

Alan smiled broadly and laughed to himself. Jeanie always had a way of making friends everywhere she went. She got her social skills and charisma from her mother. Those were things he certainly never had. Alan didn't quite consider himself to be a loner, but he also didn't go out of his way to interact with others or make friends. He always had one or two close friends, and his family. That was more than enough for him.

The rumble of the boat engine coming to life broke up his thoughts. The boat moved forward, slowly at first, and then once they hit open water accelerated to a quick but comfortable speed. Alan was surprised to find himself breaking free from his exhaustion. The cool wind that whipped up from the water of the sound invigorated his senses. He was nervous to see Jeanie, but he couldn't deny that in this moment, he was feeling extremely excited.

The boat ride was quick and smooth. Alan had only traveled by boat once or twice in his life and found himself enjoying the mode of transportation quite a lot. As they approached land, their pace slowed, and the boat landed gently next to the dock. Cameron threw a rope around a nearby pole and secured the boat.

Alan wobbled a bit as he stood. He didn't have sea legs and the feeling was not something he was used to. Once he regained his equilibrium, he made his way toward the dock. Cameron was already busy unloading Alan's hefty bag onto the wood planks. He thrust a helpful hand toward Alan as he approached. For once, Alan did not hesitate to accept, and Cameron helped hoist him onto solid ground.

"Thanks for a safe and smooth ride, Cameron. I really appreciate it. I feel terrible, I don't have any cash on me to tip you."

Cameron waved a dismissive hand in his direction.

"Oh, don't worry about that, man. Jeanie took care of all of it already."

Cameron seemed to beam with joy as he completed his thought. Alan thought Jeanie must have paid him handsomely for this late-night jaunt across the water. This time, there was nobody else there to greet Alan's arrival. He looked around while Cameron tinkered with something on his boat.

Cameron cut the engine, double checked the boat was securely tied off, and hopped onto the dock.

"I'll be taking you the rest of the way to Jeanie's house. There should be a golf cart waiting for us just up the way near the community center. They normally don't allow non-residents, like me, to even come to the island, but what Jeanie wants, Jeanie gets. But you probably already know that. Plus, I'm just dropping her guest off, no harm in that, right?"

He flashed an excited, childlike smile at Alan, and made a hand gesture to follow him up the path.

Alan extended the handle on his bag with a little *click* and rolled it over the wood planks of the dock behind him. He hoped the cart wasn't too far off. As far as he could tell, there were no paved sidewalks, only gravel trails. This heavy suitcase was going to be a real bitch to roll on the uneven ground. He should have listened to his daughter and packed light.

The gravel path led to a small community center not far off the beach. They arrived in a parking lot just south of the building. Although Cameron seemed unphased by the journey, Alan was sweaty and out of breath. Cameron spotted the cart parked close to the building.

"I'll be right back, dude. Just wait here. I'll swing the cart around and pick you up."

A moment later Alan could hear the electric twang of the cart starting up, and Cameron sped over to meet him. Alan placed his bag on the back rear-facing bench seat of the cart. He hoped the road would be smooth enough that the bag wouldn't dislodge itself and fly off. He hopped into the passenger seat and, before he could fully settle in, they were off.

They tore through the parking lot, which was also gravel and had several deep ruts. As they bumped along, Alan looked behind him anxiously at his bag, willing it to stay put. They soon reached the road, which was paved with smooth asphalt. Alan felt a wave of relief. His bag should make the trip without any mishaps. Cameron had told him it was only about a five-minute drive to Jeanie's home.

"There it is." Cameron pointed up ahead.

As Cameron's words fell from his mouth, Alan spotted the brightly lit, windows of a home nestled about five hundred yards off the paved road on the beach. On the beach side of the home, it had expansive windows that he could only imagine provided stellar views of the ocean. The other side backed to lush rainforest, with tall trees and thick green growth. To protect it from high tide, the house sat on wooden stilts.

Cameron slowed the cart to a snail's pace as they approached the long driveway. The dip from the road to the gravel driveway was significant. Alan braced himself accordingly but was impressed by the smoothness and skill Cameron maneuvered the drop with. Picking up the pace only slightly, they made their way toward the shining beacon of the home. Alan felt his heartrate shoot up and his palms were slick with sweat.

Cameron brought the cart, now covered in dust, to a gentle stop at the front of the house. He hopped out, retrieved Alan's bag, and placed it on the covered concrete porch.

"Need anything else before I take off?" Cameron asked.

"No. You've already done enough. Thanks again."

Alan extended his hand and Cameron gave it a quick shake. He turned the cart around to face the main road. Before taking off he looked over his shoulder toward Alan.

"Have a really great trip. Tell Jeanie I say hi."

Alan gave him a nod. He wasn't ready to ring the bell just yet. He wiped his sweaty palms on the front of his jeans and reached into the back pocket for his cigarettes. He'd been sitting on the pack for quite some time, and it was now mangled and flattened from the journey. He retrieved one slightly bent cigarette and slid the lighter from his front pocket.

While he smoked, he rehearsed in his head how he would greet his daughter. Everything he came up with sounded cheesy and stupid, so he snuffed his cigarette in the dirt and threw the extinguished butt in a large trash can he found on the side of the house.

He made his way to the well-lit porch and before he could chicken out again, he rang the bell. He took a small step back from the door and waited patiently. He heard the faint sound of footsteps approaching. The emotions flooding through him could not be described. As he heard the deadbolt unlock from the inside, he knew his daughter was just on the other side of the door. The door swung open, and he felt something catch in his throat as he tried to swallow.

Jeanie stood before him, tears rolling down her cheeks. He couldn't believe how beautiful she was. She looked exactly like he remembered her mother at Jeanie's age. He moved forward and embraced her in a tight hug. The joy he felt to be with his daughter after so much time was greater than any emotion he had felt in longer than he could remember. Maybe since the day she was born. Before he knew it, his body was heaving with sobs.

He was crying.

4

I

After their emotional reunion, Jeanie led Alan into the living room.

"Would you like anything? Food? A drink?" Jeanie asked. "I have water, orange juice, beer, or wine. For food I can make you something simple. I have mac n cheese. Or I can throw in a frozen pizza." Her words came out quickly, one right after the other.

Alan had forgotten he had missed dinner until just now. His stomach growled with desperate pleas for food.

"You know, I'll take you up on that frozen pizza if it's not too much trouble. I forgot to grab dinner in my rush to the airport," Alan replied.

"It's not a problem at all," Jeanie said as she made her way through the to the connected kitchen.

The kitchen, dining room, and living room were all open to one another, creating an expansive space for entertaining. She stopped at the double oven on the back wall and set the top oven to preheat to four hundred degrees. She moseyed over to the large freezer and pulled out a large frozen pepperoni pizza. She removed the pizza from its box and set it on the granite countertop.

"I'll also take a beer and a water, while you're at it, kiddo."

"Coming right up!"

Jeanie swung the fridge door open and grabbed two bottles

of beer and a bottle of water from the compartment on the inside of the door. She twisted the caps off both beers, chucked them in the trash under the kitchen sink, and made her way back to the living room. She handed her dad his drinks and sat one cushion over on the couch.

"I think I'll have one with you," Jeanie said.

They both sat in silence, sipping their beers. They had both had a long day and neither of them wanted to start the conversation. Neither of them wanted to talk about themselves. So, the silence continued until it was broken by the sound of the oven alerting Jeanie it was preheated and ready for the pizza. She slammed the rest of her beer and stood up to walk to the kitchen.

"Wait up, you can take mine too," Alan said.

Alan followed suit and emptied the remaining contents of the green, longneck bottle and handed it to Jeanie for disposal. She put both bottles on the counter and grabbed a round cooking sheet from the cabinet underneath the ovens. She unwrapped the pizza from the plastic covering, removed the cardboard bottom, and plopped it on the sheet. She carefully rearranged the pepperonis for even distribution and, once she was satisfied, placed the pizza in the oven and set the timer for twenty minutes. She turned around, retrieved the empty beer bottles, and rinsed them out in the sink.

"Do you want another one?" Jeanie's voice called out from the kitchen.

"No, I don't think I'm going to tonight. I'm pretty tired, hon."

Jeanie made her way back to the couch, dropping the bottles in the recycle bin next to the trash can on her way.

"While we're waiting for the pizza to cook, do you want me to show you to your room so you can get settled in? That way you can freshen up, change into your sweats or something, and then just crash after you eat."

"That sounds perfect," Alan replied through a yawn.

Alan slowly peeled himself from the comfort of the couch. He grabbed his suitcase from the entry way and then followed Jeanie down the hallway to the right of the living room. She entered the room at the end of the hallway and flipped on the light.

"This is the guest bedroom. The sheets are fresh and there are cold waters in the mini fridge. The closet is the door on the left and the bathroom is on the right. There are clean towels in there and some shampoo, conditioner, and body wash if you want to take a shower."

Alan looked around the room and let out a slow, high-pitched whistle.

"Wow, this is nicer than staying in a hotel. Thanks, Jeanie. A shower actually sounds amazing. I think I'm going to hop in for a quick one and I'll meet you back out there."

Alan stood in the center of the spacious room for a moment, taking in his surroundings. A modern style king-size bed sat in the center of the wall directly across from him. He made his way over to it and hefted his bag into the center of it. The weight of the bag and his tired back forced an *oouph* sound out of him. He plopped down on the bed beside his bag and removed his socks.

On the wall that shared the door to the bathroom, there was a small, built-in wet bar that contained a sink, a small stretch of granite countertop, and a fully stocked mini fridge. On the countertop sat a single cup coffee brewing machine, an electric tea kettle, and a diverse assortment of teas and coffees.

Alan browsed them for a moment before crossing to the opposite side of the room and checking out the closet. He opened the door and flipped on the light. His eyes widened with surprise as the light revealed a full walk-in closet.

He turned the light off again and headed toward the bathroom, first stopping at his bag to grab a pair of sweatpants and a t-shirt. After seeing the rest of the guest room, he was not surprised that the bathroom was very big, and very nice. It donned granite counter tops with two sinks sunk into them. They sat under an expansive, framed mirror. On the opposing wall, there was a walk-in shower with several shower heads that sprayed various parts of your body at once. Next to that sat a large bathtub.

He chose the shower and was grateful that he did. It was the most refreshing shower he thought he had ever taken.

II

Jeanie smiled and nodded before leaving the room and closing the door quietly behind herself. She couldn't explain why but having her father in her home made it feel more peaceful. She didn't think that was possible. This was her safe haven and her comfort zone. But he somehow just made it complete. She smiled to herself at this thought and made her way to the kitchen to check on the pizza. There were still thirteen minutes left on the timer.

She grabbed another beer from the refrigerator, cracked it, and leaned against the counter while she waited. She couldn't believe how settled her mind had become. Earlier she was so anxious she couldn't sit still for more than two minutes at a time, now all she wanted to do was be still. She took a long pull from her beer and let the feeling wash over her. She closed her eyes and took a deep breath. She didn't remember the last time she felt so content. So at ease. As if this moment in time were meant to happen. She finished her beer in a few more long gulps, rinsed the bottle, and added it to the recycling bin.

Alan appeared from the hallway a few minutes later, still looking very tired, but more relaxed. He let out a large yawn that contorted his whole face as he walked toward one of the bar stools at the kitchen counter and sat down.

"The pizza is almost finished. You look like you're ready to pass out, old man."

"Beat doesn't begin to cover the way I'm feeling, kid. But that was one hell of a shower. Once I get some food in my stomach, I'll be out as soon as I hit that amazing bed you got in there. What is that mattress? Memory foam? I sat on it and it damn near sucked me clean in," Alan said.

Jeanie chuckled and shook her head.

"Yes, Dad. It's memory foam. Don't tell me you still have the same mattress you've had for, like, the last twenty years?"

Alan looked up at his daughter with a flat expression.

"As a matter of fact, I do still have the same mattress. It still works just fine. It doesn't hurt my back or anything. No reason to replace a perfectly decent thing."

The timer beeped and Jeanie turned around to face the oven. She hit the button for the oven light. The bubbling cheese and golden-brown crust looked delicious. She didn't realize how hungry she was. She turned the oven light back off, grabbed the oven mitts hanging from the magnetic hook on the side of the fridge and slid them on her hands. She pulled the oven door open and slid the sheet from the rack, turned around and placed it on the counter.

"Oh man, that really smells good," Alan said.

His mouth filled with saliva as he looked over the freshly baked pizza. He watched Jeanie with anticipation as she retrieved plates from the cupboard above the stove. In search of a pizza cutter, Jeanie fumbled through several drawers. She opened the third drawer she tried, finally found it, and cut the pizza into four large slices.

"Do you care that I'm being lazy about cutting this? Do you want me to make the pieces smaller?" She looked up at Alan, waiting for a response.

"I couldn't care less. My only concern is how badly I know I'm going to burn myself shoveling that into my mouth as fast as I can."

Jeanie plated two large pieces for her father and handed him the plate across the island. She then plated herself a piece and grabbed two napkins. She walked around the kitchen island and sat in the bar stool to the left of her dad. The last time they ate a meal together was at her mother's funeral. She wondered if he was remembering that as well. She hoped he wasn't. The memory wasn't a warm one and she didn't want the joy of this trip to be overshadowed by the tragedy in their past.

They ate without speaking and Alan's prediction of burning himself turned out to be a self-fulfilling prophecy. He cursed as the molten cheese stuck to the roof of his mouth but then laughed it off, blew on the next bite, and continued chowing down. He finished his food in record time. As he wiped his face and hands he leaned back in his chair and stretched a bit.

"I can't believe I ate that like it was nothing at all. I feel so much better, thank you for taking the time to make that."

"No problem at all, I apparently needed it too," Jeanie replied.

Jeanie watched her father as he crumpled his napkin and threw it onto his plate. As he started to get up to take it to the sink, she stopped him.

"Dad. No. I've got the plates. You had a much harder day than I did. Go get your beauty rest. You are on vacation after all." She shot him a wink and a smile.

"I suppose you are correct. I'll let you take care of my mess. I'm going to jump into that bed. I've never been so excited to fall asleep." At that they both chuckled.

Before heading toward the guest bedroom, Alan walked over to the stool Jeanie was perched on, bent over at the waist, and gave her a hug around her shoulders.

"I love you, Jeanie. Thank you for planning this. I've missed you a lot. I'm happy as a clam to be here with you."

"I'm happy you're here too. Goodnight, Dad. I love you, too," Jeanie replied with a gentle smile.

She lifted her hands up to the arms that were wrapped around her shoulders and gave them a gentle squeeze. He gave her a kiss on the cheek and disappeared down the dark hallway leading to his room.

Jeanie gathered the dirty dishes, rinsed them, and threw them into the dishwasher. She checked that the doors were locked, shut off the lights, and made her way up the stairs to her own bedroom. Now that the food in her stomach had time to settle in, she could also feel her exhaustion take over her body. Her limbs all felt as if they were filled with lead, and it took all of her strength to drag them around.

As she made her way across the large bedroom, she shed her sweatpants (not before removing her cell phone from the right pocket) and cardigan, not caring about where they landed. She climbed into her king-size bed and slid under the cool sheets. She let out a sigh of relief and checked the time on her cell phone. It was just past three a.m. No wonder she was tired. She hadn't stayed up this late since college.

She plugged her cell phone into the USB port built into her bedside lamp, set the phone down on the nightstand, and rolled over. As soon as she closed her eyes, she was asleep.

III

Alan woke to his cell phone ringing. He sat up ramrod straight in bed and frantically looked around the room, trying to get his bearings in this strange place. His few moments of panic gave way to the realization that he was in the guest bedroom of his daughter's home. He took a deep breath and leaned back on his elbows. He dug his cell phone from between pillows and sheets of the bed to see who was calling. The screen read Potential Spam. Of course. He let out an annoyed sigh and plopped his head back down on the pillow.

The clock on his phone showed 10:15 a.m. He must have really needed the sleep for his internal alarm clock to let him sleep in so late. He lazily got up and made his way to the bathroom. Once he had finished his business, he sat on the edge of the bed and sent his daughter a text to see if she was awake. He stretched his arms over his head and arched his back, letting out a loud yawn. He felt great today and was ready to spend time with his daughter. They knew they would both be exhausted today, so they didn't plan to leave for Canada until tomorrow morning.

With no reply from Jeanie, he assumed she was still asleep. He wasn't ready to get dressed and was quite enjoying his relaxed mood. Staying in his pajamas, he made his way down the hallway to the kitchen. The coffee maker he spotted on the counter was far too fancy, and far too complicated for him to figure out. He wondered if she had any tea. He began poking around the kitchen and in the second cabinet he opened, found a tea kettle. He made his way to the walk-in pantry and found a section dedicated to tea. Jackpot.

He chose an Earl Grey bag and made his way back into the kitchen. He was happy to find Jeanie in the kitchen when he returned. She looked the way she did when she first woke up as a little girl. Squinted eyes and a *please don't talk to me yet* expression on her face.

"Good morning, Jeanie Bean." Alan greeted his daughter with a cheerful smile. "How did you sleep?"

"Like a rock. I haven't slept this late in ages. How about you? Did you find what you were looking for in there?" Jeanie let out a little yawn and pointed toward the pantry he had just emerged from. She tightened the tie of her robe and took a seat on a bar stool at the island.

Alan nodded and waved his tea bag in the direction of the tea kettle to show he'd found what he desired.

"I slept great." Alan gave a grin with his reply. "I have to admit, maybe it is time I got a new mattress."

He grabbed the tea kettle and walked over to the sink. A small, content smile still on his face. Jeanie returned his smile.

"Would you rather have some coffee? I know you don't mind tea, but I know you *love* coffee."

Alan set the tea kettle down gently on the counter.

"I would love some coffee, but I didn't know how to use that crazy machine you got over there." He jammed his thumb backward toward the coffee machine.

Jeanie laughed audibly and shook her head.

"You really need to come into the modern world a bit more, Dad. It isn't all bad. Put that stuff away, I'll make you a cup of coffee on this 'crazy machine' I've got over here."

She pushed herself back from the countertop and made her way into the kitchen. She made sure there was enough water in the reservoir and then followed her father into the pantry. "What kind of coffee would you like? I have dark, medium, and light roast, as well as some flavored coffees. My guess is that the flavored coffees don't interest you at all."

"You guessed correctly again, kiddo. I'll just have a good ol' fashioned medium roast please." As he responded he placed the tea bag back where he found it and watched his daughter fiddle with a turn table that housed many different plastic pods filled with coffee. She plucked one that said Donut Shop and another that he couldn't quite make out, but it looked like something vanilla flavored.

They walked back to the kitchen, and she got to work on his coffee first. She simply placed the pod in its spot, put a cup under the spout, pressed the twelve ounce button, and it began brewing. "Do you take creamer? I've got a couple flavors in here I think."

"No thanks, just plain black for me. If I would have known that thing was that simple, I could have made my own cup. I'm sorry about that." He felt slightly embarrassed at the simplicity of the machine and being so intimidated by it. A slight blush rose to his cheeks. He was used to a regular coffee maker, with a filter, and a pot.

"It's really no big deal. I was going to make myself a cup anyway."

She handed him his cup and he blew on the hot liquid before taking a sip.

"Do you approve?" Jeanie studied her father's face while she waited for his reply.

"Yeah, it's pretty good. What's that you're making yourself?"

"It's a chai latte. I'm not sure you would like it." She pointed toward her back door. "Would you like to go sit on the deck when mine is done brewing? I love enjoying the view while I drink my morning coffee."

"That sounds really fantastic. It looks like it might be a bit chilly. I'm going to run and grab a sweater from the other room."

When he returned, her latte had finished brewing. She grabbed the chiffon throw from the back of the couch in the hand that wasn't holding her drink and made her way to the sliding glass doors. "You can grab a blanket too, if you'd like one."

"No thanks, I'll be fine in what I'm wearing."

She pushed open the massive sliding glass door and they both settled into the chairs that sat on her deck facing the water. The breeze was fresh and salty. The air was filled with bird song and the gentle crashing of waves onto the beach. They sat in silence as they took in the view.

"This might be the most peaceful place I've ever been. I can completely understand why you chose to live here." Alan took in a deep breath and exhaled slowly.

He was feeling at ease but also was filled with pride in his daughter. She had done all of this on her own. It was nothing less than her hard work that afforded her these luxuries. He never wanted her to feel guilty for not making it home to visit her mom one last time. Nobody could have known she would go so quickly.

Jeanie's voice pushed the dark memory from his mind.

"Yeah, it's my little piece of paradise. I look at this every morning and damn near pinch myself to make sure it's real. I'm a very lucky woman."

They finished the rest of their coffee in silence. Simply admiring the scenery and the calmness of the morning. When they were finished, they made their way back inside. While Jeanie rinsed their cups and loaded them into the dishwasher, Alan took a seat on the couch and rested his feet on the ottoman. Jeanie made her way over and took a seat on the other end of the couch.

"Do you want to go venture across the sound and see some sights today, or would you just like to relax here? I'd like to go over our packs one more time tonight. Make sure you have everything you want."

Alan considered her offer for a moment before replying. "Honestly, I think I'd like to just relax here. Maybe watch a couple movies and prepare for the trip. Speaking of relaxing, I'm feeling a bit anxious. You got anything I can use as an ashtray? I need to go smoke a cigarette."

"Oh, I forgot you smoke. Um, I'm sure I can find something for you. I agree, hanging out here is what I'd prefer to do too. I'll be right back."

Jeanie popped up from the couch and ran up the stairs to her bedroom. As she suspected, there was a mostly empty bottle of water on her nightstand. She snatched it and trundled down the stairs back to the main level. Her father was waiting for her, gazing out the back door. "Here you go, Dad. Will this work?"

"Thanks, kiddo. Yeah, that'll be just fine. I know I need to quit these nasty things." He took the bottle from his daughter, peeled the glass door open, and took a seat on the deck.

Alan lit his cigarette and looked at the beauty that surrounded him. He felt the ocean mist on his cheeks and closed his eyes. For some reason, for a brief moment, he felt something tugging at his heart, telling him not to go on the trip tomorrow. As quickly as the thought appeared in his head, it flitted away. So quickly he may have never even noticed it.

Jeanie decided to look through her collection of DVDs and Blue-Rays and pick a few movies for them to watch when her dad came back inside. She picked a selection of five movies and would make her dad decide what they would watch first. She stacked the movies on the coffee table. Jeanie heaved one of the packs resting in the middle of the floor to a new spot against the living room wall, out of the way. As she moved the second pack to join the first, she had the slightest feeling of dread. Some faint voice in her mind telling her not to go on this trip.

At the same moment, Alan was feeling the sea mist on his cheeks.

5

I

Jeanie rolled over, eyes still closed and felt around her nightstand with her right hand until she found the source of her irritation. She picked up her cell phone and silenced her alarm. 3:45 a.m. Once her drowsiness wore off, her excitement had room to peek through.

Today was the day. She and her father were off on the biggest adventure they had ever embarked on (together or otherwise). She tossed the covers off and swung her legs over the side of the bed. She went over to the office area on the left side of her room, booted up her computer, and printed their itinerary, the checklist she created as a failsafe (so they didn't forget anything), a short list of important contacts (in case her phone died), and the plane tickets.

While her documents printed, she quickly took care of her morning routine. As she brushed her teeth, she caught herself doing a joyful dance in front of the mirror. She really needed a vacation, and she couldn't be more thrilled to spend it with her dad. She spit the paste, rinsed, and wiped the remaining bits of foam from around her mouth.

On her way out of her room she double checked all windows were locked, drapes were drawn, and lights were off. She grabbed the stack of paperwork she had printed earlier, closed the bedroom door behind her, and bounded down the stairs to the living room. The smell of freshly brewed coffee greeted her. Alan was in the living room trying his pack on and adjusting the straps to make it the way he wanted. Jeanie was thrilled to see her dad was as excited as she was.

"Morning, Dad! You ready to roll? Do you want a cup of coffee for the road? I'm going to hold off, so I don't need to stop for the bathroom during our drive."

"Good morning, sweetheart. Nope, I already had my fill this morning. Are we ready to hit the road?" Alan smiled at the sight of his daughter. He loved the way she glowed when she was happy or excited.

"Let's just run through the pack checklist one more time. Cameron is already out-front waiting with the cart to take us to the dock. Then I just have to run through one more checklist to make sure the house is squared away, and we can go." The words tumbled out of Jeanie's mouth in an excited blur.

Alan gave Jeanie a look of slight disapproval.

"We checked the packs twice last night," he said. "And that's *after* you had already checked them God knows how many times before that. Don't obsess sweetie, it's not healthy. You of all people should know that. Let's just run through your house checklist and go hop on the cart. Everything will be fine. We're only going to be out there a few days."

Jeanie let out an annoyed breath of air and crossed her arms. She thought about what her father said a moment and finally conceded.

"Okay, you're right. Take the packs out to Cameron and have him secure them. I'll start with this checklist. It shouldn't take long."

"Thank you!" Alan replied gleefully. He was giving off the excited energy of a young boy.

He took his pack that was already on his back to Cameron and returned to the living room. Jeanie was off in another part of the house, so Alan yelled out to her. "I'm going to take your pack out there and then have a cigarette. I'll wait for you outside."

He swung her pack onto his back and headed out the front door. He didn't bother to close it behind him, hoping it would hurry his worrisome daughter along. He sat in the front passenger seat of the cart with his legs off the side and lit his cigarette. He was barely halfway finished when Jeanie appeared. She closed the front door behind her, locked the deadbolt, and wiggled the knob to make sure that it was locked.

"Where are you going to put that thing out at?" She seemed annoyed but Alan knew she was just anxious. He often got that way too.

Alan pulled out the water bottle she provided him with the day before, looking proud. Inside cigarette butts sloshed around in brackish, brown water. "I still got the bottle you gave me."

"That's disgusting!" Jeanie wrinkled her nose. "You're just going to walk around with that thing?" Jeanie replied with a frown.

"I'm just going to keep it in my bag until I can find a good trash can to throw it away in. It's not going in your stuff, calm down. I'd rather have a sludge-filled bottle than litter anywhere. Now can you get your panties out of a bunch and get on this damn cart so we can finally leave?"

Jeanie took a deep breath to steady her emotions. She knew she was acting uncharacteristically up tight. She just wanted to make sure everything was perfect.

"I'm sorry, Dad. I just get anxious and want everything to be perfect." She shook her head and let out a small sigh. "Your butt bottle is not a big deal. You're right. Do you want to ride shotgun or next to the packs on the back?" She gave her dad a weak smile.

"I'll ride on the back and make sure the packs don't go anywhere." Alan stood up and embraced Jeanie in a bear hug. He leaned out, grabbed her by the shoulders, and looked into her eyes. "Everything is going to be great. I promise. Okay?"

Jeanie cracked a smile. "Okay, okay." She climbed into the front seat of the cart and greeted Cameron. "I'm sorry about that. Almost forgot another person was here with us."

Cameron smiled ear to ear.

"It's all right, Ms. Risley. I barely noticed anything at all. Are you excited for your trip? I know I would be. It sounds like you're really going to have some quality family time together."

"Yeah, it will be a lot of fun. I just hate the traveling to and from part. It makes me a bit anxious and stressed." Jeanie's reply was a bit dry and almost seemed robotic. Her posture was tense.

Cameron nodded but took the hint that Jeanie wasn't much in the mood for conversation this morning. It was only 4:30 a.m. and the sun hadn't yet made its presence known for the day. They took the rest of the short trip to the dock in agreeable silence.

This time, Cameron drove the cart down the gravel path until he reached the wooden planks of the dock. "You guys hop off with your packs and go wait for me by the boat. I'll go drop this bad boy off and be back to meet you in no time flat."

Jeanie and Alan both hopped off the cart, removed the bungees that secured their bags to the seat, and put their packs on. Alan grabbed the bungee cords from Jeanie and shoved them in his pack. When she gave him a questioning look, he shrugged his shoulders up to his ears.

"Just in case," he said and shot her a wink.

As soon as he was sure they were clear of the cart, Cameron floored it up the gravel path toward the clubhouse. Alan and

Jeanie made their way down the dock and stood next to where Cameron's small boat was docked.

After a few moments of uncomfortable silence. Alan decided he needed to cut Jeanie's tension. He cleared his throat nervously before he spoke.

"Does your pack fit all right? Is it adjusted how you want it? I can help you if you want. Is it comfortable?" Alan inquired nervously.

"I thought I had it adjusted how I wanted it, but now that it's on again…" she trailed off, and rolled her shoulders, fiddling with the straps. "Something does feel a bit off. Can you just do a quick walk around and see if I'm lopsided anywhere?"

"Sure thing, let's take a look." Alan began walking a slow circle around Jeanie and he was glad she seemed to be letting some of her excitement diffuse the anxiety. "It looks like this strap is a bit looser than the other. One sec, let me fix you up here, kid." He tightened the strap over her left shoulder until it was even with the strap on the right. "Does that feel better?"

"Loads, thank you, Dad. And hey, look, I'm really sorry for the way I've been acting this morning…"

Before she could finish her thought, Cameron appeared, jogging and out of breath.

"I'm sorry that took so long, guys." His words came in between heaved breaths. He bent over and placed his hands on his knees attempting to catch his breath. He stood up again and made his way down into the boat. He held up both arms. "Toss me your packs and hop in."

Alan and Jeanie did as they were instructed. Alan climbed down first making sure to give Jeanie a hand for support as she got in. Cameron pulled the rope that held the boat in place from the dock and started the engine. They pulled away from the island. As the light from the island dock faded, the ride became dark with the exception of the small lights on the front of the boat.

Jeanie found herself suddenly a bit frightened of the darkness and the never-ending blackness of the water that surrounded them. She wished Cameron would pick up the pace, but she knew that would frighten her too. Why was she feeling so on edge? In an attempt to shake the fear from her mind, she gave a small shiver. She was glad nobody would notice in the dark. To her relief, the lights of another dock appeared and were rapidly growing brighter.

Had she been zoned out for that long?

II

Cameron slowed a bit as he approached the dock. His landing was just as smooth this time as Alan remembered from his first ride with Cameron. Alan was feeling a bit queasy after this trip and was ecstatic to be near land again. The boat ride was silent, and he wondered what Jeanie was thinking about. Maybe he would get the chance to speak to her about it later. For now, he thought it was best to just let her be.

Once Cameron had the boat secured and the engine was cut, Alan climbed out of the boat onto the solid wood of the dock. He held his hand out for Jeanie and she accepted. Cameron handed the bags off to them one at a time, and then deboarded himself.

He wiped his palms on the side of his jeans and nodded at them. "So, I guess this is it. Looks like your car is already up there waiting for you guys. I'll meet you back here on September sixth?"

"Yes, that sounds great. We will be here at around one p.m. on the sixth. Thank you so much for doing this for us and for putting up with my snotty attitude this morning. You're truly a saint." Jeanie sheepishly smiled at the young man with a sincere apology in her eyes.

"Oh, it's no big deal, Ms. Jeanie." Cameron waved a hand and blushed scarlet from his neck to the top of his forehead. "Everyone has good and bad moments in a day. It's what makes us human. Now you guys go have some fun! I'll see you soon."

Cameron flashed his boyish grin and waved both of his hands in front of him in a shooing gesture. Alan and Jeanie both chuckled and waved as they walked away from the dock toward the SUV that was patiently awaiting their arrival.

As they approached the large, black SUV, a large statured man emerged from the driver's side door. Alan squinted against the LED headlights to try to identify the driver of the vehicle. He continued walking and placed his hand over his brow to try to shield some of the light, but he could still only make out the man's silhouette.

Once they were within earshot of the mysterious man, he called out.

"Hey there, Jeanie girl! It's been too long since I've seen that pretty face. Nice to see you again, too, Alan!"

The booming, yet polite voice was unmistakable to Alan. It was the man he had met at the airport. Terrance gave Alan a firm and friendly handshake, paired with his brilliant smile. For Jeanie he opted for a hug. This man was truly pleasant at all waking hours, Alan thought. He was growing quite fond of him.

"Don't worry with your bags," said Terrance.

He opened the front and rear passenger doors and made a hand gesture for them to enter the vehicle. He opened the back end of the SUV and placed both packs inside before closing it again with a heavy thud. He entered the driver's seat, buckled his belt, and adjusted the review mirror.

"We have about a two- and half-hour drive ahead of us today, my lovely passengers. So, please get comfortable and let me know if there's anything I can do to make the ride more pleasurable for you. Don't hesitate to tell me if you need any breaks along the way. I can honestly say, I'm happy to have you two as passengers for this long drive."

Jeanie, who had chosen to ride shotgun, gave Terrance a toothy smile. "We're happy to take the ride with you behind the wheel, Terrance. And please, just because my dad is here doesn't mean you have to be so formal. You've been my driver for the last year, and I consider you a dear friend of mine."

Terrance's famous smile appeared brightly across his face.

"Thank you, Jeanie. That means a lot to me. Let's get this show on the road, shall we?"

He shifted the SUV into gear and moved the vehicle gently onto the main road away from the marina.

III

About an hour into their journey, Jeanie's stomach began to loudly protest against its emptiness. "Terrance, can you pull off at the next gas station? I'm going to use the bathroom and get some snacks. I'm starving."

"Absolutely, girl. It looks like there's one about five miles up ahead," Terrance replied.

"Sounds great." She moved her seat back to the upright position and began searching for the shoes she had kicked off along the floorboards.

As she searched beneath the seat, she caught a glimpse of her father in the side mirror. She couldn't remember the last time she had seen him so content. And because his joy was her joy, she smiled.

Terrance took the next exit off the highway. The gas station was immediately off the interstate and the SUV pulled into the parking lot. Terrance glanced at the various numbers and gauges on his dash.

"I might not need it, but I'm going to go ahead and top the tank off while we're here. Better safe than sorry." He pulled into the bay of the nearest pump, placed the vehicle in park, and killed the engine.

Jeanie climbed out the front passenger seat. Before closing the door, she poked her head back inside.

"Are you coming inside with me, Dad?"

"Yeah. I'm just a lot slower about it nowadays," Alan replied.

As she waited for her father, she clasped her fingers together and stretched her arms as high above her head as they would go, leaning first to one side, and then the other.

"It does feel damn good to be up and walking around," Alan's voice came from behind her.

They walked into the convenience store together, both stiff from being in the car. The automatic sliding glass doors granted them access once they got close enough. They made their way to the back of the store between the aisles of assorted candies, jerkies, and chips. The familiar hum of refrigeration systems grew louder as they passed through an opening between coolers filled with sports drinks, soda, and beer on the right side and ice creams, frozen pizzas, and bags of ice on the other.

"Damn, there's only one stall. Can I go first?" The pleading look and small dance Alan presented his daughter reminded her of a small boy.

She laughed and nodded her head.

"Well hurry up then! Go, before I change my mind!" Jeanie giggled as she replied.

Alan disappeared behind the bathroom door. Jeanie, trying to stay patient, passed the time by pacing the small hallway until her father emerged.

"Okay, it's all yours, kiddo. I'm going to go browse the snacks. Meet you out there."

Jeanie opened the heavy door and closed it gently behind her, making sure to push the round button on the knob in until it clicked. The cleanliness of the interior of the bathroom was less than desirable but Jeanie hadn't expected anything better.

She maneuvered her way through the pieces of toilet paper stranded on the floor by previous occupants. She used the toilet without sitting. As she hovered over the bowl in an awkward squat, she was thankful for the *Butt Burner* workouts she'd been doing at home recently. She flushed the toilet with her foot, hopping on one leg. When she made it over to the sink, she was disappointed to see that it was not motion activated. She would have to touch it to turn it on. She washed her hands thoroughly and turned the faucet off using a paper towel. She opened the door handle using the same paper towel method, held it open with one foot, and tossed the paper towel into the trash can across the small bathroom. As the discarded paper towel disappeared into the receptacle, she made a gentle *swoosh* sound with her mouth.

Jeanie made her way into the main area of the store. She picked up a water, a sports drink, a few bags of chips, and some gummy bears. Satisfied with her selection, she checked out with the clerk at the counter. When she didn't see her father anywhere in the store, she headed outside. The SUV wasn't parked at the pump any more. She casually scanned the parking lot until she spotted the SUV on the far side, where the asphalt turned to dirt.

Her father was leaning against the back, smoking a cigarette.

Alan waved as Jeanie grew closer.

"Sorry, we moved on you, I wanted to get a smoke in before we hit the road again." He took the last hit from his cigarette, extinguished it in the loose dirt, and chucked the butt in the water bottle that now acted as his portable ashtray.

"It's okay, you were easy to find." Jeanie opened the front passenger door with her free hand and climbed inside. "Thanks for being patient while we took care of business, Terrance."

"Not a problem at all. Just let me know when you need to again." As always, Terrance's reply was polite and professional, but also friendly. He had an inviting aura about him.

Once Alan was safely back in the vehicle, Terrance started the engine. Jeanie kicked her shoes off and pulled her legs into a crisscross on the seat. She grabbed a bag from the floor and opened it in her lap, gleefully looking inside at her newly acquired food treasure. She fumbled around with the contents of the bag until she found something that struck her fancy. She removed a bag of chips and placed the rest of the treats in the bag on the floor again. Soon, her crunching filled the silence of the car.

"You didn't get anything to eat, Dad?" Jeanie turned around slightly and glanced into the back seat.

"I grabbed one of those pre-made breakfast sandwich things from the hot case at the gas station and wolfed it down before you came out." He gave a shrug and sideways smile. "I guess I was a lot hungrier than I thought."

Jeanie returned her father's smile and faced forward in her seat again. She finished her snack and cracked open a bright blue sports drink. She washed the chips down with half the bottle. She wasn't completely full but was satisfied enough and reclined her seat.

IV

About twenty minutes later, they arrived at the ten-lane checkpoint that signified they had reached the United States–Canadian border. Their early morning departure seemed to work in their favor, as the lines were not very long. Jeanie estimated that they would likely be across in about thirty minutes.

Jeanie returned her seat to the upright position. "Hey, Dad, can you grab me the passports? They should both be in the front zipper of my pack."

Alan unbuckled his seatbelt, turned around, and fished Jeanie's pack from the rear space of the SUV. He dragged it over the back of the seat and plopped it down into the seat next to him. He unzipped the front pouch and retrieved the passports. Jeanie reached her hand around the rear of her seat and grabbed the passports from her dad.

"Thanks, Dad," Jeanie said.

"You're welcome, kiddo. I was starting to doze off there for a moment but now I'm really getting amped up. Before we know it, we'll be in the great wide open!" Alan was grinning ear to ear.

His energy was buzzing, and Jeanie thought she could see him practically bouncing in his seat. This also retrieved one of Terrance's famous smiles.

"I'm excited too." Jeanie gave a grin and glanced out the window at the cars slowly inching along in the lines, all anxious to cross the border.

She wondered if the people in these cars were also excited and going on a vacation, or if they were heading to a job, or to see family. She found herself dozing off. The bob of her own head would wake her. She retrieved another bag of chips from the floor in front of her in an attempt to wake up.

Thirty-two minutes later, they arrived at the front of their line. Terrance rolled his window down and provided the two passports and his own Nexus card. Terrance frequently took passengers across this border for his work. He had a few different people he drove for, but Jeanie was always his favorite, although lately his least frequent.

Their luck continued and their vehicle was not chosen for a random search. They passed through the checkpoint and were on their way again. Jeanie reclined her seat and when she felt herself dozing, this time she let sleep take her.

V

Jeanie was woken by the gentle shake of her father's hand on her shoulder.

"Hey, sweetie, we made one last stop before the airport for a bathroom break. Do you need to go?" Before Jeanie had the chance to answer, Alan was closing his car door behind him.

Jeanie opened her eyes, slowly lifted her head, and looked around.

"Yeah, I do. How close are we to the airport?" She stretched her arms directly in front of her and yawned. She fished her shoes from under the bags filled with her snacks and pulled them on without untying them.

"We're about twenty minutes to the airport but Alan really needed to pee, and we are doing good on time, so I didn't see an issue with a little pit stop. Thought it might help you wake up a bit before we got there, too." Terrance shot her a wink and climbed out of the driver's seat.

Jeanie unbuckled her belt and got out of the car. The morning air was crisp, and it felt good in Jeanie's lungs. The sun was finally beginning to show signs of making an appearance, and the sky was now a faint purple at the horizon. She walked inside the gas station and to the bathrooms. She was happy to see this station had separate men's and women's rooms. The women's room had several stalls and was kept in much better condition than the last.

When she was finished, she was not surprised to find the SUV on the outskirts of the parking lot, her father perched at its back end, puffing his cigarette.

"Hurry up and finish that thing. I'm ready to be done with this car ride."

Jeanie entered the SUV while Alan hurriedly put his cigarette out. The ride the rest of the way to the airport was quiet but you could feel the excitement starting to build in the air as they got nearer to the next leg of their journey. Jeanie was now just as excited as her father. She couldn't help but give herself a mental laugh. Just a couple of grown kids, she thought.

6

I

By the time they reached the airport, got their boarding passes, and got through security, Alan was starving. The sub-par gas station breakfast sandwich he chowed down earlier felt like a lifetime ago.

"You want to find something to eat on the way to our gate? I don't know about you but I'm dying over here." He hoped Jeanie was just as hungry as he was. They had about forty-five minutes until their plane would be boarding. He was fairly certain they would be the only two passengers on the small plane.

Jeanie looked at him and gave an exaggerated head nod. "I agree, I feel like I haven't eaten in ages. Those chips did not cut it. I think there are a few different fast-food options, if that works for you."

"That's perfectly fine with me. I don't care what it is, I just need a meal before we get on that plane." Alan patted his stomach.

Hunger wasn't the only reason for Alan's stomachache. He was a very nervous flier and the small aircraft made him even more anxious. He knew he was the reason his daughter was always wound so tightly. He had passed a curse along with those killer blue eyes. It made him feel guilty. Jeanie's mother always told him it wasn't his fault and there was nothing they could do but get her proper care from someone who could help her and support her throughout life.

As they arrived at their food destination, Alan shook the past from his mind.

"You go ahead and order first, I'll pay for both of us." Jeanie gave him a reproachful look. "Seriously. I know you're miss money bags, but I'm not so completely broke that I can't buy my daughter breakfast. Even if it is just shitty fast-food." Jeanie put her hands up in a defensive gesture and stepped forward to order her meal.

Alan hadn't intended for that to come out so mean, but he was still her father damn it. There was no need for her to treat him like some charity case all the time just because he didn't make the big bucks like she did.

Alan ordered and paid for their food. They drifted off and found a table that wasn't too far away so they could hear their order number being called when their food was ready. The small round table was covered in crumbs and Alan could see Jeanie's unease as she sat down.

"Hang on. Stand back up for a sec." Alan waved his hand in an upward motion and Jeanie obliged.

He jogged lightly back to the fast-food restaurant and grabbed a few napkins from the dispenser next to the drink station. He did the same little jog back to the table and wiped it clean.

"There you go." He gave her a small smile that said, 'sorry for being a dick earlier.' She returned the smile, and he was relieved that she didn't take his words too harshly.

"Thanks. Man, I hope this food comes out quick. I didn't realize how hungry I was until I smelled those hashbrowns when we were ordering." As if her words had summoned some magical force, the worker behind the counter shouted their number at them.

"I got it. You want ketchup for your hashers?" Alan stood and waited for Jeanie's reply.

"Yes, please!" Jeanie's reply was cheerful and excited.

Alan retrieved their food from the 'pick-up' side of the counter. He grabbed a hand full of ketchup packets and napkins and returned to his daughter. He was barely able to set it down on the table before Jeanie tore into the grease-saturated paper bag. She grabbed and sorted the food and laid it out on the small, wobbly table. Space at the table was limited so, before sitting down, Alan grabbed the now empty bag from her and threw it in the closest trash can.

When Alan sat down and unwrapped his bacon, egg, and cheese breakfast sandwich, Jeanie was already halfway through hers. It didn't take him long to catch up. Their ravenous eating left no room for conversation, so they ate in silence with the exception of a few grunts of approval.

When they were finished, Alan balled up their trash and deposited it in the same trash can the bag had gone to. He brushed off the excess crumbs from the front of his shirt with both hands as he walked back.

"Okay, Dad, we should probably get going to the terminal. We might be the only passengers, but I still don't want the pilot to have to wait on us. But first…" – Jeanie pointed toward a location just past the fast-food restaurant – "let's hit the bathroom."

"Sounds like a plan, Stan," Alan replied.

II

They made it to their gate at the exact moment the young woman at the podium announced boarding. Alan felt this was one of the most pointless actions he had seen in a very long time, since it was obvious there were only two passengers, and they were standing directly in front of her.

He also took a moment to recognize the smoothness this trip had had. Absolutely nothing stressful had happened. No glitches or hiccups. He was grateful, but being the person he was, he was also suspicious. He was secretly waiting for everything to fall apart. Traveling is never one hundred percent flaw free.

The woman at the podium scanned their boarding passes and wished them a safe flight. Instead of traveling through a large makeshift hallway to board their plane, they were directed outside. They descended a steep flight of stairs onto the tarmac where there was a small passenger plane waiting for them. Alan could see the pilot was already on board. An attendant waiting outside the plane took their packs and placed them in a storage compartment before ushering them to the open door.

Once inside, they were each handed a headset so they could still communicate with each other and the pilot during the noisy flight. As he adjusted his headset to fit properly, Alan's stomach began to churn. He couldn't wait for this part of the trip to be over. Every second felt like five minutes, and he couldn't help but wonder what the hell was taking this pilot so long to get moving.

Alan jumped when the pilot finally brought the engine to life. The pilot was a large, broad-shouldered man with shaggy, dirty blonde hair. He wore mirrored aviator sunglasses that made Alan automatically assume he was a bit of a douche. The man seemed to notice Alan's distress and decided to finally grace them with an introduction.

"Hey, guys, I'm Tom and I'll be your pilot today. I know a lot of people get nervous on these smaller planes, but rest assured it'll be a smooth ride and I'll get you there safely. We've got clear skies and no wind to fight us, so once we're in the air it should only take about half an hour. Remember, I can hear you just fine through the headset so if you need anything from me, just let me know. Here we go, folks."

The small plane lurched forward and then smoothly maneuvered over the black top. After about three minutes of what felt like pointless driving around. The pilot came to a gentle stop and the end of a runway. Alan was not used to being able to see everything happening outside the airplane. His heart raced and he felt sweat begin to drip down his back. He hoped his daughter didn't notice how nervous he was. How embarrassing for a grown man to be so terrified of a plane ride. If she did notice, she didn't show it and he was thankful for that.

The plane moved forward slowly at first and then picked up speed at, what was to Alan, an alarming rate. Alan hadn't noticed that at some point he had squeezed his eyes shut and when he opened them again, they were in the air. His tension eased slightly, and he took a deep breath.

Only thirty minutes of this left, he told himself.

You can do it.

III

Alan experienced the smoothest landing of his life. Pilot Tom might have been a douche, but he was talented in his craft. Alan and Jeanie shook his hand, thanked him for a great flight, and left their headsets on their seats before departing the plane. Tom also deboarded and popped a storage hatch to retrieve their bags for them. He handed their packs over one at a time and then lit a cigarette. Alan's heart jumped at the sight, and he waved to get the attention of the pilot.

"Are we allowed to do that right here?" Alan asked the pilot, anticipation dripping from his voice.

Tom the pilot gave a conceited chuckle and nodded.

"Yeah, man. This airport is basically just a runway and a shitty run-down room they like to call a terminal." He made air quotes with his fingers around the word airport, a smug look on his face.

Wow, this guy really is a tool, Alan thought.

He shifted his attention to his daughter and put on the most innocent, sweet face he could.

"Do you mind if I smoke really quick?"

She laughed and shook her head.

"Why would I care? That was a short flight, and we are finally *here*, Dad."

The emphasis she put on the word here made Alan remember they weren't in some commercialized place any more. They were in the place he always pictured as his 'happy place.' Although the weather was quintessential for the pacific northwest, Jeanie's smile made it feel like it was eighty degrees and sunny. She beamed. In that moment, he couldn't have felt more proud to be her father.

Alan snagged his pack of Reds and lighter from his hoodie pocket. He lit a cigarette and exhaled relief. He normally didn't make a big deal out of needing a smoke, but the last hour of his life seemed exceptionally stressful. As he smoked, they wandered closer to the small building this island considered its airport. The sides were lined with windows and inside was filled with about ten blue, vinyl chairs and a long desk with one person behind it on the back wall. The lone employee smiled and gave an excited wave. Alan guessed they didn't get many people traveling through. He also guessed this level of exclusivity was only acquired due to his daughter's deep pockets.

Alan put his cigarette out on the slightly damp concrete and chucked the butt in the trashcan near the door. They both used the restroom and when Alan emerged from the men's he saw Jeanie, deeply concentrated on her cell phone.

"What's up? You look worried." He knew it wouldn't go off without a hitch.

"No, no. I just thought our ride would already be here, so I'm just shooting him a quick text." Movement outside the large windows prompted her to look up from her cell phone screen. "Oh, never mind. He's here now!"

Alan followed his daughter's gaze to a door on the other side of the small building. A tall, handsome man in his mid-twenties entered the building. He had skin the color of dark honey, thick black hair that was perfectly tousled, and his light brown eyes had flecks of bright green tossed throughout them. When he saw the two of them standing there he rushed to their side.

"Jeanie, I'm so sorry. I didn't mean to be late. I was just making sure everything was perfect on the boat and lost track of the time. I'm so sorry." He spoke so quickly, everything almost sounded like one long word in a foreign language.

The man was out of breath and Alan thought he must have run from his vehicle. Actually, he sounded like he'd been running everywhere he'd been in the last hour. Jeanie only smiled and put her hand on the man's shoulder.

"Hey, breathe. It's all right. We haven't been here very long at all." She made a hand gesture toward Alan. "This is my father, Alan. Dad, this is Kai. He's a fisherman by trade and lives here on the island. I met him by chance at a farmer's market back in Washington. He was there visiting family. He's going to take us to our location by boat. It'll be a lot faster than driving to the other side of the island."

Alan shook Kai's hand and gave him a slight nod.

"Nice to meet you, Kai. Thanks for helping us out on our little trip."

Kai returned Alan's nod. His dark skin crinkled pleasantly around his eyes as he smiled.

"Shall we get going?" Kai held his arm out in a you-can-go-first manner.

Jeanie led the way and Alan followed. Kai caught up with them and was in the lead of the pack before Alan knew it. He stopped at a small, beat-up truck. The light blue paint had rust spots near several of the wheel wells from years of existing in the damp, salty air. He opened the driver's side door and slid in.

"Hop on in, guys, I'll drive us to the dock," Kia spoke at them through his driver's side window, which was open a crack.

IV

Kai's boat was bigger, much older, and much more used than Cameron's little boat. But he trusted Jeanie and, after only knowing Kai for a short time, he trusted him too. Kai jumped aboard like the seasoned professional he was, and Jeanie followed. Alan's attempt at not embarrassing himself failed. He clumsily climbed on to the bobbing vessel, almost falling. Jeanie reached out and steadied him before he could face plant onto the deck.

The air had a slight nip to it, but it wasn't frigid. Alan guessed it was hovering somewhere around the mid to low sixties. They had replaced their hoodies with rain jackets to keep the sea spray at bay. Alan looked out over the water and was happy it seemed to be a calm day. He wasn't sure if he could handle a choppy ride, even for a short distance.

Kai brought the boat engine to life. He looked back at Alan

and Jeanie.

"I'm going to take you around to the other side of the island, near where the trail you want is located. Should be about twenty minutes, tops. It's not well traveled and not maintained, so it might be a bit tricky to find. There isn't cell service there either," he had to yell over the motor.

Alan thought the man looked a bit tense. Anxious. Jeanie returned his intense look but hers said *stop being stupid, we will be fine*. Kai hit the throttle and they were off.

V

The boat arrived at a beach littered with fallen driftwood and large clumps of sea kelp. Although it appeared abandoned as they got closer, Alan could see there was a small, haphazard dock. It didn't look like it was very stable, but it would keep them dry and out of the water. Beyond the beach, thick forest blanketed the island. Evergreen trees, underbrush, and moss covered the Earth in an array of greens and browns.

Kai pulled carefully up to the dock but didn't risk tying the boat off or cutting the engine. He idled as Alan and Jeanie strapped their packs on. Kai raised his voice so they could both hear him clearly.

"I'll be back here in three days to pick you guys up. This exact spot at three o'clock in the afternoon. That should give you guys plenty of time to hike back to the beach from wherever you decide to camp. I know you guys are experienced, but please, for my own sanity and your own safety, don't wander too far from the trail. Game trails can look similar, and you could really get lost in there. It's beautiful country but it's also dangerous."

Alan gave a thumbs up and made his way onto the dock first. The bleached, semi-rotten wood threatened to give way under his weight but held.

"I don't think this thing is going to safely hold the weight of us both." He yelled over the boat engine and the waves crashing into the coastline. "I'm going to head off to the beach. You think you're okay to get off without a hand?"

Jeanie smiled, nodded, and waved him away with a gesture of her hand. Alan carefully departed the wooden structure onto the sand. Once safely on land, he turned around to keep an eye on Jeanie while she made her way to him. She was still on board, talking to Kai. Their expressions and body language were tense. Once their conversation ended, she departed the boat with a grace that surprised her father. She made her way toward Alan with a smile from ear to ear.

"Can you believe we're here? Are you ready for an adventure?" She spoke with so much excitement, Alan thought she was about to break into laughter at any moment. "We should probably get moving so we can find a good spot to set up camp."

They turned to face the forest. Alan was more excited than he had been in his entire life. But there was another feeling lingering in the back of his mind. A concern had begun to grow there. He was excited and happy for the amazing location, but it was truly isolated. They were alone. As they made their way toward the tree line, Alan cleared his throat.

"Why was Kai so concerned? Is there something more I should know?" Alan asked.

"Nothing like that at all. He just wants to make sure we're safe, that's all." Jeanie didn't look at Alan but pressed ahead keeping her eyes on the trees. "We need to keep our eyes peeled for the trail marker. Kai said they have one but since this area isn't regularly maintained, it may be grown over."

"Okay, I'll keep my eyes peeled," Alan replied.

Jeanie's answer didn't do much to put Alan at ease. She was the one who planned this trip, so he needed to trust her. Once they reached the edge of the forest, they stopped to assess where they were at on the tree line. Alan stopped a moment and took a deep breath. The smell of the salty ocean air mixed with the alpine forest was magical. And the view – he couldn't believe this was real. As they surveyed their location, the clouds began to break allowing a small amount of sunshine to filter through.

"According to Kai's directions, we should be damn near on top of the trail. Let's spread out and look for it. I'll go right, you go left, deal?" Jeanie looked at Alan waiting for confirmation.

"Deal. I'll holler if I find anything," he replied.

Alan headed down the direction Jeanie aimed him in and kept his eyes on the forested side, looking for the trail marker, or a sign of the trail itself.

Only a few minutes later, Jeanie was shouting from behind him. He couldn't make out her words, but could see her jumping up and down, waving her arms above her head. He assumed that her aerobics meant she had found their trail head. He made his way over to her, walking with purpose. The beach was beautiful, but he wanted to get into the forest. Most of all, he wanted to get to camp. He wasn't sure why, but he was feeling exposed out here. Unsafe. Like they should be hiding from someone, or something. He kept feeling like they were being watched.

As he approached, he could see a small wooden sign post next to where Jeanie stood. Moss had overgrown most of it and what might have once been letters or words had completely faded. Looking past the sign into the forest, there was clearly a trail cutting through the thick throng of plant growth and trees. They had found their entrance to the forest.

7

I

Jeanie climbed over the large fallen tree that blocked the entrance of the trail head. Once she was on the other side, she tried to grab her father's hand and help him over. He playfully swatted her hand away.

"I know I'm old, but I'm not that old," he said.

Jeanie smiled and put her hands up in surrender. She took a step back and folded her arms across her chest. She placed her weight on her right leg and jutted her left hip out slightly. A stance that was meant to say *okay, old man, let's see what you got*. Jeanie knew her dad was in fairly good physical condition for his age, but she also knew he was not the most coordinated person she had ever encountered. Her whole life she watched him stumble, knock things over, bump into walls (always followed by a little *oop!*).

Alan shimmied his way on top of the fallen tree and into the sitting position. He swung his legs over the other side. He gently slid to the ground, brushing his backside free from moss, bark, and other debris as he walked past Jeanie.

"Show off!" Jeanie's sarcasm made them both laugh.

They walked side by side on the trail, soaking in the beauty that surrounded them. The sun wasn't fully out but was filtering through the thin clouds, making it just warm enough for Jeanie to shed her rain jacket. She tied it around her waist. The trail had a slight incline but was mostly flat and the hike was easy and enjoyable. The underbrush was lush and thick. The biggest evergreen trees she'd ever seen grew closely together and shot up into the sky. Roots and rocks were covered in moss, and mushrooms showed themselves shyly through the debris of fallen pine needles, dirt, and decomposition that made up the forest floor.

The mood was light, but Jeanie could sense her father didn't fully believe that her conversation with Kai was about nothing. And Jeanie had to admit that Kai's level of concern had her subconscious telling her to be wary. She shook the thought away. This was going to be a perfect trip. It already was. *Any* trip into the wilderness had an aspect of danger.

Kai had warned her that the island was home to many predators. Black bears, cougars, and wolves called this place their home. But there were also an abundant number of deer, rabbits, squirrels, and birds (just to name a few). The wildness of this place is one of the biggest things that drew her here. They both had first aid kits, flare guns, bear mace, air horns, etc. Their cell phones picked up a weak signal from the beach. If they ran into any issues, they would make it out just fine. Still, Jeanie couldn't seem to shake the feeling that she needed to be alert. Always. The feeling that they were being watched.

II

"So, kiddo, is there a set destination on this hike with a campsite already scoped out, or are we truly just riding the wind?" Alan looked down at his hiking boots as he spoke, idly kicking a bit of mud off the side of one boot with the toe of the other. "I don't mind either way, just genuinely curious."

They had been hiking for a little over an hour now.

"We are truly to the wind," Jeanie replied airily. "I figured we would hike in a ways, and then start poking around for a good spot for camp. Do you want to start looking? I've kind of been keeping my eyes peeled and, honestly, everything is so thick, I haven't seen anywhere decent to pop the tents up."

She stopped and looked around. There was nothing but thick, overgrown forest as far as the eye could see, in every direction.

"This is still pretty thick stuff. Let's take a rest here for a few and then hike in a bit further to see if we can find a nice clearing," Jeanie said. She thought her voice sounded slightly uncertain and she hoped her dad hadn't picked up on it.

Alan looked around, unclipped and swung his pack off his back. He sat on a boulder just off the side of the trail. Jeanie didn't remove her pack but checked a nearby log for rot, and then perched herself on top of it. Alan unzipped his pack and pulled out his cigarettes and lighter. As he lit up, he noticed Jeanie's look of disapproval. He smiled and wagged his finger in her direction.

"Hang on. Hang on. I know what you're thinking. But I have a place to safely put my butt without littering." Alan was digging through his pack. His cigarette hung from the corner of his mouth; eyes squinted to shield them from the stream of smoke rising from the tip.

"Aha! Look!" he finally said. Triumphantly, he raised the water bottle from his pack. Ghosts of cigarettes past floated through the murky brown water as he raised it to show his daughter.

Jeanie's face was one of both wonder and disgust. Her mouth hung slightly ajar, brow furrowed.

"You still have that thing? I thought you ditched it at the last gas station before the airport. How did you get that through security?" She couldn't help but be slightly impressed by her father's smuggling skills. Disgusted, but impressed. She let out a little laugh accompanied by a head shake. "You never cease to amaze me."

III

Jeanie was starting to get a bit concerned that they weren't going to find a spot to set up camp. If there were no clearings, they would have to create one themselves. She didn't like the idea of not leaving the forest exactly how she found it. They would also need time to get it cleared, set up camp, and get a fire going before any afternoon storms rolled through.

They had hiked two more hours since their break. The forest hadn't thinned, and the sun was no longer peeking through thin clouds. Jeanie needed to make a decision soon. The trail had completely leveled, and the hike remained easy, so it wouldn't hurt them too terribly for them to press on a bit. She could feel her father beginning to lose faith in her choices.

"No fucking way."

Jeanie looked up from her boots at the sound of her father's voice. He turned around to face her and started laughing. She tilted her head slightly and stared at him, confused. "We did it, Jeanie Bean. We hit the campsite jackpot!"

Jeanie power walked to close the gap in the trail between her and her father. Just beyond where she could see, the trail dipped, and just below was a picture-perfect meadow. It was just big enough for an amazing campsite, filled with lush, green grass. The relief Jeanie felt made her eyes well briefly with tears.

"Let's not get too excited before we get down there and check it out. It could be completely swampy or something,"

Jeanie said.

She tried to hide her own excitement for the location, but she feared the tone in her voice had given it away.

Trying to contain her great expectation, Jeanie led the way down the hill. It was a bit steep, and she didn't want her dad blowing a knee, so she took it slow. The meadow was just to the left of the trail at the bottom of the dip. They arrived in only a few minutes, but it felt like an hour to Jeanie. She paused a moment to look around the surrounding area.

The trail continued past the meadow in a slightly downhill angle, but not steep. She could hear running water somewhere nearby but not close enough to create a danger of flooding if it rained. The ground beneath the grass was slightly damp but not flooded. There were no large rocks they would have to move. It was absolutely perfect, in every way.

"All right, Dad, this is it. Welcome home," Jeanie said, beaming with joy.

IV

They were both excited and made quick work of setting up their individual camp areas. They each had their own one-person tent. Jeanie was still pumping up her twin-sized air mattress and arranging her sleeping bag when her dad poked his head in.

"Looking good in here." Alan looked around the inside of Jeanie's tent and nodded his head slowly. "I'm going to go try to find some tinder and wood dry enough to get a fire going. I'm bringing my flare and my air horn. That covers me for wildlife and getting lost. Be back in a jiff."

Before Jeanie could reply or protest him going alone, he was already trundling through the underbrush into the forest. That man was so loud and ungraceful, no wildlife would get close to him. She mostly just worried about him getting turned around, but her father was not a dumb man, he knew his limits. He would stay close. She hoped.

She told herself to quit worrying so much and worked on finishing making her temporary home as comfortable as possible. When she emerged from her tent, she saw that her father not only set up his tent, but also created a perfect fire ring out of medium and large stones he found in the surrounding forest. She could always count on him to get things done at back breaking speeds. He also never cared to make his temporary living space as homey as she did.

While she waited for her father to return with the firewood, she retrieved the ultra-light chairs from each of their packs and set them up around the fire ring. As she was finishing some set up around camp, she noticed there were already two cigarette butts in the ring, waiting to be burned in the fire. She shook her head.

The joy she was filled with being here with her dad was insurmountable. She hadn't felt this feeling in her chest since long before her mother died. She sat in her chair, closed her eyes, and inhaled deeply through her nose. A faint smile graced her lips as the sounds of the forest flooded her ear drums. She let happiness and relaxation flow through her. This is exactly the way she pictured this trip. No stress. No worries. No sadness.

In the distance she heard an animal cry. It was far off, and she couldn't quite place what it was. She opened her eyes slightly and listened, hoping she would hear it again. It came again, more distant this time. She thought it might be a bull elk bugling. It was a bit early for that but not out of the realm of possibility. Rutting season was only a week or two off. She tried to play the sound in her mind again. Something about it made her feel uneasy.

She brushed off the feeling and decided to go through the meals she brought and make a decision on what they would eat for dinner. If she was hungry, she knew her father would be too.

V

Alan bounded into the forest with a mile wide smile plastered on his face, blue eyes blaring with excitement. His movements were childlike, but he remained aware of his footfalls. He knew he wasn't the most coordinated person (and in no way a spring chicken) and didn't want to ruin the trip with a tumble in the forest because he was acting like a schoolboy. Bent at the waist, hands on his knees, he looked around and caught his breath.

"Wow, this place is fucking gorgeous," his voice reached out into the forest. "All right, Alan, enough dicking around. Let's find some stuff to burn."

The conditions here were fairly wet, but he had done his research. He was confident that he could find some decent kindling. He searched the area until he found the old stump of a fallen fir tree. He kicked at the stump until he could reach the center pieces of wood within the stump. He untied the small bag he brought with him and filled it with the pitch wood from the stump, humming to himself as he gathered.

A wild cry tore through the forest. Alan's humming ceased and he froze, trying to listen for the sound again.

It's okay, dude, you're fine. It didn't sound predatory. Probably just an elk or moose or some shit. And it was far away.

Even as he reassured himself, his heart pounded in his chest. It didn't sound like a bear or wolf, but it also didn't sound quite like any animal he had ever encountered before.

The animal sounded again. Alan's unease mounted and he went from frozen, to hauling ass. His fight or flight instinct kicked in. Whatever made that sound was far away, but he didn't know for how long. And he didn't want to find out. He had left Jeanie alone with no fire. It was only late afternoon, but the cloud cover had increased, creating an eerie greenish light within the thick forest.

He quickly searched the area and found a tree large enough that its branches shielded the underbelly from a great deal of moisture. He dove under the tree and gathered as many twigs and branches as he could stuff into the bag with the pitch. He hadn't heard the sound again, but his mind began playing tricks on him, and his anxiety heightened. He backed out from underneath the tree, not caring that the branches scraped at the back of his head and his jacket.

As he quickly made his way back toward camp. He scanned the area for any more dead branches that might be dry enough to burn. He snapped dead branches from trees as he walked. He knew it was stupid to be so alarmed, but he always listened to his gut. And his gut was telling him to get as far from whatever made that noise, as fast as he could.

Relief washed over him as the bright orange of Jeanie's tent became visible through the trees. He slowed his speed as he approached. He didn't want Jeanie to know he had gotten spooked out there. And he didn't want to make her uncomfortable either. As he entered camp, Jeanie greeted him with a warm smile.

"Got some decent wood to get a blaze started!" His enthusiasm was overexaggerated, but Jeanie didn't seem to notice. Without getting up from her seat, she raised her hand above her head.

"Put it there, partner!" Alan slapped her palm with his own.

"I'm going to grab the folding saw and cut some bigger pieces of wood, and then I'll get us a fire going."

"Okay, no rush. It's not super cold. Do you want to eat something when you're done?" Jeanie replied lazily.

"Yeah, I'm pretty hungry."

Alan didn't feel very hungry at all after his scare, but he wasn't going to mention that to Jeanie. He thought he was doing a decent job at acting natural. He fetched the folding saw from the vestibule of his tent and went to work chopping firewood.

When he had several good pieces, he took them near the fire pit with the pitch wood and kindling he had gathered in the forest. He found his pack of cigarettes. As he lit his cigarette, his hands trembled, and he hoped his daughter didn't notice. If she did, he would blame it on low blood sugar.

"Hey, Dad."

The sudden sound of Jeanie's voice made him jump slightly. He closed his eyes briefly. He took a breath, opened them, and turned around to give Jeanie a slightly forced smile.

"I brought some fire starter to make this easier on you. Let me grab it really quick." Jeanie patted him on the shoulder as she jogged past him.

She returned with a fire starter briquette and handed it to Alan.

"Thanks, kiddo, this will definitely help me out. It's wet here."

He tossed his cigarette butt into the pit and began work. He placed the briquette in the pit and took out his pocketknife. He feathered the end of a few pieces of the pitch he had gathered. He lit the briquette and then the end of each of the feathered ends, with the small flame going, he added some of the dry tinder.

They had fire.

VI

Making the fire gave Alan's fear some time to abate. Thinking back on it, even just a short thirty minutes later, he felt foolish.

What an old idiot you are, Alan.

He placed one hand on his knee and shoved himself to a standing position. He brushed his pant legs off and sat in the chair Jeanie had set up for him.

"You ready for some food?" Alan asked Jeanie.

"You read my mind! Let me go grab the pot and a couple of the MREs. I'm curious about the chicken gumbo. Is that good with you, or do you want something else?"

"Gumbo sounds just fine," he replied.

Jeanie returned with the food and a pot of water, and a portable 'stove.' She placed the titanium pot on the stove to boil and sat in her chair.

Alan could hear Jeanie speaking to him but wasn't fully listening to her words. Instead of understanding or responding to her, Alan simply nodded in agreement. He wasn't lost in thought but rather lost in a void of thought. He stared into the fire, hypnotized by the flames.

VII

Jeanie removed the top of the MRE pouch and poured the boiling water inside until it reached the fill line indicated on the inside of the container. She pinched the top together and folded it down. She repeated the process with the second pouch. It would take about ten minutes for the dehydrated meal to come to life.

Jeanie wasn't always a heavy drinker, but she sure wished she had a beer right now. Since she heard that strange animal in the forest earlier in the day, she had been on edge. Since her father returned to camp, her anxiety had eased itself a bit. But it was still there; lurking in the back of her mind and the bottom of her stomach, ready to pounce at any moment.

Something else was nagging at the back of her brain. Her father was acting odd. Since his return from the forest, he seemed nervous. He was on edge and jumpy; even zoned out. She could tell he was trying to hide it, and he was doing an okay job of it. But the anxiety still peeked through the veil, impossible to completely conceal. She decided she wouldn't mention what she heard and that it frightened her. She didn't want to deteriorate his mood any further or make him worry more than he already might be.

The timer on her watch buzzed, letting her know their meal was ready to be consumed.

"Dinner is served, Dad," Jeanie said.

Her words pulled him from his fire-induced daze, and he reached across the span between them and grabbed his meal pouch from her. She handed him a metal spork.

"Thanks, kid," Alan replied.

As he opened the top of his pouch, steam rose toward his face. He closed his eyes and inhaled through his nose.

"It actually smells great. I didn't know I was so hungry."

Jeanie mirrored her father's actions and grabbed a sporkful of the gumbo. She blew on the bite until its temperature wouldn't scald her tongue. At the smell of food her mouth filled with saliva. Her stomach growled in a rejoice. She took her first bite and was pleasantly surprised. After a long day of physical activity, it was delicious. As if he could hear her thoughts, Alan spoke over a mouthful of his dinner.

"Great choice on the food selection. This is hitting the spot," he said.

Once their bellies were full, they burned their trash. Jeanie boiled a bit more water and washed he sporks, dried them and put them away. She climbed into her tent and opened her pack. Now that she wasn't stressed about getting set up, and her hunger was at bay, it was time for comfort. She dug out her favorite t-shirt, sweatpants, and a crew neck sweater from her pack. She undressed to her underwear. After she was dressed in her new outfit, she folded her dirty, sweat-stained clothes, and placed them in a plastic bag inside her pack.

She ducked through the doorway of her tent. When she fully emerged and looked up, the chair her father had previously occupied by the fire was empty. She could hear rustling coming from inside his tent. He must have had the same idea she did, Jeanie thought. No use in stewing in the uncomfortable sweat of the day. Now it was time to relax. She took her seat next to the fire, the slight movement of her father's tent still in her peripheral vision.

Although the cloud cover had obscured the sun from view for the entire afternoon, it was now clear that it was making its descent toward the horizon. The lavender hue of twilight was beginning to settle over the forest. The sounds of bird song were settling down for the day and there was in increased crispness in the air. Even with the drop in temperature, Jeanie was still quite comfortable in her sweats near the fire.

Alan emerged, donning his sweats, a beanie, and mischievous grin. Jeanie gave him a what-in-the-hell-are-you-up-to look as he moved toward the fire. He walked with both hands shoved into the front pocket of his hoodie, a cigarette hanging from the corner of his mouth.

"You didn't think dear old dad would forget to bring a little fun with him, did you?" Alan's tone was playful.

He removed his right hand from his pocket, holding his lighter. As he lit his cigarette, his left emerged to reveal a flat, plastic bottle of whiskey. He shook it side to side gently. He showed off his dance skills by moving his hips side to side.

Jeanie threw back her head and laughed.

"Woohoo! I thought about bringing some but didn't want to make either of the packs too heavy with unnecessary shit."

"My dear, alcohol is never unnecessary shit. Especially, on vacation." He unscrewed the cap and took a sip from the bottle. He winced as the liquid burned down to his stomach. "I've got another one of these. Had to get the cheap shit so it would be in plastic. Easy to dispose of and a lot lighter."

He handed the bottle to Jeanie. She didn't want to get too drunk, but a decent buzz would be a welcome friend. It would help her relax and would help her get some sleep, if the twinge of fear decided to creep back in again. She took a few sips before handing the bottle back to her father. He placed the bottle in his empty chair and flicked his cigarette into the fire, which had begun to burn down. He placed the last few cut logs into the pit.

"I'm going to cut up more wood to last us through the night," Alan said through a thin veil of cigarette smoke.

Jeanie nodded in agreement.

From his tent, he retrieved a tarp and spread it over the ground. He sawed wood until the stars in the sky shone brightly. Once he was confident the pile had accumulated enough to keep the fire fueled until morning, he grabbed a few logs from his stock. The rest he wrapped in the tarp to protect from any impending rain. Before taking his seat, he placed one more log on the fire. The other two he left on the ground nearby. He wanted to keep the fire well fed. He needed the hottest bed of coals he could get to combat the moisture.

Even with nightfall, the temperature was still in the sixties and the heat of the fire was making Jeanie sweat. She moved her chair back a few inches. She held out her left arm and made a pinching gesture with her hand. Alan obliged and handed her the whiskey, as requested. She loved that words weren't always necessary when she was with him. They were both comfortable simply being in the presence of one another, enjoying a peaceful moment. The whiskey was working as she intended. A warmth and calmness swept over her body as she sat with her father. The only sounds were the crackling of the fire and the breeze gently caressing the treetops.

VIII

They watched the fire and gazed at the abundance of stars overhead. They couldn't believe how many shooting stars there were flashing across the night sky. It seemed there wasn't a single stretch of sky you could look at without seeing at least one streaking past. Jeanie didn't think there was a meteor shower that was supposed to happen, but she made a mental note to look it up when she got home. They snapped a few goofy pictures together on Jeanie's cell phone by the glow of the campfire light. They drank more than Jeanie expected them to, roasted marshmallows (which her father also snuck in his bag to surprise her with) and reminisced about her childhood. Most importantly, they laughed. It was the most Jeanie had laughed in years, and she guessed the same was true for her father.

When the roaring fire Alan built was burnt down to glowing coals, they both decided it was time to turn in for the night. Jeanie wished her father goodnight and made her way to her tent (but not before making a quick pitstop to pee). Once inside, she removed her sweatshirt and sweatpants before climbing into her sleeping bag. Her cheeks were warm, and her head swam slightly under the fluorescent glow of her battery-operated lamp. She drank more than she originally intended but she wasn't at all uncomfortable. She made sure she drank plenty of water throughout the night to avoid a hangover in the morning. She giggled to herself and shook her head slightly.

Any worry from earlier in the day had completely dissipated. She reached an arm from her sleeping bag and cut the power to her lantern. She slipped into a perfectly sound, dreamless sleep.

8

I

Alan woke just as the sun was starting to make its presence known for the day. Despite the whiskey he drank the night before, he felt well rested and refreshed. The faint light of an impending sunrise gave everything in his tent an odd glow. He stretched his arms as far as they would go over his head and inhaled deeply.

He unzipped his sleeping bag and flung the flap of material covering his torso back. There was no need for him to get dressed yet, he wanted a slow morning. He grabbed his hoodie and pulled it on, removing the hood from his head once it popped through the hole. He patted the front pocket with both hands in search of his pack of cigarettes. Once his hands felt the familiar outline of the rectangular box, he opened the door of his tent and ducked out into the open.

The air was crisp, but not cold. He found the pot and portable stove Jeanie had used the night before and put on water to boil. His morning ritual always consisted of a cup of large coffee (or tea on occasion) and a cigarette. Being in the wilderness wasn't going to change that for him.

While he waited for the water to boil, he decided to get the fire stoked back up. He lifted the tarp covering the wood pile, shaking the condensation from the top as he did. He grabbed an armful of wood and replaced the tarp. He was happy to see his bed of coals was still nice and hot and placed the pieces of wood in a cone shape in the pit. He placed a bit of kindling in the center and blew gently. It didn't take long for the fire to ignite.

Satisfied (and slightly impressed) with his fire making skills, he looked up toward Jeanie's tent to see if there was any movement yet. He didn't think there was and decided to leave her sleeping for a bit longer. As he stood up, he noticed the absence of the two chairs they had left around the fire the night before. He did a quick scan of their camp and noticed them folded and neatly leaning against a tree opposite their tents.

I guess Jeanie must have put them up before she tucked in for the night.

It was a perfectly viable explanation, but Alan couldn't help feeling the tug of unease at the back of his mind. There couldn't be another explanation for it. They were the only two people out here. He brushed the feeling away and grabbed the chairs, one under each arm, and set them up near the fire. The water he placed on the stove was now boiling, so he retrieved two cups and instant coffee. He whipped up a cup of Joe for his daughter and then one for himself. He placed his cup in the holder of his chair and, with hers still in hand, approached her tent.

"Time to wake up, kiddo!" He gently rattled her tent with his free hand. "Come on! I made you some coffee."

"I'm up, I'm up," Jeanie mumbled. Her reply was soft, but she sounded cheerful.

"I'll leave it in the holder of your chair. No need to rush, I'm in chill mode."

Alan was pleased to hear the relaxed happiness in Jeanie's voice. Every time he'd spoken to her on the phone in recent years (although it was not often), there was always the presence of stress or strain in her voice. She always seemed tense. He wasn't sure if it was her dedication to her work that made her sound that way, or the loss of her mother at such a young age, but it always broke his heart to hear it.

He plopped down into his chair and took a careful sip of his coffee to test the temperature. When the liquid didn't scald his mouth, he took a bigger gulp and let out a satisfied *ahhh*. Leaning back into his chair, he lit a cigarette and waited for Jeanie to join him. He was looking forward to exploring the area with her today and hoped they would see a bit of wildlife too.

II

Jeanie woke feeling amazing. If there was anything she expected out of this trip, it wasn't a good night's sleep. Although shocked, she was also extremely grateful. She didn't remember a time in her adult life that she had ever slept so soundly. As she stretched her arms and legs, she realized how stiff she was. It wasn't a painful stiffness, just the kind that happens when you're in your thirties and you didn't move even a wiggle all night long.

She climbed from her makeshift bed and into a large sweatshirt and sweatpants. Something didn't quite feel right as she moved around the tiny interior space of her tent. She let herself fall back on her butt and she studied her surroundings. Her lantern was next to her bed when she fell asleep. She knew it because she turned it off from the comfort of the interior of her sleeping bag. The space it once occupied was now empty. Without standing up Jeanie turned around, swiveling at her hips to see behind her, first to the left and then the right. The LED lantern was sitting by the entrance of her tent.

I must have gotten up to go pee in the middle of the night and left it there.

She instinctively scratched her head, which was cocked to

one side. Her brow furrowed in deep concentration, trying desperately to remember. There's no other explanation. We are the only two up here and if Dad would have come in to use it for whatever reason, it would have woken me up.

"You coming? Coffee's getting cold!"

Alan's voice broke Jeanie's trance. She shook her head, trying to make the confusion and concern go away. She let out a little sigh and unzipped the door of her tent. She grabbed her tennis shoes from outside the door and shoved them onto her feet without untying them. Carefully ducking so her head wouldn't catch on the tent door, she made her way to meet her father near the fire.

As she approached, Alan gave her a questioning look. The confusion must have still been showing on her face.

"Everything okay?" Alan inquired with concern.

"Yeah. Yeah." She gave a little wave of her hand, furrowed her brow, and shook her head. "I just can't remember part of last night, I guess. I don't know if I was sleep walking or what."

Alan responded with a tilt of his head, resembling a curious puppy. Then he laughed a little. Jeanie opened her mouth to say something, but the words stuck in her throat. She put her hands out in front her, palms up and let them fall into her lap.

"I don't know. The last thing I remember last night was turning my lantern off before bed, from my bed." Her brooding expression deepened as she tried again to remember. "But this morning, I found it next to the door of my tent. I must have gone out to use the bathroom and left it there when I came back. I just don't remember it."

Jeanie shrugged, adding a slight shake of her head. She searched her father's face but found nothing but a smile.

"You must have drank more than you thought, girl," Alan

said. His tone was light as he teased her. After letting out a small barely audible chuckle, he nudged her arm with his closed fist and took a drink of his coffee.

Her father's good mood helped ease Jeanie's anxiety. She allowed her shoulders to relax, and she sat back in her chair, picking up her coffee and holding it close to her chest with both hands. She took a long drink, swallowed hard, and inhaled deeply through her nose.

III

As much as he didn't want to admit it to himself, Alan was feeling freaked out. Without trying to be obvious, he scanned the rest of their campsite with his eyes, making sure to keep his head still.

Was anything else moved?

Was anything missing?

Or did Jeanie truly just do a little sleep walking last night?

Alan was tempted to mention the chairs to his daughter. But what was the point of upsetting her further when it could have been nothing but a simple case of sleep walking? It was just sleep walking. There's no other explanation. He landed on the conclusion that he would keep the chairs to himself. He would also pay close attention to the items around camp. He wanted to make sure nothing else was moved in the night.

"Do you want to go exploring today? We could hike further down the trail and see if there's anything cool close by." Alan looked over at Jeanie, who was sitting with her eyes closed, soaking in the morning.

She slowly opened one eye and looked at him, squinting.

"Absolutely. Let's go enjoy some nature." As she replied, she stretched her arms high above her head, simultaneously stretching her legs out in front of her so her body resembled a giant letter X. "Let's eat some breakfast first, though."

Jeanie put another pot of water on the stove to boil and then disappeared from Alan's view. He could hear her lightly humming while she rifled through their food stash.

"Scramble or oatmeal?" she called out to Alan from somewhere behind him.

"I'll take the scramble, please! I'm going to get dressed really quick," he shouted back as he poked at the fire with a long, sturdy branch he had found the day before.

Jeanie appeared in his view. She placed the two packages that contained their breakfast in the seat of her chair.

"I'm going to poke around out here until the water is boiling so I can get our breakfast cooking," she said.

Alan nodded his acknowledgement and withdrew into his tent. Jeanie could hear the faint sounds of his body brushing against the slick material of the tent as he changed into his day wear. While she waited to prepare their food, Jeanie walked slowly around the campsite, hands thrust into the pockets of her sweatpants. As she walked past a large tree on the edge of camp, closest to the trail, something caught her interest out of the corner of her eye.

She stopped and backed up a few paces, squinting to see the tree with more clarity. Still unable to confirm exactly what she was seeing she approached the tree. Standing closer she could now see what looked like a carving in the bark of the tree.

The carving was high enough that she had to stand on tiptoes to touch it. She ran her fingers over the surface of the symbol. Its curves were intricate, and she was impressed that anyone would be able to pull off such a clean carving into the bark of a tree with a simple knife. Even the sharpest pocket or hunting knife would have had difficulty completing the task. The curves tangled together forming a knot. When she finally pulled her fingers away, they glistened with fresh tree sap. She rubbed the tips of her two forefingers together with her thumb. Sticky strings formed as she pulled her fingers apart. She thought it was her imagination, but it felt as if the sticky goo was charged with electricity. Like when you touched a light switch and the energy built up gave you a tiny zap, or the feeling you got sticking your tongue against a nine-volt battery.

In her curiosity, she had completely forgotten about breakfast. She could hear the voice of her father calling out to her, but her concentration wouldn't allow her to hear it fully. He sounded far away, his voice was faint and muffled, almost like she was submerged in water.

"Whatcha got over there?" Noticing he was being ignored, Alan's expression hardened with a slight annoyance. His voice adopted a slightly higher pitch as he spoke again. "Hello! Earth to Jeanie!"

The sizzling sound of water on open flame pulled the attention of them both. Jeanie's dazed trance broke, and she spun around quickly to find the source of the urgent noise.

"Oh shit!" she yelled as she jogged over to the stove.

She quickly yanked the sleeve of her sweater down over her hand and removed the pot from the heat. Placing the overboiling pot of water on the ground, she shut off the portable stove. Without breaking stride, she retrieved their meals from the seat of her chair. She ripped the top from the packet containing her father's requested breakfast scramble and began pouring boiling water into the cavity.

"Are you really not going to fill me in on what the hell was so interesting over there?" Alan's tone was worried and peppered with a hit of annoyance.

Jeanie stopped mid-pour and looked up at her dad. What had she been doing over there? What did she see? She thought she had found something unusual, something captivating, but now she strained to remember what it was, if anything at all. Her brain must still be fogged from last night's whiskey.

"Nothing. It was nothing. I must just be out of it from last night. I was zoned out. Sorry about that, Dad." She gave him a weak smile and finished filling their breakfast pouches with hot water, folding the tops down to seal them shut. "I'm going to get dressed while this food hydrates. I'll be back in two shakes of a lamb's tail, Pops."

IV

To Alan's pleasant surprise, his breakfast scramble was quite delicious, and he ate it with record speed. After breakfast he made sure the campsite was clean and secure, grabbed his walking stick, and laced up his hiking boots. He was excited to explore with his favorite adventure buddy. As he waited for Jeanie to finish getting prepared for their hike, he poked at the fire to ensure it was only coals before they left. Jeanie emerged, also donning her hiking gear. On her back she wore a small pack that housed water, granola bars, and some beef jerky.

"Hey, Dad, look what I brought!" Alan turned around in his chair and noticed Jeanie holding up two small, collapsible fishing poles in her hand. "I thought we could try our hand at catching dinner. I was told there are some good fishing spots on the island, so I brought these in case we come across one."

Alan rose from his chair. His eyes were filled with childlike excitement.

"What a kick ass idea! You just reminded me to grab my small pack before we take off. I have to fill up a water bottle to throw in it, and then I can strap the poles to it too." He did a slight jog over to his tent and retrieved his pack.

Jeanie waited patiently for her father to fill his water. She gazed in the direction they would need to walk to hit the trail. She didn't know why but she felt a great and distinct unease. She didn't want to walk in that direction but was glad she didn't have to do it alone. Her thoughts were interrupted by her father's presence next to her.

"Ready to go?" he asked.

Jeanie nodded her head and gave him a smile. "I think we want to hit the trail in that direction, right? You wanted to see where it leads beyond our camp?" Jeanie pointed in the direction of the trail they came in on.

"That's what I was thinking," Alan said. "But if you have a different idea or a direction you would rather go, I'm game for that."

"No, no. I think sticking to the trail isn't a bad move at all."

"Plus, I'm pretty sure I heard some running water in that direction when I was gathering wood, so maybe it will lead us to a decent body of water we can fish at." Alan patted his daughter's shoulder.

As if they had established a psychic connection, they both began walking toward the trail. It didn't take long before they were comfortably hiking along at a decent pace. The trail continued to dip gradually past their site and the meadow was met by more thick forest. The day was overcast but the clouds were not thick, and the sun was trying its hardest to reach the Earth below. There were small sections above where the sky wasn't completely obstructed from view, like a thin white veil over blue backdrop.

Alan walked with his face toward the sky, binoculars slung around his neck. He wasn't quite smiling, but his face exuded joy. The pair walked in silence. Only the sound of their boots on the gravel, and the steady plunk of Alan's walking stick could be heard from them. The mood was light and, although the prospect of finding water was on his mind, it wouldn't ruin his day if they were unsuccessful in their search. Once in a while he would stop and put the binoculars up to his anticipating eyes. He was fascinated by the variety of birds that presented themselves on this one island. He closed his eyes and listened to their songs winding their way through the treetops.

The trail began to turn to the right and cut back up into the forest. They both paused at the curve. Jeanie put her hands on her hips and surveyed the area.

"I know it's smartest to stick to the trail, but I really want to know what's down there." She pointed in the direction opposite to the trail. The decline wasn't straight down but its steepness increased dramatically from the grade they experienced on the trail. "I'm going to just shoot down there and take a peek. I won't go far. I just want to see if I can see anything worthwhile. If I find anything cool, I'll yell up to you."

Alan watched his daughter carefully cut through the forest. At the steepest points, she turned sideways and considerably slowed her pace, making sure her foot placement was secure. When she was lost from Alan's view, he moved forward so he could see further down the slope. She was visible now but just a small black figure in the distance. He put his hand up, making his thumb and forefinger parallel in front of his face, and viewed her through the opening between them. He squinted his right eye and opened and closed his fingers a few times, pretending to squish her like an ant. He laughed a little to himself and shook his head.

His childish antics were dissipated by the jumping of the tiny figure that was his Jeanie. Alan grabbed the binoculars that rested on his chest and through them could see she was waving her arms over her head. He couldn't tell if she was in trouble or just summoning him (the binoculars were shit) but he immediately began making his way down the slope. He was sure to pay close attention to his footing. If she was in trouble, he wouldn't be able to help her if he was also injured. And if she was excited about something, he wouldn't want a poorly placed boot to ruin the fun.

When he was about halfway to where Jeanie was waiting, he thought he could see that she was not in trouble, but she was instead, very happy about something. This made him throw caution to the wind (but only slightly). He sped his pace. Loose gravel trundled down the earth in front of him, but the most dangerous ground was the damp moss and rocks, which were very slippery in places.

Once he was within ear shot of his daughter, his patience ran out.

"What is it? You're not hurt, are you? Did you find something?" He noticed he was now doing an odd, lopsided jog down the face of the slope, frantically blurting out questions like a madman.

When he reached the bottom, Jeanie's face was amused, and she spoke to him around a small laugh.

"Dad, I'm fine. Quit focusing on me and *look*."

She put a hand under her father's chin and led his face in the direction she was pointing. Alan's eyes widened. He gave a loud "Ha!" and shot his fisted hands straight up above his head. Just through the trees, he could see the shimmer of a body of water, and once he was quiet, he could hear small waves lapping at the rocky shore.

Jeanie had found them a lake.

9

I

To their delight, the lake was rather large and appeared to be quite deep in places. That meant big fish. Alan used his binoculars to check out the shoreline for the best place to cast from. They decided on a spot close to where they emerged from the forest on a sandy shore. Although there looked to be better places to try their luck at picking up a real lunker, they decided they better stay close to their entry point. No sense in taking the risk of getting lost.

Alan swung his pack from his back and plopped it onto the wet sand (which was really more like gravel). There was a slight wind, but it wasn't strong enough to make the water overly choppy. It wasn't exactly ideal fishing weather, with flat still waters, but it would do. Alan handed Jeanie her pole and began assembling his. They only had one or two lures each, so if they got lost quickly, that would be the end of their fishing on this trip.

Alan was about to throw out his first cast when he noticed Jeanie struggling to get her rod in working order.

"Been a while since you've used that huh?" He chuckled and held a hand out toward her. "Give it here. I'll do that for you."

He made quick work of the task and it didn't take long for Jeanie to throw out her first line.

The sun revealed itself fully and Jeanie thought that was lucky. She took it as a sign from the universe that they were meant to be there, in that exact moment, on that exact beach. She wedged her pole between two large rocks and sat down, not caring that the rear end of her pants was soaking up the dampness of the ground. She leaned back on both hands and held her face to the sky, her long ponytail wagging behind her back.

"Jeanie! You got something! Your line's tugging!"

Her father's urgent voice brought her attention back to her pole from her sun-soaking daze. She shot up to her feet and quickly made her way to her pole. A few specks of gravel fell on her way over, but the rest stayed, clinging to the butt of her pants like barnacles on the bottom of a boat.

At first, she thought a wave had gotten her line tangled in the various plant life that lingered below the surface, triggering her pole to wobble. As she reeled in the line, her disappointment turned to nothing less than giddy. There was resistance at the end of her line, and it felt like whatever was hooked there, was not ready to go without a fight.

After a few minutes of strategic reeling, Jeanie's opponent was too exhausted to go on fighting and was brought to shore successfully. It wasn't the biggest fish in the world, but it was much larger than anything she had expected to catch. She gave the fish a quick painless death and then held it up to examine it. It was a Rainbow Trout and by her estimation, probably weighed about seven or eight pounds.

"Hey, Dad! Grab my phone out of my pack. I want to take a picture."

Alan wedged his pole and completed his daughter's request.

"Hold it way out in front. I heard that's supposed to make it look bigger in a picture." He shot her a wink.

Jeanie did as her father instructed. With her fingers hooked in the fish's gills, she extended her arm fully and waited for her father to snap the photo. A photo that would capture her proud moment for the rest of her life.

II

After another hour at the lake with no more luck, they decided it was time to start heading back to camp. Alan gutted and processed Jeanie's fish at the lake. To further mitigate any smell from the fish that might attract predators on their journey back, they wrapped the fish in a couple of disassembled Ziplock bags before placing it inside Jeanie's day pack. With Jeanie in the lead, they began their ascent.

Alan had to admit, he was feeling very uneasy walking around the wilderness with fresh fish strapped to his daughter's back. From the speed of her walk, he could tell Jeanie was feeling similar discomfort. He wasn't one hundred percent positive which predators called this particular island home, but he knew they were there. Black bears and mountain lions at a minimum, he suspected wolves, as well.

He was thankful they weren't terribly far from home base. It had only taken them somewhere around thirty minutes to reach the lake this morning and then their pace had been nothing short of lackadaisical. Now their feet pounded the Earth at a hasty pace, their arms swinging quickly at their sides. Alan's calf muscles were tight and burned furiously. He didn't care enough to slow his speed, but he did make a mental note that when he returned home, he would start working out more.

Jeanie looked over her shoulder at her father. "How are you doing back there, Dad?"

"I'm fine, kiddo, just keep going."

Neither Alan nor Jeanie mentioned their fear. It was as if they both silently agreed that if it wasn't spoken aloud, it couldn't become a reality. Alan had concluded that they would cook the fish for lunch, not dinner, and as soon as they reached camp. He wanted that damn thing gone. He had never felt so afraid in the wild before and part of him felt absolutely ridiculous for it. But the other part of him, the part where the fear lived, told him it wasn't ridiculous at all. They were a traveling lunch bell, leading every predator in the area directly to where they were sleeping.

"Jeanie, I don't think we should take that thing all the way back to camp. We need to cook it and eat it somewhere else."

Alan could hear the fear in his own voice. It trembled terribly and he hoped his daughter didn't pick up on it. He was starting to panic. It was as if someone was whispering in his ear, feeding his fear with worst case scenarios.

Jeanie didn't stop moving forward as she answered her father.

"That might not be a bad idea, Dad, but how are we going to get a fire away from camp? We have no supplies. We have nothing to cook with. We have nothing to eat with. We will walk back to camp with fish-covered hands, leading whatever predator straight to us anyway," Jeanie said to her father.

She sounded on the verge of annoyed. Her breathing wasn't quite labored yet, but she was beginning to sound winded. She didn't slow down. Something in her gut told her it was not safe out here.

She wanted nothing more than the safety and security of camp, the comfort of a roaring fire. She felt exposed and the last thing she wanted to do was slow her pace or stop to look for a spot to eat. Jeanie felt as if hundreds of eyes were watching her, boring holes into her back. She felt like a blinking beacon, beckoning the dangers that lurked in the recesses of the forest. Her paranoia was growing into panic. She hoped like hell her father wasn't picking up on it and so she pressed on as hard and fast as she could, trying to hide it.

Get it together, Jeanie. Why are you freaking the fuck out right now? Just breathe, keep moving, and try to keep logical.

Just breathe.

People catch fish and eat them while camping all the time. They don't all die a horrific, predator-induced death.

Chill. Out.

Her internal dialogue did little if nothing to comfort her as they made their way along the trail. They were getting close to camp now. It felt like some magnetic force was pulling them there, urging her to pick up speed. It was a feeling similar to when she was a child, and her grandmother would make her go get something from the basement. She would creep into the dusty, dank of the basement, hastily flipping every light switch on as she went. Once she retrieved the item her grandmother had requested, she would flip the light switch off and bolt as quickly as she could from the darkness, knowing that something horrible would surely consume her if she didn't get the hell out of Dodge. She would take the stairs two at time, skipping every other rickety wooden stair with long strides. When she finally reached the top, she would turn the light at the top of the stairs off and close the door behind her briskly, keeping whatever evil that lurked behind it at bay.

Alan was breathing like he had just finished a marathon. But he didn't care. He felt an unnatural force, pushing him forward. Encouraging more speed with every step. After he had told Jeanie he wanted to stop and eat this fish away from camp, something in his mind told him that was all wrong. Getting back to camp was the best option. The only option. Jeanie was right. They had to just keep going. To get there pronto.

Step it up, old man. You can do this. You have to get back to camp, where it's safe.

You'll be safe back near the fire.

Just keep breathing and, whatever you do, keep moving.

He inhaled deeply through his nose and the urgency increased. The smell of a smoldering campfire. They were close and he suddenly had the urge to run. He didn't know why he felt camp was the safest place on Earth. Like a forcefield surrounded it and nothing bad could happen there. After all, it was in the same wilderness they were in right now. The same wilderness they were fleeing from. The same wilderness that filled them with childish fear. But something pushed those thoughts away. Something told them camp was safety, camp was comfort, and camp was the only place they needed to be.

She didn't know when she had quit but Jeanie was no longer walking. She was jogging toward the bright orange beacon of her tent. As she passed through the last tree and into the meadow, she stopped. Immediate relief washed over her. She turned around to check for her father. She bent over, hands braced just above her knees, trying to catch her breath. She was glad to see her father was just behind her.

As Alan entered their campsite, he mimicked Jeanie's exhausted position. He held onto his knees, desperately trying to catch his breath.

"We made it," he spoke through labored breaths, staring at the ground in front of his feet. "Holy shit, we made it."

Jeanie, too out of breath to form a response, nodded her head gently, in agreement.

As the words slid from his lips, he realized how absurd they were. They weren't in any true, immediate danger. They had no real reason to believe they were being chased or hunted. Not to mention, if they were in any real danger, camp would not be any safer than it had been just outside of it.

But Jeanie felt it too. She moved with more urgency than even he had. She *ran* into camp. Were they just feeding off each other, amplifying one another's fear until it manifested as panic? Maybe. As Alan tried to evaluate the last thirty minutes in his mind, he found he was having trouble remembering everything. He remembered being away from camp, in the woods, but it was very foggy, like trying to remember the night before when you've drunk too much. Just small bits and pieces coming back, all viewed through a white mist.

While Alan was doing his best to recount his memories, Jeanie had swung her pack onto the ground, removed the fish, and made sure it was on the side of camp furthest from their sleeping arrangements. She grabbed a piece of braided nylon rope, tossed it over a sturdy tree branch, and strung it up by the gills. She then began work on the fire. She grabbed a few logs from the tarp-covered pile and strategically placed a few logs onto the hot coals. Before long she was welcomed by the *whoosh* of the flames catching.

This brought Alan back to the present. Still feeling the effects of the journey back to camp, he made his way to the chair set up near the fire and plopped down in a daze. After Jeanie was finished with her chores around camp, bouncing back and forth like a pinball, she joined her father. She sat on the edge of her chair, elbows on her knees, face in her hands. She rubbed her face and sat still for a moment.

What the hell just happened?

It was as if the last hour elapsed within ten minutes. Maybe less. She felt more mentally drained than physically. The worst part was the intense confusion she was experiencing. She imagined this is what it would feel like to be roofied. She needed to lie down.

"Dad, I think I'm going to go take a nap. Are you okay out here without me?"

Alan slowly looked over at his daughter. He nodded his head. He felt unable to form the words to respond to her. Jeanie got up and walked to her tent and without closing the door behind her, crawled to her bed. She didn't bother to remove her dirty clothing or her boots. Dirt and stray pine needles followed her in and trailed across the tent floor. She did not climb into her sleeping bag. She slithered her way on top of the bag and the mattress and almost immediately fell asleep.

III

When Jeanie woke, darkness had settled into the camp. She was still fully clothed and face down on her bed. She rubbed her eyes with loose fists and rolled onto her back before forcing herself into an upright position. Her body was stiff and sore from the deep, motionless sleep of her nap. She flipped the switch on her lantern and looked around the interior of the tent. The small bag she took on their hike earlier was nowhere to be seen. She must have left it outside in her earlier daze.

An abundance of bugs had gained entry to her tent through the door she left hanging open. She let out an annoyed sigh.

Going to have to deal with that later.

On all fours, she crawled from the tent. Once outside, she got slowly to her feet, her body popping and cracking with protest on the way. She immediately noticed the fire was nothing more than a smoldering pit of hot coals. Her father was still sitting in his chair where she left him.

"Dad?" Jeanie's question rose into the open air. She moved slowly toward his chair.

Although he wasn't an elderly man, he wasn't a young buck and when she didn't receive a response, she feared the worst. Had his heart given out? Her own heart began to pound as she inched toward the chair containing her father.

When she reached her own chair, the soft sound of snores

could be heard coming from Alan's mouth. She let out the breath she didn't realize she had been holding the entire time. She nudged her father's shoulder gently with the tips of her fingers.

"Hey, Dad. Wake up." He stirred slightly but still didn't wake. She closed a gentle hand on his shoulder and shook. "Dad!" Jeanie yelled in a sudden panic.

Alan woke with a start and looked around, first to his left and then his right. When his gaze fell on Jeanie, a look of clarity, but also panic and sadness, washed across his face.

"I guess I fell asleep. How long was I out? What time is it?"

"We were both out cold. For exactly how long, I'm not sure. Obviously, at least several hours." Jeanie gestured to the darkness that grew deeper by the minute, hugging them in its cold embrace. "I can't find my pack. What time does your watch say?"

Alan lifted his left arm and pressed the button on the side of his digital wristwatch. The back light came to life, turning Alan's face a bluish white that made him look ill. He peered down at the screen. "Holy shit. It's 8:13. I don't know what time we got back to camp but it couldn't have been later than one or two in the afternoon. We were asleep for at least five hours." He looked up at Jeanie, shocked and scared. His blue eyes were wide, but his brow was furrowed. "Jeanie, what the fuck?"

IV

Jeanie wrapped her catch of the day in foil. She used a stick to move a pile of coals to the side of the fire pit and placed the fish on top to cook. She sat in her chair and let her sight settle on the small fire that occupied the other half of the fire pit. As the flames danced in her eyes, her mind raced with questions and ached with the impossible answers to those questions. Her father sat next to her in silence, and she thought he was likely suffering in the same way she was. There was no logical explanation to what happened to them earlier. What her father didn't know is that something similar had happened to Jeanie before they even left camp.

She thought she remembered seeing something carved on a tree near camp. Did it hold some sort of significance? She couldn't be sure but something in her gut told her it did.

But what does it mean? Was this some kind of supernatural occurrence or were there people somewhere in these woods playing some kind of horrible trick on them? Deep down, she knew there was no way a human being could have done this to them. This wasn't a trick. This was a nightmare.

Jeanie shook her funk for long enough to flip the tin foil pocket containing their dinner. A faint sizzle could be heard from the interior of the shimmering receptacle. Tiny streams of steam escaped from the seam where the foil was folded over onto itself, and Jeanie would be lying to herself if she didn't think the aroma rising with the steam wasn't delicious. Alan shifted in his seat to her left and cleared his throat.

"Smells pretty damn good. I didn't know I was so hungry," he said.

They hadn't spoken for quite some time and the sound of his voice – though it seemed a bit hollow – was welcoming and comforting to her ears.

"Yeah, it does smell good. Should be done pretty soon. It's not very much food, should I boil some water and make something else, too?" Jeanie asked in a flat tone.

"No, I'm hungry but…" Alan's voice trailed off and his brow furrowed deeply. A frustrated sigh escaped his chest, and he shook his head. "Never mind."

Jeanie opened her mouth to speak but the words wouldn't come. She knew exactly how her father was feeling. With the smell of the cooking fish, her hunger was aroused but the anxiety was still ever present. She would eat because her body commanded it, but the amount she would be able to put down was questionable. Her father had not brought up another word about their experience. She hadn't either.

It was a subject she wanted to breech, one she knew they would eventually absolutely have to talk about, but she couldn't find the strength to put it into words yet. As if her brain was intentionally blocking her from saying the words out loud, because that would mean she truly believed the conclusion she had settled upon. They were prey and the hunter was not human. But the hunter was not animal either. She did not believe the whatever-it-was, was from this place. Where it was from, she was not fully certain, but she knew in her heart it was not from this Earth. It was not natural.

10

I

"Honey, why don't you come up to bed?"

Alan opened his eyes slowly. His heart raced. He looked around the room, trying to gain his bearings. When his eyes came into focus, he could see he was in his living room. But he was not in the house he left behind to go camping with his daughter, he was in Jeanie's childhood home.

The television set directly across from him was on. The volume was low and the kind of infomercial that plays late at night was playing on the screen. The comfort of his favorite recliner was unmistakable. He ran his hands along the velvety, burgundy fabric of the puffy arms of the chair. The right arm conveniently contained a hidden compartment underneath that housed various items – magazines, batteries, and the remote when it was not in use. In this case, the remote was laying across his lap.

"Earth to Alan. Hello? Am I invisible over here?" Alan turned his head slowly. Standing between the living room and the kitchen to his left, was his wife.

Alan's heart thundered in his chest.

I'm dreaming.

This can't be real.

None of this exists any more.

She is dead.

The room was silent with the exception of his heartbeat and the television. Some man was peddling what he called a 'miracle' kitchen appliance. His cheesy salesman voice was saying, "*For just four easy payments of $32.95, it could be yours!*"

"Are you really going to just sit there and stare at me like that? What is wrong? You're acting like you've seen a ghost." She raised her eyebrows at him as she spoke.

Cassandra was standing with the full weight of her body on her right leg. Her left hip jutted out and her hand was resting on it. Her head cocked slightly to the side, causing her light brown hair to pool over her right shoulder. She widened her hazel eyes and jutted her head forward slightly, clearly riding on the edge of full-blown annoyance.

Alan slowly opened his mouth and when he spoke, his voice crackled in his throat.

"Sorry—I-I'm just a little confused. I think I'm having a lucid dream or something. You, um." He shook his head and put a closed fist to his mouth before clearing his throat. "You're dead."

Cassandra's head immediately snapped backwards, and laughter glided from her throat, toward the ceiling. "Alan Michael Risley, you have lost every marble in that beautiful head of yours."

She walked over to where Alan was still sitting, now slightly turned in the recliner to face her, and placed one hand gently on his shoulder. Her touch made him jump slightly. He could feel the warmth of her hand through his shirt. He could *feel* her. Maybe this wasn't a dream, after all.

"Alan. I'm not dead. I'm standing right here in front of you. Behold me in all of my pajama clad glory, my dear." She took a step back so he could see her full frame.

Her black silk robe was tied loosely in the front, the hem resting at her mid-thigh, revealing her slender well-toned legs. The top of the robe was open enough to reveal her weathered t-shirt. It had a few splotches of oil paint on the fabric from when she wore it while she finished her last art project. She moved both hands up and down as she turned in a circle, trying to further validate her existence to her husband.

Alan's chest tightened and as he tried to swallow, his sandpaper-dry throat seemed to stick shut. He felt the hot sting of tears fill his eyes. When his throat finally opened, it gave way to a loud sob. His head fell into his hands, and he let his emotions completely take control.

Cassandra rushed from where she was standing to comfort him. She knelt next to the recliner and put both arms firmly around her husband. The chair was still set to recline, and the foot portion of the chair was fully elevated, forcing her to hug him from an awkward side angle. Her chest pressed against his left shoulder, while her hands wrapped around his right.

"Oh, babe. It must have really been a bad dream. A really horrible, bad dream. You really believed I was dead. I'm so sorry. I'm right here. It's okay."

Her eyes were wide with concern and Alan was not surprised to see them brimmed with tears when he lifted his head to face her. She was always the most caring person he had ever known. A true empath. His pain was hers. He also noticed her eyes were more of a blue green today than brown. Her eyes always did that when she was in a good mood.

"Will you please come up to bed? I promise you'll feel better if you do." She gave him a sweet, sideways smile. She wiped the remaining tears from his face, then placed a hand under his chin and kissed his cheek.

"Okay." Alan's voice was gravelly and thick. And when he tried to speak again, his body betrayed him by instead heaving in a large, shaky breath from his crying. He closed his eyes and exhaled slowing. "Just let me check the doors, shut everything down, and get a glass of water. Go on up. I'll be right behind you."

He tried to put on a brave face and forced a weak smile. She planted another kiss on his cheek before heading up the stairs toward their bedroom. Once she was out of sight, Alan took several deep breaths. He pushed the foot of the recliner in with both of his legs and planted his feet on the ground. He turned off the television and leaned forward with his elbows on his knees. He stared at the slightly worn beige carpet between his feet. There were a few speckled stains where he had spilled his morning coffee in the process of sitting down.

I think I'm losing my mind. I've sincerely gone fucking crazy.

He pinched himself firmly on the top of his left thigh through his basketball shorts.

See, that hurt.

You felt that.

Just like you felt her hand on your shoulder and her lips on your cheek.

Snap the hell out of it.

He stood up slowly from his recliner and shook his body trying to relieve himself of the confused, painful feeling that was filling him to the brim, not unlike a dog trying to shake itself dry. He placed both hands on the small of his back and bent backwards. He was rewarded with a few cracks and pops from his spine.

He made his way to the front of the house. He made sure the front door deadbolt was slid into the locked position and checked that the porch light was on. When he was sure the front of the home was properly secured, he shut off the lights in the living room. As he passed the staircase to the second floor, he flipped on the light switch that operated the light in the upstairs hallway. He no longer had to worry about the light waking Jeanie. She was grown and gone now.

He entered the kitchen and passed directly to the rear of the home, where he made sure the sliding glass door was locked. He looked behind the drapes to see the broken broomstick was in position in the track behind the door (you can never be too safe). His bare feet padded across the wooden floor to the cabinet to the left of the black refrigerator. He opened the cabinet with his left hand, covering a large yawn with his right. Sleepily, he grabbed a large plastic cup and filled it with water from the fridge.

He indulged in a few large gulps of the cold liquid before turning the lights off and making his way toward the stream of light provided by the upstairs hallway. He stopped at the bottom of the stairs and gazed up toward the hallway that led to the place his wife was tucked into bed.

My dead wife.

His dead wife who was actually, clearly, very alive.

If her death was in fact a dream, it was a very vivid and detailed one. And it spanned the length of years, instead of mere hours. Alan's skin broke out in goosebumps. The hair on his arms and the back of his neck stood on end.

This feels so real.

Quit dwelling on your nightmare and just go up to bed. Once you're tucked in there, everything will feel better.

Listen to your wife, Alan.

He exhaled a deep breath and climbed the short staircase. There were two small bedrooms that occupied the right side of the hallway. The first was Jeanie's room. The walls within were still painted a soft pink and plastered with posters of bands she loved (and might still love) and pictures of her adventures with her high school friends. A twin-sized bed clad with a white down comforter covered in small pink flowers, a four-drawer dresser, and a small vanity with a mirror also occupied the cozy space.

The second was the guest bedroom. This room had little to no decoration but was equipped with a comfortable queen-sized bed that Cassandra always kept fitted with clean bedding, just in case someone needed it. The small closet doubled as storage for miscellaneous blankets, pillowcases, and board games the family had acquired over the years.

The left side of the hall contained a bathroom (that also used to be 'Jeanie's'). Jeanie had taken any decorative items, as well as her towels when she left for college. A sink occupied the center of the ample counter space. To the left of the sink was the toilet, followed by the standard tub-shower combo. A light tan towel currently hung from the rack parallel from the toilet.

The master suite was located at the very end of the hallway. Alan flipped the switch at the top of the staircase. The faint glow of a sensored night light plugged into the outlet between the bedrooms led his way. The door of the master was cracked, and he could see the unmistakable light of the television flashing behind it. He and Cassandra often fell asleep watching TV. Experts recommended against such habits, but it was one they were never able to break even into their older adult years.

He gently pushed the door open and, as he entered the room, Cassandra greeted him with a warm smile. His heart swelled as she looked up at him through her thick lashes. She was sitting upright in bed with her back against the headboard. The lamp on her nightstand was lit and she had a book in her right hand. The

TV flashed silently in front of her. She had it on most of the time as background visual or audio. It was comforting to her.

Alan returned her smile and closed the bedroom door behind him. He placed his cup of water on his own nightstand before making his way to the bathroom. The bathroom was nice, but modest. It had decent counter space with two sinks (one for him, and one for her), a large soaking bathtub, and a separate shower housed in glass. The toilet was in a small water closet with its own door. The small walk-in closet was just beyond the toilet room.

The tile floor was cold under Alan's feet as he used the toilet. When he'd finished, he washed his hands in the sink designated for him and looked in the mirror. He looked younger than he remembered, but not enough to be alarmed by it. It was the kind of 'younger' a person looks when they've been well rested and they're happy.

The memory of his nightmare was fading quickly.

He climbed into bed next to Cassandra. The familiar cold of his sheets was inviting, and he could feel the warmth radiating from his wife's body to his right. The sheets warmed to his body temperature and the chill left on his feet from the bathroom floor began to lift. He fluffed his pillow a bit before settling down onto his side with his knees slightly tucked, his body facing the direction of his wife.

"Do you want me to turn the volume on? Or the light off? You trying to sleep?" her voice was gentle and warm. It was soothing.

He knew she truly cared what his answer to her questions would be. She *wanted* him to be as comfortable as possible. Alan lifted his head slightly to see his wife. She hadn't looked away from her book as she asked her questions. She sat reading as she waited for his reply.

"No, nope, and not yet. I can read the subtitles. There's something relaxing about it. Keep reading, honey. If I'm tired enough, I'll fall asleep through anything."

She chuckled in agreement but didn't speak. Contentment flowed through Alan as he lay there reading the subtitles for some true crime docuseries about a woman poisoning her husband. It was on *his* bedroom television. *Their* bedroom television. He was home and everything was just as it should be.

Life was *perfect*.

11

I

Jeanie woke to the smell of bacon frying. She could hear the faint sound of birds chirping in the early morning light outside. She stretched her arms and legs out as far as she could and let out a small groan. She lay still with her eyes closed and breathed deeply.

How is Dad cooking bacon right now? We're in the middle of the fucking forest.

She slowly opened her eyes and was immediately hit with a wave of utter confusion. Not a wave, a tsunami. She found herself cradled in a familiar bed but one she hadn't slept in for *years*. She was wrapped in a white down comforter. It had small pink flowers scattered over the surface. It was housed in the bedroom she lived in when she graduated high school, before she left for college. The soft glow of the pink walls was only broken by the few band posters tacked to the walls (the same posters also had a few lip gloss stains, where she had kissed the face of the band member she thought was the hottest).

"Knock, knock. You awake in there?" The woman's voice was accompanied by a gentle rapping of knuckles on the exterior of the bedroom door.

Jeanie sat bolt upright in her bed. She knew that voice. It was a voice she was sure she would never hear again, not in person at least. Her alarm increased as the worn brass knob on the door turned, and the door began to swing into the bedroom. The woman who entered the room was naturally beautiful. Her almond brown hair cascaded down to her shoulders and her hazel eyes were bright and cheerful. Her face was void of makeup, but her skin still seemed to emit a dewy glow. She wore a pair of faded jeans and an old t-shirt that had several spots of paint on the front.

Despite her dressed down look, her bare feet showed toes that were painted perfectly in a shade of apple red. The nails on her hands were perfectly manicured in the matching color. She stood and smiled at Jeanie for a moment before she turned into a look of awkward confusion.

"Look, I know you haven't been back to visit for a while, but I know I haven't aged that much. Have I?" She paused a moment, giving a sarcastic smile and waiting for Jeanie's reply. "Seriously. Why the hell are you looking at me like that?"

The woman's face fell slightly, going from joking and happy, to mildly concerned.

In Jeanie's frozen state, she hadn't noticed that her mouth had fallen open slightly. Her eyes were wide and were beginning to dry out from the lack of blinking.

Don't panic, don't panic, don't panic.

It's just a dream.

"Mom?" Jeanie finally let the words pass over her dry lips.

"That would be me. Since the day you were born. You're being *really* fucking weird." Cassandra gave a sideways smile and a chuckle that came out as more of a chuff than a laugh. "Hopefully you haven't started doing drugs or anything crazy like that. Come downstairs, breakfast will be ready any minute."

As the last line floated through the air toward Jeanie, the door was already closing behind her mother. Jeanie's heart hammered in her chest. Her mother was dead. She had cancer. Terminal. There was a funeral. There were years of grieving and pain.

She was suddenly too hot and threw the blanket from her body. She swung her legs over the side of the twin-size bed and rested her feet firmly on the floor. Nausea began to overwhelm her, and she bent her body in half and placed her head between her knees. She took several deep breaths and when she was sure she wasn't going to lose the contents of her stomach, she slowly rose to a normal seated position again.

Okay, Jeanie.

This is just a dream, so roll with it.

Just roll with it.

She stood slowly and her knees wobbled slightly. She made sure she wasn't going to fall before she worked her way forward. Her hand approached the doorknob with caution, like she was checking to make sure the hallway wasn't somehow ablaze. Her movements were slow motion and she felt like she was trying to move under water.

She managed to make her way across the hall into the bathroom. Morning light filtered through the skylight, painting the bathroom in a soft blue glow. She couldn't believe how real everything felt. She could feel the cold of the toilet seat on the back of her thighs as she sat down and the water running over her hands after she was finished.

Was she currently in a dream or was what she considered reality the dream?

Did I have a fucking psychotic break?

Fall into a coma?

Both?

She would accept either option over her mother really being dead.

Please be a coma. Please be a coma.

As she repeated her silent prayer over in her mind, she made her way down the stairs. Her movements were becoming more fluid, and her pace was closer to normal. When she landed at the bottom of the staircase, she took a left and rounded the corner into the kitchen. Her eyes welled with tears of joy and a warmth crept from the center of her chest and worked its way into her limbs.

The sight of her parents standing side by side, cooking a meal was almost more than she could handle. She didn't know this amount of joy was possible to feel all at once. She stared at their backs, silently watching them for a moment. The conversation was an inaudible murmur, but her father's laugh rose and filled the room like a warm spring breeze. He gently bumped her mother with his hip, and she returned his laugh with a sweet giggle.

Jeanie cleared her throat and captured the attention of her parents. They both glanced over a shoulder to peek at their grown daughter. Her mother's smile filled her to the brim with warmth and comfort. She made a hand gesture toward the kitchen table that was nestled in the dining nook.

"Sit down, sweetheart. This will all be ready in just a sec."

Jeanie took a seat in 'her spot.' She sat in that spot for every meal as a child. Her father always sat at the head of the table to the left of her and her mother to his left, directly across from her. The table was already set with three plates, napkins, silverware, butter, and syrup for pancakes. A plate heaped full of bacon also rested in the middle of the table. Jeanie absently plucked a piece from the stack and took a bite. It was just the way she liked it; crispy but still with a nice chew to it. She closed her eyes while she chewed.

The gentle clink of a ceramic plate hitting the table forced her eyes open again. Her father was placing a plate piled high with fresh pancakes in the center of the table. Her mother was close behind with a platter of scrambled eggs in one hand, and hashbrowns in the other.

"Dig in, kiddo!" Her mother smiled at her as she set the food onto the table and took her seat.

"Anybody need ketchup or hot sauce while I'm up?" Alan pulled tongs and large serving spoons from the drawer near the stove.

"Um, some hot sauce would be great. Thanks, Dad." Her own voice sounded alien and unfamiliar to her. It reminded her of when you watch a video of yourself and realize that's the way your voice sounds to rest of the world. She cleared her throat and tried again.

"Thanks for making breakfast. This looks delicious. It's clear that Mom was the one who cooked the bacon." Her voice was her own again. Her mother shot her a wink from across the table, as Alan set an assortment of hot sauces onto the table in front of her.

Jeanie picked up her fork and stabbed a pancake. She shook it from her fork onto the center of her plate. The appearance of the morning time feast in front of her made her realize that she wasn't just hungry, she was ravenous. And her parents had made her all-time, absolute favorite meal. She paired her pancake with a heaped portion of hashbrowns, a generous portion of scrambled eggs, and four pieces of bacon. She picked up the bottle of green Tabasco (her favorite) and shook it over her hashbrowns. Her mouth watered as the droplets of transparent green liquid splashed over the surface of the golden-brown potatoes.

She ate the hashbrowns and eggs first because she didn't want to get syrup mixed in with the items that contained hot sauce. Once she was done, she spread warm butter over the surface of each pancake on her plate and drizzled a healthy amount of syrup over the top of them.

"Plenty more where that came from, kiddo. Have seconds if you feel like it. We haven't had a family feast in too long." Cassandra was filling her own plate as she spoke to her daughter.

II

Jeanie ate until she felt it was impossible to swallow another bite. Each morsel of food was as delicious as the last. Her exciting morning was catching up with her and she let out a yawn. Her full stomach and her childhood home provided the comfort she needed.

"I think I'm going to go take a nap. I guess I didn't sleep very well last night," Jeanie addressed her parents as she carried her plate to the kitchen. Her mother met her halfway to the sink and grabbed the plate from her hands.

"Don't worry about your plate. You got in late last night and traveling will take it out of anyone. Go get some rest. We'll see you in a bit."

"Thanks. I'll be back down in a little while."

Jeanie's heart soared as she made her way upstairs to her bedroom. She felt as if she was floating up the staircase. Where her room was confusing and frightening earlier, it was now radiating warmth and comfort. She closed the door softly behind herself and climbed into bed. She closed her eyes and pulled the covers up to her chin, a joyful smile on her lips. She took a deep breath and was dead asleep before she was finished exhaling.

12

I

Jeanie and her father ate in silence. She only ate because she knew she needed to. It was a robotic motion from plate to mouth as she stared blankly off into the depths of the fire in front of her. She tasted nothing. Her mind was far off. She thought only of the dream she had woken from. It felt so real. Her senses were on fire the entire time. She could taste the breakfast her parents cooked. She could feel her blanket as she was falling asleep in her bed.

She would give anything to go back to that moment. To feel that level of joy again. Jeanie's concentration was broken by the sound of twigs breaking in the distance. Her head snapped upward. The only areas of the camp that were not hidden under the shroud of darkness were those that were grazed by the soft glow emitted from the crackling fire in front of her.

She strained her eyes to try to see into the darkness of the forest in the direction she heard the snap come from. More twigs snapped in the darkness and a shadowy figure moved in the direction of the camp, slowly and steadily making its way closer. Jeanie's heart pounded in her chest so hard she could feel it pumping in her ears. She slowly stood up from her chair. Her legs trembled and her palms burst into perspiration.

As the figure broke into the dim circle of light of the campfire, Jeanie charged. Her right fist connected with the figure, and she *knew* she wasn't dreaming. She cried out like a warrior heading into battle and began whaling on the figure with both of her fists, prepared to fight, even if she was going to die. Hot tears streamed down her cheeks.

II

"Jeanie! Whoa, Jeanie! Calm down, it's just me! It's Dad!" Alan held up his hands to defend himself. Between the blows he struggled to yell out at this daughter. "Stop that! God damn it, Jeanie, I said stop!"

He felt his frustration and rage boil over and grabbed her by the shoulders. He shook her hard twice, her head snapping back and forth in the opposite direction of her body like a rag doll. He quickly let her go and put his arms up to cover his face. He was ashamed of his behavior. He could not ignore the immensity of his fear.

What was going on?

Why was she attacking him?

As he retreated into his thoughts, he waited for the next fist to come crashing down, but it never came.

Alan eased his defensive position and found Jeanie crumpled on the ground. Again, he thought she resembled a rag doll. One that had been discarded carelessly onto the floor by a child who had found something more interesting to play with. He cautiously moved forward and knelt beside her.

"Jeanie." He paused for a few seconds, waiting for a response.

"Jeanie Bean." He slowly reached out and placed his hand on her back.

She jumped slightly at his touch but then relaxed. She slowly rolled over and turned her face up toward her father's. The places where her tears had made their way down her cheeks were now covered with mud. Stray pine needles and debris from the forest floor clung to her hair.

"I'm so sorry, Dad. I don't know what's wrong with me. I didn't even know you had left camp. I thought you were sitting there next to me." She spoke quickly, her words tumbling out one after another.

She was crying again. She sat up and wiped the fresh tears from her face with the back of her hand.

"I thought you were..." Her voice cracked slightly. Her words broke off sharply as they tried to escape from her mouth. "I thought something was coming to..." Her words caught in her throat again. Frustration filled her suddenly and her voice rose to almost a yell. "I thought someone, something, was coming to kill us!"

Jeanie's breath was uneven and coming to her in ragged gasps. Tears now flowed freely down her face and onto her neck. She had her right hand flat on her chest and her blue eyes were wide and wild. Alan sat quietly staring at her, unsure how to comfort her. They sat together on the damp forest floor, eyes locked in shock and bewilderment. The distant flickering light of the slowly dying fire danced across their faces.

"I know you're upset, Jeanie, I am too, but we really need to make sure that fire stays burning." After about thirty seconds, Alan stood and held his hand out to Jeanie. She took his hand and he helped hoist her to her unsteady feet. He locked his arm with hers to help steady her as she walked. He helped lower her into her chair by the fire.

He made his way to the edge of the camp site, lifted the tarp, and unveiled the stash of firewood he had collected the day before. He quickly grabbed several large logs from the pile, chucking each log toward the fire as he went. He replaced the tarp and retrieved the logs he had tossed. While he worked to collect firewood, the flames worked on burning out. As the light grew dimmer, Alan's heartbeat grew faster. He used his hatchet and split two of the logs into smaller pieces but, in his panic, he did not bother wasting time splitting the other logs. He was moving quickly now, not quite running (more of a power walk), carrying as much wood as his arms could carry.

He was relieved to see a small flame still dancing in the embers. He wiped a drip of sweat from his brow with the back of his hand and carefully placed the split wood in a cone shape in the middle of the pit. A few nervous moments passed before the wood caught with a *whoosh*. Relief washed over Alan. He was not satisfied with the size of the fire yet but was happy it took so easily. It hadn't gone out, and that was the most important thing.

He glanced up at Jeanie. She retained her zombie-like trance, sitting perfectly still, staring into the newly lit flames.

"Jeanie," he said calmly.

She made no indication that she heard her father's voice. He knelt in front of her, so they were face to face, and gently placed a finger under her chin, moving her face in his direction. When her eyes landed on his, he raised his eyebrows and made his I'm-dead-fucking-serious face. She had only seen it a few times in her life. It seemed to grab her attention properly.

"Jeanie, I need you to snap out of it and listen to me right now. Are you hearing me?" Jeanie gently nodded her head in acknowledgement.

"I'm going to make this fire as big and as bright as I possibly can right now, and I'm going to keep it that way for the rest of the night. Before your incident, I was out in the woods because I needed to use the bathroom. I finished my business as quickly as I could because as soon as I left camp, something felt wrong."

Alan paused and waited for Jeanie's nod, letting him know she was still with him, that she was listening.

"I brushed it off as just being paranoid because I'm in the middle of nowhere, in the very dark forest, alone. But on my way back…" He broke off and shook his head slightly.

Jeanie pushed her head forward slightly and widened her eyes, impatiently waiting for her father to continue.

"On my way back, I heard branches snapping. I got frightened but didn't run, thinking it could be a mountain lion or something that would take me down immediately if I took off. I felt like I was being followed. So, I turned around. And I saw someone. No, not quite human… some*thing*."

"Dad, what do you mean?" Jeanie's voice was urgent and shaky.

Alan's eyes drifted toward the forest. It was Jeanie who pulled him back to reality this time.

"Dad!" Jeanie's eyes brimmed with tears. She placed her hands on her dad's shoulders and gently shook him. Her voice was thin and pleading. "What did you see?"

Without taking his eyes off the forest, Alan shook his head slowly.

"I don't know." He slowly turned his head back toward Jeanie, as if he forcibly had to rip his attention away from the blackness beyond. "But whatever it is, I know it's out there. And it's hunting us. But first it's toying with us. Like a cat plays with a mouse before it finally kills and eats it."

They both stared at each other, fear filling their eyes.

13

I

Alan fed the fire until it was what he would have considered to be a certified bonfire. The heat it radiated was immense and he and Jeanie both had to remove their jackets after a while. But the bright flames made them both feel a bit safer, and that was all that mattered. He would need to go collect more wood tomorrow, once the sun was up.

"I think whatever is out there can get in our head. I think it's been fucking with us since the moment we got here." Jeanie's voice was no longer weak. She sounded scared. But she also sounded damn angry.

Alan looked over at his daughter and took a moment to digest her words. He agreed. He also knew that if that was the case (and he was pretty sure it was) they would need a serious game plan. He looked over at his daughter. She was searching his eyes for confirmation, for an answer.

"Yeah, I think you're right, kiddo." Alan slowly nodded. "I think first things first, we need to tell each other everything we think has happened to us since we got here. Every detail. I think it'll help us better understand what's happening to us." Alan paused and sighed heavily. He couldn't believe he was about to say what he was thinking out loud. "I think it'll help us *survive*."

Jeanie stood from her chair and crossed her arms in front of her chest. She surveyed the area briefly. "I'll get the whiskey."

Before Alan could speak again, Jeanie was headed to her tent. She was taking longer than Alan expected but he could see her tent rustling as she dug through her bag, so he tried not to let himself worry. When she returned, whiskey in hand, she was also in her comfortable nighttime clothing (which consisted of sweatpants and a pull over sweatshirt). She sat down and took a long pull from the bottle of whiskey.

Alan reached his hand out across the small gap between their chairs. Jeanie picked up on his please-pass-the-bottle cue and handed it over. Alan took a drink and handed it back. He wanted to feel the comfort of the alcohol, but thought it was wise for him to stay mostly sober. He didn't plan on sleeping much tonight.

"I'm going to go change too. Take it easy on that bottle. I don't want you too fuzzy. This shit isn't a joke, Jeanie." His tone was slightly irritated. He tossed another log into the pit and to feed the hungry flames.

"I know it's not a joke. I'm just scared. You have no idea how it felt, how it feels. Dad…" She paused and took another small sip. "I could have fucking killed you. If I had chosen to get some kind of weapon instead of using my hands – I didn't have any clue that it was you I was attacking. And that was *before* I had even fully come to the conclusion that there is something out there that wants us dead."

Tears were running down her face again. She wiped them away with a few quick swipes. She made a shooing gesture with her hands.

"Go change your clothes. But please hurry. I don't want to be out here alone." Her words were forced through shaking vocal cords.

Alan jogged back to his tent and tore the zipper open as fast as he could. He ducked through the opening and stumbled over the flap of the half-zipped doorway. He tore through his bag and yanked out his sweatpants and a t-shirt, not bothering to try to keep things organized or neat. He undressed as quickly as humanly possible. When his stubborn pants caught on his legs, he plopped onto his back in frustration and kicked his legs until they were finally free. He pulled his comfortable clothes on in a more graceful process than the undressing. He was still tugging his sweatshirt the rest of the way on as he was moved out the door, back to his daughter. She was scared and in danger, and he would stop at nothing to protect his little girl in a way he wasn't able to protect her mother.

II

"Did you dream about Mom when you were asleep after the lake?" Jeanie's voice seemed to have taken on a permanent watery quality.

Alan nodded solemnly.

"I did. But that's not where we need to start." He looked up at Jeanie.

She had gotten warm enough, either from the fire or the booze, to take her sweatshirt off and was now in a plain gray t-shirt.

"When was the first time you thought something might be a bit... odd?" He paused briefly before speaking the last word, seeming to search for the most fitting word to describe what he was trying to say.

Jeanie stayed silent a few minutes, but Alan didn't pressure her. She was clearly playing the motions of the last two days over in her head. Searching for the exact moment. Finally, she broke her silence.

"If I really think about it and I'm honest with myself, I think it was the moment I stepped foot onto this island. The moment I left that dock. I wanted so badly for it to feel exciting and fun, but there was this sense of fear and danger in the back of my mind almost immediately. I thought it was just Kai getting to me. He told me the native people of this island believe there is something horrible in these woods." Her bottom lip began to quiver again, and she covered her face with her hands. "Dad, I'm so sorry. I should have never brought us here. I should have listened."

She had quit bothering to wipe her tears. They were nearly constant now. Alan processed the information he had just received. Now he understood what was happening on the boat, why Kai held Jeanie back to speak with her. Kai was warning her, begging her, not to come to this part of the island. Alan gave a contemplative nod.

"Okay, so we know that Kai warned you about his place. Did he give you any details about why the locals find it so dangerous? Did he give you any specific details about what we would be up against?" Alan was now deeply invested in what was being said. He was leaning forward in his chair with his elbows on his knees, looking intently at Jeanie.

She furrowed her brow and shook her head, clearly disappointed in herself.

"No. I didn't want to know. I was so damn dead set on this trip, so set in my ways, I basically told him to fuck off. In a nice way, of course. I didn't want to hear it because I didn't want it to taint the vision I had for this place. And so obviously, I didn't ask any questions either. I fucked us. I'm so sorry, Dad."

"No more saying sorry." Alan gave his daughter what he hoped was a reassuring look. "This is not your fault. We are not fucked. We are going to get out of this. We are smart and we are tough. I think it's safe to say we both had a sense of immediate danger. And we both chose to block it out. I thought I noticed some things moved around camp this morning. Did you notice anything like that?"

Jeanie's eyes lit up.

"Yes! I thought I was losing my mind!" She was now standing, looking over their campsite.

"The chairs were moved. They were picked up and put away."

Alan watched cold fear wash over his daughter's face.

"Dad." She looked up at him. "Things inside my tent were moved. My lantern. I know it was right next to my bed because I turned it off from inside my bag. When I woke up this morning, it was by the door. I thought I had just gotten too drunk somehow and forgotten I moved it in the middle of the night."

She was pacing between her chair and her father's, visibly shaken by her recent realization.

"I feel sick. Whoever, whatever the fuck that thing is, was that close to me while I was sleeping." Her voice was shaking again, she was talking with her hands in big, animated gestures.

"We don't sleep alone any more. You'll move into my tent. If we don't have to, we don't sleep at the same time. Actually…" Alan paused and gave his daughter a deeply serious look. "I think it's best we don't go anywhere alone any more. Not just at night, during the day too."

"I'm completely on board with that." Jeanie stopped pacing to retrieve the whiskey from the ground beside her chair. She took a small swallow. "God, this is so fucked up. I can't believe this shit is happening."

"Well, kiddo, believe it or not, it is happening. But we will always be on guard now. Always prepared. That's why I need you

131

to quit with that stuff." He pointed at the bottle. "You've had enough for tonight."

"Okay, you're probably right." Jeanie obliged her father and put the bottle back down. The bottle sat on a small rock and fell over with a small clink as it hit the gravel. Without noticing or caring, she continued to pace between the chairs, her hands on her hips.

"This morning I think I remember something else weird but it's fuzzy, like it might have happened to me in a dream," she said.

Alan looked at his daughter expectedly. "Well, what the hell was it?"

Jeanie still didn't respond immediately. She stopped in front of her dad with a distant look on her face.

"I think before we went down to the lake, I found a weird symbol carved into one of the trees on the outskirts of camp. I touched it and it made me feel…" She shook her head as if to help clear the fog in her memory. "It made me feel like I was far away from myself. Like I was completely out of it. As soon as I quit touching it and walked away, everything cleared up again. There might have been more to the experience, I just can't remember."

"Where was the tree?"

Jeanie pointed to the far edge of the site, toward the hiking trail. Though their fire was large, the light it put out couldn't penetrate the darkness of the area she pointed to. Alan gazed in the direction his daughter pointed for a moment.

"I think we should check it out, but I think we should wait until morning. If this thing has been getting inside our heads, I have a feeling it's always listening. Always watching." Alan's voice began to shrink as he finished his statement. A cold shiver ran through him. Goosebumps flashed across his body. The hair on his arms and the back of his neck stood on end. "I've also considered there may be more than one. It could be *they*. In fact, I think that's the most likely scenario."

Jeanie gave her father a blank expression, and then nodded slowly. "I don't see how there could only be one. But I also don't know what the hell it is. If the little information Kai provided me is true, it has been here a *very* long time."

"So basically, we know something is out there. It is extremely old, equally intelligent, and has supernatural abilities that it uses to mess with us – to hunt us." Alan threw his hands up in frustration and let them fall back into his lap. "We don't know shit about this thing." He brought his hands back up to his face and rubbed his temples gently.

The fire had burned itself back to a level that didn't resemble a deep woods frat party. Alan let out an exhausted sigh as he made his way over to the wood pile. Jeanie continued her pacing while Alan aggressively chopped wood. Once he had enough to fill both arms to their maximum capacity, Alan waddled his way back toward the fire, stretching to see over the stack of wood in his arms. He plopped them all down in front of his chair, breaking Jeanie's concentration and making her jump slightly. He threw four new pieces of wood on the pile and brought it back to a higher glow.

"I know you want to sleep in shifts, but I think we both need to try to get as much sleep as we can." Jeanie's voice made Alan jump. Alan looked up at his daughter. Her expression was determined. "We need our wits, and we need our strength. We have two more nights and two more days to survive out here. And the last day, we have to get back to the beach. We have to go through the damn forest."

"We need a plan," Alan said.

"I think you're right about sleeping in one tent. Or at least trying to sleep. If anything crazy happens tonight, tomorrow night we will sleep in shifts. We need to make sure we each always have some sort of weapon. I have a decent knife. You have your saw and a hatchet."

"I agree. I also think we don't ever leave without the other. If you go, I go. And vice versa," Alan said.

Jeanie nodded in agreement.

"Our best course of action is to just face this bastard head on. If it gets aggressive, so do we. If not, we hunker down and wait it out. Day after tomorrow we pack up as fast as we possibly can, and we damn near run to that beach. It doesn't matter how hurt or exhausted we are when we get there, as long as we're alive."

"That's all we can really do at this point." Alan picked up the bottle of whiskey from the ground and looked it over for a moment. He took a small sip. "I'm going to make this fire a bit bigger and then I say we just try to get some sleep. Even if we don't sleep the whole night, you're right, sleep deprivation makes the situation that much more dangerous."

Alan threw the remaining firewood into the fire. He began to walk back toward Jeanie's tent. "Come on, kid, let's grab your sleeping bag, pack, lantern – whatever else you might need. Rule number one, if you go, I go."

III

After they hauled Jeanie's items to Alan's tent and got everything settled, they both zipped into their bags with the lantern in between them.

"Should we open the door? So we can see if anything is out there?"

Alan shook his head in response. "No, kiddo. If there's something out there, we won't know anyway if we're sleeping. Hell, we might not know if we're awake. But what we're going to do, is sleep."

Jeanie tightened the grip on her knife. She wouldn't be doing anything without it now.

"Do you have a weapon with you?" she asked her dad, a bit of panic in her voice.

Alan picked up his small hatchet and waved it side to side before laying back down on the other side of his sleeping bag.

"Okay. Goodnight, Dad." She still sounded uneasy.

"Goodnight, Jeanie Bean." Alan switched the knob on the lantern to the off position.

"Wait!" Jeanie's voice was urgent. "Can we sleep with the lantern on low please?"

Alan couldn't help but think of the little girl he tucked into bed all those years ago. The girl who requested the night light in the hallway. He couldn't help but smile at the memory.

"Sure thing." He leaned over and turned the knob to low. "Get some sleep." He did his best to sound reassuring, but he wasn't sure if he pulled it off.

Jeanie let out a small yawn and rolled over. With her back now to Alan, he stared at the ceiling of his tent, wondering if he would take his own advice and sleep. Would it even be possible? He closed his eyes and tried to focus on his breathing. To his surprise, he thought he could hear gentle snores coming from Jeanie's side of the tent. That whiskey must have helped after all. And that was the last thought Alan had before he was asleep, too.

14

I

The sound of birds loudly chirping woke Alan. He cracked his eyes slowly, blinking against the sharp brightness that filled the bedroom. He rolled over and looked at the clock on the nightstand next to his bed. 8:43 a.m. shone back at him in bright red, block numbers. The sound of the door opening made him open his eyes fully and begin to sit up.

"I was wondering if you were ever going to get up. You're very late for work, mister." Cassandra entered the room carrying a mug in each hand. From the smell, Alan assumed both contained freshly brewed coffee. She was still wearing her robe. She sat on the edge of the bed beside him. "Made you some coffee. Want it?"

Alan cleared his throat and nodded.

"Yes, it smells wonderful. Thank you, sweetie."

He sat up fully in the bed and she handed him one of the steaming mugs. He leaned in as she did and gave her a kiss on the cheek. Warm spread through his body and he couldn't help but feel like the luckiest man on the planet. His concentration was broken when he noticed Cassandra giving him a suspicious look. She cleared her throat loudly at him. Had he forgotten something important?

"What?" He gave his wife a blank but nervous face.

"Are you going to work today? Or did you plan a day off and

forget to tell me about it?"

"Oh shit, what day is it?" Alan set his mug down on his nightstand and began searching the bed for his cell phone.

"It's Thursday."

"Uh, well, huh." He gave up his search for his phone and looked back toward his wife. "I guess I thought it was the weekend." He gave one more distracted look around the bed, hoping to catch a glimpse of his phone.

Cassandra placed her palm on Alan's forehead with a worried look on her face. "Are you feeling all right?"

"Yeah, I'm fine. I don't know. I was just having a really strange dream, I think. Or maybe some kind of nightmare." Before he could continue, Cassandra shushed him by placing her pointer finger on his lips. A smile spread slowly across her face.

"What if…" She drew the sound of the f out and then paused for a moment. A contemplative, playful expression was present on her face. "What if you pretended to not be feeling well? And stayed home with me today? Just the two of us. We could stay in our pajamas, eat junk food, and watch movies all day." She grabbed Alan by both hands and made her best please face, puppy dog eyes and all.

Alan laughed gently. "Fine. Twist my arm why don't you?" He shot her a quick wink. "But that means you have to help me find my damn cell phone so I can call the boss. I've somehow lost it in my sleep."

He tossed the down comforter to one side, and then the other.

"Oh, don't bother!" She wagged a hand at Alan. "You don't need it for our day in anyway. Here, just use mine really quick." She pulled her phone from the pocket of her robe and plopped it on the bed in front of him.

Weird.

She would never insist I don't have my phone. And she would never carry hers around with her, especially in her robe pocket. He shook his head. Maybe I'm just letting that dream get to me more than I thought.

Alan grabbed the phone and dialed the number for the office attached to the door shop where he worked. He was thankful it went to voicemail when he was transferred to his manager's line. He didn't want to have to answer the barrage of questions his employer would surely have for him (Alan never called off work, even if he was sick). He knew without doubt he would have to convince everyone that he was not dying, he just simply felt under the weather and wanted the day to get rest and feel better.

He handed Cassandra her phone and she placed it back in her robe pocket. "Better keep it on me unless the boss decides to call you back." She leaned forward and gave Alan a gentle kiss on the forehead. "I'm so happy you decided to stay home with me! What should we watch?"

Alan gave his wife a small, boyish grin. "Harry Potter marathon?"

Cassandra lit up and threw herself into Alan's arms. "Yes!" she squealed with excitement. "You grab the necessary blankets and pillows from up here, and I'll start a batch of chocolate chip pancakes."

Cassandra practically flew from the bedroom. Alan stood up and stretched his arms over his head with a loud yawn. He took a drink of his coffee and made his way into the bathroom. After he took care of his morning business with the toilet, he washed his hands and brushed his teeth. As he was brushing, he glanced into the mirror.

His reflection made him stop brushing. He bent over and gently spit the toothpaste from his mouth. Not bothering to rinse his toothbrush, he set it on the counter next to the sink. He slowly raised his head and stared back at himself in the mirror. He looked good, great even. His hair was fuller than he remembered and had a bit of a shine to it. His skin looked younger and supple, with very few wrinkles at all. He was radiant.

He shrugged and made his way back into the bedroom to collect the items Cassandra had requested from their bed. He cautiously walked down the stairs, arms full of pillows and blankets, careful not to go tumbling headfirst down to the bottom. Something about carrying so much at once made him feel a familiar tingle in the back of his brain, like it wanted him to remember something. He suddenly felt dizzy and a bit nauseous.

Maybe I really did need to take a sick day.

"You made it! I was wondering what was taking you so long." Cassandra was standing at the stove, flipping a large pancake in a pan. "These are almost done. Is there anything else you wanted? Eggs? Bacon?" She turned around to look at him, spatula in hand. She gave him a small smirk.

"Do we have whipped cream?" Alan asked.

"We sure do. Two cans I think."

"Then just the pancakes and some coffee for me. You know chocolate chip pancakes with whipped cream is one of my biggest guilty pleasures." He smiled at her before walking to the adjoining living room and piling the couch high with the contents he brought down from the bedroom.

"One or two pancakes?" Cassandra called over her shoulder at him as she removed a completed pancake from the pan onto a plate.

Alan contemplated this for a moment.

What the hell, might as well make the best of the day.

"Two please!" As he called back to his wife in the kitchen, he could hear the sizzle of fresh batter hitting the pan. He inhaled deeply. His stomach growled fiercely. It smelled amazing. He couldn't remember the last time he had eaten a chocolate chip pancake.

While he was waiting for Cassandra to finish up in the kitchen, he stood in front of the bookcase on the far side of the living room which held a decent sized DVD collection (it even had some VHS tapes, though he wasn't sure they had a VCR any more). He hummed to himself while he scanned the rows of movies, searching for the collection he had agreed to watch.

"Aha, found you," he whispered to himself.

All eight movies were together, neatly in a row on the same shelf. He carefully slid The Sorcerer's Stone out of line with his pointer finger. He was placing the disk in the DVD player just as Cassandra was arriving with a tray piled with two plates, two hot mugs of fresh coffee (black for him, vanilla creamer for her), and a can of whipped cream.

Alan grabbed the proper remotes from the coffee table. He grabbed the mugs of coffee from the tray and placed them on the table (on coasters, of course, since Cassandra was present) and sat next to Cassandra on the couch. They both sat cross-legged, with the tray in between them. He topped his stack of pancakes with a generous helping of whipped cream and pressed play.

He was so content. He couldn't even attempt to describe how warm he was feeling if someone were to ask him. The opening scene of the movie started, and he closed his eyes as he chewed a mouthful of chocolate chip pancake and whipped cream. He inhaled through his nose, a faint smile gracing his lips. These were the best pancakes he had ever eaten.

Just as he was at the peak of his enjoyment, he suddenly felt a low rumble coming up from the ground and reverberating through the couch. His eyes snapped open. The power in the house cut off and what was once a sunny morning, seemed to have turned dark and gray in the very short time he had spent with his eyes closed.

He turned to Cassandra, but she was gone. The contents of her plate were spilled across the couch and floor. Sticky footprints made their way out of the living room and into the kitchen. Alan picked up his plate from his lap and planted his feet on the floor in front of the couch. As he was placing his plate onto the coffee table, movement caught his eye. The plate was now a solid moving mass of pancake mush and maggots. He let out a small yell and dropped the plate just short of the table.

He suddenly felt as if his insides were crawling and ran toward the hall bathroom. He tripped over a tangle of his own feet and fell short of the bathroom. He lost the contents of his stomach in the hallway just outside the doorway. When he was finished, he pushed himself back up to his feet. The ground shook with more ferocity and he had to use the wall to brace himself. Loud cracking could be heard from outside as concrete, and asphalt began to break apart and separate. He looked around with wide, wild eyes as knick-knacks and photos began falling from shelves. A large crack shot across the ceiling of the living room.

We live in Colorado. There aren't earthquakes here.

An earsplitting booming made him lose his balance and fall to the floor. He covered his ears as a second boom sounded.

What the fuck is going on?

"Cassandra! Cassandra!" He had to shout so loudly it made his throat sore.

He pushed himself back onto his feet as he screamed for his wife. Every footstep he tried to take was unsuccessful and he was knocked forcefully back down to the floor. His core filled with nausea and fear. Tears streamed freely down his cheeks and his eyes stung as debris and dust fell around him.

15

I

Jeanie stretched her arms high above her head, forcing her feet in the opposite direction and arching her back slightly. She couldn't remember the last time she had taken such a wonderful nap. She slept soundly and she felt incredibly rested. She actually couldn't remember the last time she had woken up without hearing the obnoxious tone of her alarm blaring from her cell phone.

She stared up at the light pink ceiling of her childhood bedroom and let out a deep sigh. She smiled slightly. The pure relaxation that filled her body began to give way to her emotions. Joy radiated from her center. She compared this feeling to how you feel when you find out the boy you have a crush on likes you back when you're in high school. She was practically giddy. Her stomach fluttered. Not a care in the world.

Jeanie rolled onto her side and plunged her hand beneath her pillow. The cool that resided there greeted her skin as she searched aimlessly for her cell phone. She pulled it out and hit the side button to check the time. The screen didn't obey her command. She impatiently pressed the button a few more times.

Damn, I let it die.

In any other situation, Jeanie would have placed more importance on finding her phone charger and plugging it in. But in this moment, here and now, she couldn't have cared less. Honestly, she wasn't even sure where her bag or any of her stuff was. She got to her feet and plopped the lifeless cell phone onto the now empty bed. Bending forward, she flipped her long blonde hair over her head and let it dangle as she wrangled it all into a messy ponytail. Before standing up, she straightened the pant leg of her sweatpants.

She made her way across the hall into the bathroom. When she was finished, she stopped in the hall briefly to listen for her parents before heading downstairs but was received by dead silence.

I wonder if they decided to take a little nap too.

Oh God, I hope that's what they're doing. Please don't let me walk in on something I don't want to see.

Jeanie made the decision to descend the stairs in the loudest way she possibly could. Her every footfall was exaggerated and close to a stomp. She walked through the kitchen and into the living room, but the main level was empty. She retrieved a glass from the far kitchen cabinet and poured herself a glass of water. As she sipped the cold liquid, she let her mind wander through memories of her childhood spent here. Spaghetti dinner nights, birthday parties, her first love, prom, her first break up.

Movement from the backyard caught her eye through the sliding glass door. She set the glass down with a gentle clink and went to investigate. She slid the door cautiously, only opening it about a foot. She poked her head out and looked right and left. That's where she found her parents. Her mother was lounging in a hammock, reading a beat-up copy of a novel she couldn't quite make out the name on.

Her father's shadow must have been what caught her attention. He was lovingly tending to his small vegetable garden. Meticulously pulling weeds, watering, and harvesting what appeared to be very large zucchinis. He looked over his shoulder and gave a surprised, but excited smile and wave in her direction. She returned his smile and forced the door the rest of the way open.

She stepped out with her bare feet. The warmth from the concrete on the soles of her feet brought back more memories. Summer breaks from school spent back here – eating ice cream, water balloon fights, and practicing her cartwheels in the grass while her parents sipped glasses of wine or beer. She must have been letting her mind drift too far. One minute she was sliding the door closed behind her, the next she was seeing her father's worried face running toward her. She felt herself falling and knew she must have completely missed the stairs and stepped directly off the side of the patio.

Darkness.

II

Jeanie's eyes shot open in alarm. The sun shining through her father's bright orange tent gave everything inside a sickly glow. Normally, she kind of liked the odd light it produced, but today it made her feel sick to her stomach. She wanted more than anything for the last twenty-four hours to be nothing but a nightmare, a long, drawn out, horrible dream. Looking over at her father, it was clear that it hadn't been a dream at all. She was here, in her father's tent, feeling scared and hopeless. The memory of the dream she had just woken from filled her with a black sadness, deeper than anything she had ever felt.

Jeanie picked up her father's watch that lay on the ground between their two sleeping bags. 1:00 p.m. Panic filled her gut. She ripped open her sleeping bag, forcing the zipper open and making a loud *zzzzrrrp* noise. She clumsily crawled over to Alan.

"Dad!" She shook him gently. "Dad, wake *up!*"

She shook him again, but this time with a great amount of force. His body flopped back and forth, sweat rolled off of his forehead and down the side of his face. A droplet landed in his ear. She began to cry and shook him harder.

Alan's eyes snapped open. He sat upright so quickly Jeanie had to propel herself backward to avoid taking a painful headbutt to the nose. Still on her knees, she leaned back on both arms. She stared at her father with wide eyes, like a deer caught in the headlights of an unsuspecting vehicle. Sweat rolled off his face and down his neck in streams. His shirt was completely saturated. His breath came in sharp broken inhales, like he'd been crying hard.

Is that sweat coming off his face or tears? Both? Jeanie thought to herself.

Alan looked around like a wild animal caught in a trap. He quickly slithered backwards out of his sleeping bag and pulled his knees into his chest. He reminded Jeanie of a scared child. There was silence between them. Jeanie stared silently at her father for what seemed like an eternity. A large fly noisily buzzed around the interior of the tent. She wished it would die.

Alan's breathing slowed to a normal pace and his shoulders and back began to relax. He let out a heavy breath and released his legs from the powerful grip of his arms. His eyes fell on Jeanie.

"I'm sorry. I was having a really fucked up dream." As he looked at his daughter, he began to realize his unsettling arrival to awareness wasn't the only thing bothering her. "What's going on? What's wrong, Jeanie?"

Without a word she tossed his wristwatch at him. It landed at his feet and he leaned forward to pick it up. She gave him a moment to adjust his eyes and look at the time.

"What's wrong is that we just slept thirteen fucking hours somehow. What's *wrong* is that we are being tortured and hunted by something we can't even begin to try to understand. That's what's wrong, *Dad*."

Her emphasis on the last word was almost venomous. Her anger toward him she couldn't comprehend. He hadn't done anything to deserve it, but it was there, and it was on fire. Her heart pounded in her chest. She could feel her pulse in her head, behind her eyes. She brought her hands to the sides of her head and rubbed her temples with the heels of her hands. She was never an angry person. She needed to calm down. She was starting to feel out of control.

Alan gently touched his daughter's arm. "Whoa. What can I do to help you right now?" She shrugged his arm away. "Look, Jeanie, I'm just as scared as you are. This is what those things want to happen. They're getting in your head. You can't let them. You can't let the fear take over."

Jeanie took a deep breath and exhaled slowly. It seemed to help slow her heartbeat. She repeated the process until the red veil over her vision was cleared. She looked up at her father with tears brimming her eyes. She shook her head slowly.

"I'm sorry. I…" She took a sharp and unsteady breath in. Her breath came in short, severe inhales. "I don't know why I'm acting so crazy."

"Don't apologize. We both know why you're acting out of character. Just breathe in through your nose and out through your mouth. Once you get settled down, we need to go get that fire ramped back up. I hope the coals are still hot enough to make an easy fire, but I'm not counting on it." Alan gave his daughter's shoulder a brief, gentle pat.

Jeanie nodded slowly in agreeance. She closed her eyes and inhaled deeply through her nose, and out through her mouth slowly. She repeated this process several times. She stood up and held her hand out to her father.

"I'm ready now. Let's go."

Alan gripped his daughter's hand and stood beside her. He embraced her in a hug and pulled her away from him, with his hands on her shoulders.

"We're going to be okay. These things aren't stronger than us. Okay?" Jeanie nodded weakly. "I love you, Jeanie Bean."

"I love you too, Dad."

Alan unzipped the tent door and looked over his shoulder at Jeanie. She gave him a firm nod and they both made their way outside. Alan stood just outside the tent door, placed both hands on the small of his back and stretched. When he turned around, his face fell, expressionless. Any color remaining drained away.

Jeanie emerged and immediately noticed her father's expression. It was fear and disbelief. She turned to see what the cause was. When she saw it, she inhaled sharply and put her hand to her mouth.

"Holy shit," Jeanie said.

Her voice was barely a whisper.

16

I

The father and daughter duo looked out at their campsite in disbelief. Anything that had been left out was neatly packed up and put away. Jeanie's tent was disassembled, and the components were neatly placed next to each other on the ground. The chairs were folded and leaning against a tree near where Jeanie's tent was previously pitched.

Alan cautiously approached the stone ring that held their campfire. The coals appeared to still be smoldering, but the fire had long since burned out. He turned back to Jeanie who was frozen in place. He wasn't even sure she was breathing. Alan, on the other hand, was shaking violently. He hoped his knees wouldn't buckle and send him to the ground. His whole body was vibrating as his adrenaline surged. He felt too many emotions all at once. Most importantly, he felt a primal need to protect his daughter.

His mind was racing trying to figure out what needed to be done next. Surely, they couldn't just sit here like sitting ducks, could they? But the boat wouldn't arrive on shore until tomorrow evening. They just had to survive until then. The biggest question that swirled in Alan's mind – *is it safer to stay at camp, or should we take our chances with the forest today and camp on the beach?*

"Jeanie. Take all the time you need to process the situation, but I'm going to get this fire going again."

Jeanie slowly turned and stared blankly at her father. She was crying again. Silent tears streamed down her cheeks. She nodded at her father and moved slowly toward the folded camping chairs. Her movements were robotic and stiff, her eyes remained blank and emotionless, but the tears still streamed steadily down her face and neck. She dragged the two chairs behind her, one in each hand, and set them up near the fire.

"I know it seems impossible, but we need to eat something. We're going to need our energy." Jeanie's voice sounded far off and foreign, even to her own ears.

Alan nodded solemnly.

"Do you want to make it or should I? I don't mind doing it." Alan asked his daughter, concern in his voice.

"I need a moment. If you don't mind putting the water on, I'll take care of the rest," Jeanie replied without breaking her gaze from the ground in front of her. Alan wasn't even sure she was blinking.

Alan finished splitting the pile of wood he was working on and hastily brought the fire back to life. Once it was a decent size, he put water on the camp stove to boil and sat in his chair near his daughter. His shaking had subsided slightly, but his breathing was rough and uneven. He wasn't a young man any more and his body was reminding him.

Alan plopped into the chair next to his daughter and attempted to regulate his breathing. He dropped his cigarette on the ground as he attempted to retrieve it from the pack. He picked it up. He had to hold his left hand with his right to stabilize it enough to successfully light the end. After he finally got it lit, he shook his arms, hoping it would help relieve the remaining shaking that filled his limbs. He looked over at Jeanie, who was still in a trance-like state in her chair.

"Okay, kiddo, water's boiling. Do you want to finish up the

cooking or do you want me to?" He didn't want to nag her but he needed to try to snap her out of her current mental state. He desperately needed her to be present.

Without responding, Jeanie got up and dug two dehydrated breakfast scrambles from her pack, and began preparing them. Alan thought Jeanie's movements looked like they weren't her own. He imagined a marionette on strings, only moving when the puppet master commanded. In just a few minutes their meals would be brought back to life, as if the hot water were magic.

The duo waited in silence. They did not look at each other. Jeanie stared at the ground. Alan stared into the firepit, feeding its flames as soon as they showed signs of growing even a fraction smaller. When their food was finished re-hydrating, they ate slowly and methodically without conversation.

II

Jeanie struggled to finish her meal. Every chew required maximum effort and each time she swallowed it felt as if she was swallowing a rock covered in thick paste. She forced the sticky, masticated chunks down with water.

After finishing her meal, she had to admit it did make her feel better. Her energy seemed to be rebounding and the fog that coated her mind seemed to be lifting slightly. She tossed her trash into the fire and watched it melt into nothingness. Her father tossed his in after hers and the collision of his trash with the bottom of the pit did its best to break her concentration and she flinched.

"I'm glad we decided to eat. I'm starting to feel better. Are you doing okay?" Her father's voice pulled her the rest of the way out of her daze. She looked up at him and gave him a weak smile.

"I'm feeling a lot better, actually. I feel like I just need to get up and walk a bit and I might feel almost normal again."

She got up from her chair and began to slowly pace between her chair and her father's, in her usual pattern. She clasped her hands behind her back and her face fell into a look of deep concentration. Alan was pleased to see his daughter look more like herself again. A healthy pink color began to form in her cheeks and the sallow grayish color started to lift from her skin.

"Okay, Dad. It's time to make a game plan and outsmart these fuckers." She didn't look up at him or break her look of concentration. She continued to pace slowly.

"I don't think we can stay and fight. We don't know what they look like physically but I'm not sure that will matter since they can mind fuck us so hard. I think we need to pack all of our shit up and make a break for it." She looked up at her father and stopped walking, waiting for his response to her proposal.

"I'm glad you said that, Jeanie Bean." Alan furrowed his brow and nodded with intent. "Let's fucking rally. I think these things, whatever the hell they are, only live in the forest. Something tells me if we make it to the beach, they can't touch us. I don't think they like the water or the openness of it." He squinted his eyes slightly and shook his head. "Don't ask me how I know, it's just a gut feeling. Honestly, I'm pulling this out of my ass."

"I don't care where you're pulling it from, it sounds legit to me. We're running out of daylight fast. We better hustle. The last leg of our journey will be in the dark as it is."

Jeanie made her way to her already disassembled items and began hastily shoving them into her pack. She looked over her shoulder and pointed to the fire pit.

"Putting the fire out is dead last. It's definitely some sort of protection."

Alan nodded in agreement and began emptying the contents

of his tent. He hastily threw the smaller items out the door and opened up the air mattress to release the air. He rolled back and forth on the mattress until it was flat and began to roll it. Jeanie poked her head into the tent.

"Thanks to our asshole neighbors in the woods, I'm already done packing. I'm going to start working on getting the stuff out here in your pack."

"Sounds good. I don't care if it's neat. And if it doesn't fit and isn't vital, leave it. I know it's not best practice and I love Mother Nature, but this is life or death, kiddo. Time is not on our side."

Jeanie gave a curt nod and disappeared again.

III

Twenty minutes later they were both standing near the fire, packs on their back, ready to embark on the worst journey of their lives. Alan poured water onto the fire and watched as the flames began to shrink. Once they had disappeared completely, he turned to his daughter. He hugged her tightly and let out a single, gentle sob.

Jeanie pulled away from her father and grabbed him by the shoulders.

"Don't you dare do that. Don't fucking hug me like you're saying goodbye." Jeanie's voice was harsh and serious. "We're going to make it to that beach. You have your hatchet?"

Alan nodded and raised his right arm. In his hand was the small, sharp hatchet. Jeanie patted her right hip, which was equipped with her hunting knife.

"If they try anything, we fight. But until then, we choose the flight option. By my approximation, we have about three and a half hours of daylight left. We need to go. Right now."

17

I

Jeanie looked over her shoulder at her father. He was doing a decent job of keeping pace with her but had started falling behind in the last ten minutes or so. She slowed her pace to a quick walk. She had barely noticed how quickly she was moving (it was damn near a steady jog). She reminded herself that her father was not a young man any more, and if she was being honest, he was not in the best of shape. The extended years of cigarette smoking were catching up to him.

As much as everything in her body told her to keep moving, no matter the cost, she knew she needed to give her father a small break. She slowed until she was walking at his pace, and they walked side by side for a bit.

"We've been going pretty hard for about an hour, Dad. I know you don't want to, but I think I need a short break. Have a quick bite of a protein bar, some water, and a little rest. We've really been moving so I think we might be almost halfway to the beach."

Without a second thought, Alan nodded in agreement. They did not risk straying from the trail, even the slightest bit and instead took a seat smack in the middle of it. Jeanie dug through her pack and found two protein bars and handed one to her father. They both sucked from the straws attached to the water compartments on their pack (careful to reserve enough for the remainder of their trip).

Alan took the snack from his daughter and began searching through his own pack. He retrieved his lighter and pack of cigarettes from the front pocket. As he was lighting his cigarette, he noticed his daughter's look of disapproval. She was trying to hide it, but it was still there.

"I know this is probably the last thing I need right now, but quite frankly, I don't fucking care. If this is going to be my last day on this planet, I'm going to have a damn cigarette if I want to. I won't smoke the whole thing. How about that?"

The underlying hostility in her father's tone alarmed Jeanie. He was not a naturally grumpy man, even in stressful situations. She couldn't help but wonder if this was her father feeling stressed or something else entirely. Surely, they saw them leave their campsite, and it would be foolish to think they hadn't been following them. Jeanie's stomach began to knot. She wrapped the rest of her uneaten snack in the wrapper and put it back in her pack.

"Oh, so now you're not going to eat? You're going to pout like a little baby?" Alan smashed his cigarette into the ground, breaking it in two. He stood up and ground the still smoldering part of the butt into the dirt angrily with the toe of his boot. "Fine. Let's fucking get on with it then. Get up!" He spat the last words out as if they were venom. A few pieces of stray saliva clung to his chin.

Jeanie withdrew slightly, eyes wide with shock and fear. She stood slowly, not taking her eyes off of her father. They had been stopped for too long. She couldn't be one hundred percent sure, but she had a feeling it was easier for them to control them, to enter their minds when they were stationary. Her father's exhaustion was sure to make him the easier target of the two. It was the only explanation she could think of for why he was behaving this way. They needed to get moving.

Jeanie knew snapping back at her father would do nothing but worsen the situation, so she kept her thoughts to herself (mentally flipping him the bird) and began walking down the trail. She felt a small surge of anger and the urge to go at her own pace.

Who cares if he can't keep up? Sounds like his problem to me. Old asshole.

Jeanie shook her head, surprised at her own horrible thoughts. Were they her own thoughts, or was she being manipulated by outside forces? These creatures must think I'm stupid, she thought to herself. She projected her next thought out into the forest, hoping it would reach them.

I know what you're doing.

I'm just as smart as you are.

You're trying to turn us on one another.

You want me to be angry with him so I leave him behind, so there's distance between us, because that would make easy prey for you. Well, guess what assholes?

It's not going to happen.

She tried her best to make sure her projected tone was unwavering and angry. She didn't want them to think she had any fear of them. She flipped the mental bird again and slowed her pace to match her father's. She was determined to keep her mind strong and clear. She wasn't going down without one hell of a fight. She knew as long as they didn't take any more breaks, and kept a decent pace, they could make the beach before the sun went down. In her gut, she knew if they got stuck on this trail, in this forest, in the dark, they would not come out again.

She took a deep breath and they pressed forward. She could

feel fear begin to trickle into her mind, like a slow and steady leak.

Drip. Drip. Drip.

She knew they were getting closer and that they needed to go faster, but her father seemed to be set on one speed. When she went faster, he did not follow suit. He didn't even try.

They had him now. Maybe not all of him, but a decent portion of his mind and parts of his physical being along with it. They would not let him go faster. Jeanie knew she could not leave him because they would take the opportunity to strike. They would take her father. And then they would take her, too.

II

Alan wanted to move faster but his limbs felt as if they were filled with heavy, wet sand. He used every ounce of his energy to move forward at the slow, arduous pace he was currently holding. His chest screamed in pain with every breath that filled his tar laden lungs, but he desperately wanted to keep moving, and to keep up with Jeanie.

Something in the back of his mind told him to stop for another break. Stop for another smoke. That's really what he wanted. That's what he needed most right now. He knew his priorities were skewed but he could not control the thoughts and urges overwhelming his mind.

Red warning lights flashed in the part of his mind that was still his own. Sirens wailed trying to tell him to just keep moving, to fight the influence that was taking hold of him. He kept trying to break free but every time he focused and struggled to break the compulsion, the black tentacles wormed their way further into his mind. Every time he tried to speak about what he knew was happening out loud, to tell Jeanie, his voice was stifled, and red-hot anger flared in his chest. It was like psychic quicksand.

I know it's hard, Alan, but you can't give up, man.

Keep moving forward.

This isn't you, it's them. It's all in your head.

He took a deep breath and forced his heavy legs to continue moving. It took all of his effort to keep cheering himself along in his mind. They were trying to stop that, too.

One foot in front of the other. One step closer to freedom. Keep going.

The sound of his own voice in his head was starting to grow fainter. With every minute that passed, it was getting harder to hear himself. A flood of negative emotions filled him to the brim. Fear, sadness, and most of all, anger. The tiny voice of his conscience told him that if the anger kept growing, he would have to tell Jeanie to run, to leave him, because they weren't just trying to take him, he was now aware that they wanted him to kill her first.

His grip tightened around the handle of the hatchet.

III

Jeanie could feel the negativity radiating off her father. She could almost feel the heat of it. Worry filled her heart. She tried not to show her fears outwardly. She knew it would be unwise to let her father know what she was thinking or feeling now. He was becoming one of them. He was their eyes and ears because they were still too far away to know everything she was thinking.

They still weren't able to penetrate as deeply into her mind. She was still able to hide things from them.

She continued at his slow pace with her head down,

watching her feet. The only sounds were the crunch of the Earth beneath their feet and the labored, heavy sound of her father's breathing. She wanted to cry. She wanted to fall to the ground, kicking and screaming like a toddler throwing a tantrum. But she knew she needed to stay calm and level – at least outwardly.

Could they have enough control over his body to give him a heart attack?

Could they kill him from a distance?

Jeanie couldn't help but notice the eerie quietness of the forest around them. Not a single bird call could be heard, nor a breeze through the trees. It was completely silent and still. Jeanie found a moment of braveness and looked up and into the forest that surrounded them.

Is it getting dark faster than we had planned?

Without changing her pace, Jeanie reached to the side pocket of her pack and removed her dying cell phone to check the time. There was certainly no way she was going to ask her father to check his watch. She couldn't alert him in any way.

3:47 p.m.

It shouldn't be this damn dark yet. Can those fucking things control everything?

She felt frustration start to rise from her stomach and into her chest. She pictured it in her mind's eye. She envisioned a classic cartoon, where the character gets angry and the red rises from their feet to the top of their head and then suddenly, steam emits noisily from their ears, or their top completely blows. She took a deep breath and closed her eyes, letting the heat subside.

You can't let them win, Jeanie. Stay focused, stay calm. Keep walking with Dad.

She replaced the cell phone into its place in her pack and took the opportunity to glance back at her father. What she saw, she did not expect. He looked nothing like the man she had known her whole life. His eyes were much darker than they normally were. They weren't piercing, icy blue any more but appeared to be a harder hazel color. They were intently focused on her. A deranged smile was plastered on his face. The knuckles of his right hand were white from the tight grip they kept on his hatchet.

As she turned back to face forward, the dam in her mind ruptured. Fear flooded every ounce of her being. She felt like a bomb that had been slowly ticking toward detonation, and the time was finally up. Her arms and legs began to shake as her heart thundered in her chest. Her vision blurred slightly, and she blinked her eyes hard to fight against it.

That is not Dad any more, Jeanie.

Oh fuck. Oh fuck.

What do we do? We can't just leave him because somewhere in there is Dad.

Try to calm down and just keep walking.

Her eyesight wavered in and out. Darkness began to creep into view from both sides. Her head felt like it was filled with a swarm of loudly buzzing bees. Bright white spots flooded across her field of vision.

Oh God, Jeanie. Do not pass out right now.

She forced her legs to remain in motion. She hoped like hell he couldn't see her knees shaking with every step.

No.

Not he.

It.

She now realized her father had lost the war waging inside him. Whatever creature (or creatures) they were running from had taken complete control of him, mentally and physically. She hoped there was still some part of her father inside; able to at least distract it. Her mind was reeling. She needed to come up with a plan, but she also needed to keep moving.

She knew she only had two real options. The first option was to take off and leave him behind. The second, was to stay with him and see what would happen. Would she have to possibly fight with her own father? Would she win? It didn't matter because in that situation, there was no real winner. No matter how she looked at it, they were both going to die.

IV

The war waged on inside Alan's body. Every step forward was now agonizing. A searing, white hot pain filled his limbs with every movement. The voice urging him to slaughter his own daughter was growing louder. It wasn't a whisper any more but a deafening scream. His hand gripped the hatchet so tightly that it ached clear up to his wrist, but no matter how hard he tried, he couldn't loosen it.

Why won't she just leave me?

She saw me and I know she knows something isn't right. So why won't she just fucking run?

She wouldn't leave him alone. Alan knew that, deep down. He would just need to keep fighting. Maybe if he could just take a quick break and talk to her, it would help him break free of this monster's control. He needed to break free just long enough to tell Jeanie to go. Alan forced his eyes shut and took a deep, ragged breath. Talking on his own would be a difficult task, if not impossible. But he thought he could do it if he forced his voice out with all of his remaining energy.

"Jeanie! We need to stop for a break."

His voice came out as a loud burst at first and was quickly drowned into something gravelly and weak. The creature was choking him back into silence. His eyes bulged from his head as he tried to fight against the compulsion.

V

Jeanie was surrounded with the most unease she had ever experienced in her life. She was mentally preparing herself for a physical battle with her own father, and a mental battle with something she couldn't wrap her mind around. Their pace had slowed to an extremely slow walk. She dragged her feet along the trail in an exhausted shuffle. She could sense that something devastating was rapidly approaching.

Behind her, she could hear her father suck in a large gasp of air. When he released the large breath, he was asking her to stop for a break. The sound of his voice made her nauseous. It sounded like her dad when he initially said her name and then it was something else altogether. It was the sound of a man possessed by something otherworldly. She had only heard someone speak that way in horror films.

Goosebumps broke out across her entire body. Every hair was standing completely on end. The air was thick and charged and it felt like at any moment Zeus himself would strike them down with a fierce and powerful bolt of lightning. Jeanie slowly came to a stop. Fear froze her in a front facing motion. She did not want to see her father's face again, not like that.

As she slowly turned around, she could hear his ragged and labored breathing. When she was finally facing him, he had thrown his bag to the ground carelessly and was busy lighting a cigarette. He was shaking violently as he struggled to light the cigarette hanging from his lips.

Jeanie put her hand over her mouth. She wasn't sure if she was trying to fight against vomiting or stop herself from screaming. Alan's skin was beginning to turn an odd grayish blue color. It made him look hypothermic. She could see the cuticles around his fingernails were darkening and turning black. His left thumbnail was completely missing, sloughed off somewhere along the way. Clumps of his hair appeared to be falling loose from his scalp, and other sections began to turn gray.

Alan looked up, locking eyes with Jeanie. His eyes had gone completely black, as if his pupil had grown so large it swallowed the entire eye whole. He squinted slightly and blew a stream of smoke toward her. She forced herself not to flinch. She was positive no part of her father remained behind those devilish eyes. His mind was completely overtaken. His body was being used as a vessel.

He threw his head back and laughed. The sound made her skin crawl. He locked eyes with her again. A wide sick smile spread across his face, revealing a rapidly decaying set of teeth. The gums were turning black and most of the teeth were a dark yellow or brown color. Not breaking his eye contact with Jeanie, Alan opened his mouth wide and reached his fingers into the back of his mouth. After a few seconds he slowly pulled his hand away, revealing a large molar held between his thumb and forefinger. The fingernail on his third finger was now barely hanging on.

Jeanie could not contain the contents of her stomach any longer. She pivoted to the right just fast enough to miss her boots with the spray of vomit projecting from her mouth. She wretched a few more times, recovered, and wiped her mouth with the back of her hand. She stood up straight and returned the creature's gaze.

She wasn't afraid any more.

She wasn't sad either.

The only emotion she could conjure was anger.

"Get the fuck out of my dad, you nasty piece of shit." She grabbed the hunting knife from her hip and held it out in front of her.

The creature laughed uncontrollably, throwing Alan's body into a coughing fit. He spat chunks of black tar at Jeanie's feet. She held her ground, her only movement was the slight squinting of her eyes. Her anger now grew into white hot rage. Her breathing was quick and uneven, her skin flared with heat, turning her neck splotchy and red in places.

"Oh, child." The creature laughed quietly, looked down at the ground, and shook its head slowly. "Do you really think you will hurt us? Can you bear to stab your own father and risk his life? Just to possibly extract our consciousness from his lump of flesh?"

The voice coming from her father's throat was not singular, but several vocal tones at once. Jeanie felt the bile rise in her throat again and swallowed hard to push it back down to her stomach. She did not lower her weapon. She took one step closer to her father's possessed body.

"Well, since you won't listen to reason, little girl." Alan's body shrugged both shoulders toward his ears.

The creature smiled its disgusting smile, clearly enjoying every moment of torture it was providing to Jeanie and Alan. It reached behind its back and retrieved the hatchet from where it had been stored in the belt of Alan's pants in order to light the last cigarette.

"Let the final battle begin, *kiddo*." The creature's voice lowered an octave on the last word, openly mocking Jeanie.

It raised the hatchet above its head. Jeanie let herself give in to fear and began a slow, backward retreat. She held her hands out in front of her in a defensive gesture. Her 'father' advanced on her slowly.

PART II

DAY 1

1

I

Kai threw up his hands and released Jeanie's arm from his grip.

"Fine, go. I hope you have a fun trip. I mean that. But don't say I didn't warn you about what's in there." Kai jabbed his pointer finger in the direction of the forest and rolled his eyes slightly.

He was tired of trying to convince her. If she wanted to risk her life, and her father's life, that was on her shoulders now. Jeanie looked over her shoulder before leaving the fishing boat for the rickety wooded dock.

"I'll be fine. We will be fine." She smiled sweetly and winked. "I pinky promise. See you in a few days."

He watched anxiously as Jeanie departed the boat and landed gingerly on the old wooden dock (that was less of a dock and more of an old rotten landing strip, for old rotten boats). He waited with the engine of his fishing boat idling until she was safely planted on the dark, golden sand of the wet beach. Once he was sure she was safe (as safe as she would allow herself to be, he thought) he backed his boat away from the dock and headed out into the open water.

As Kai drove back to the other side of the island, he let his mind wander. No matter where his thoughts began, they always seemed to land on Jeanie. He was immediately attracted to her the day they met in the farmer's market on the mainland. She was as intelligent and charming as she was beautiful and although it wasn't clear if she returned his affections (and he was always far too nervous to tell her his true feelings) he was always very happy they stayed in contact and became friends.

They would text almost daily. Any time he found himself on the mainland, which he admitted happened more frequently since meeting Jeanie, they would meet up for a coffee or a bite to eat. She was easy to talk to and conversation always flowed freely when they were together. Not to mention, she had the most amazing eyes he had ever seen. Kai smiled to himself at the thought of them.

He sighed deeply. He just didn't feel right dropping them off at that place. The dangers might only be legend but when he got there, his internal alarms began to scream. It felt genuinely dangerous. He pounded the butt of his hand on the steering wheel.

Damn it, Kai. You fucking idiot.

He considered turning around and catching them before they got too deep into the forest. He shook his head. They would already be into the forest far enough that it would be dangerous for him to follow them in without being properly prepared. He needed to move on and let them have their trip. He knew how much Jeanie was looking forward to the time with her father and the last thing she wanted (or needed) was him crashing the party.

He focused on the cold sea mist caressing his cheeks and did his best to clear his mind of all thoughts of Jeanie, and of any and all thoughts of monsters that might be lurking in the forest. The rest of the short ride to his home marina, he focused on letting his mind settle on absolutely nothing. He watched birds float in the gray sky and breathed the salty air deep into his lungs.

He pulled into his assigned space at the small marina that

housed several other fishing boats, as well as some boats that were reserved for pleasure rather than business. He shut off the engine and as he was securing his boat to the dock, his mind found its way back to Jeanie. Jeanie was in trouble. He could sense it. He needed to do something to help.

Well, I guess you're invested in a little adventure of your own, Kai. You fucking idiot.

2

I

Kai hurried through his front door. He removed his shoes without stopping, not caring where they landed. In the process, one of his socks slipped halfway off his foot. He pressed forward without fixing it. He threw his keys haphazardly into the coin dish that lived on the bar countertop separating the kitchen from the living room, rushed down the hallway toward the guest bedroom (which also doubled as an exercise room, an office, and a place where his general clutter came to disappear).

With a surprising amount of grace, he plopped himself into his office chair and swiveled around to face the desk. He had his laptop open before he had even come to a full stop in his chair. He thrummed his fingers over the keys thinking of where to begin his search for answers. He started out with a vague search, hoping at least a few of the results would lead him to some key words that might help him narrow his search criteria.

In the search engine he typed in 'forest monster folklore.' As he suspected, this returned a massive number of unusable information. He sighed heavily and tried to narrow his search by adding 'North America.' This seemed to get him closer to what he was looking for, so he decided to start diving deeper within his search.

I'm going to need some serious caffeine for this. It's going to be a long night.

Kai pushed himself away from his desk and headed into the kitchen. His home was small and humble, but he enjoyed its comfortable charm. It was one level but had a crawl space for extra storage. It had two bedrooms – the guest (office, exercise, junk room) and the slightly larger master bedroom. The master had an attached bathroom with a standing shower and walk-in closet. There was an additional bathroom in the hall with a simple tub-shower combo, toilet, and one sink for when he had guests (or didn't want to walk all the way to his bedroom to relieve himself).

The kitchen didn't have much wiggle room but had countertops that lined the entire perimeter of the square room, giving it a much larger feel. The wall of the kitchen that was shared with the living room had a cut out with a breakfast bar, making the kitchen open to the living room and easier to entertain (or in his case, watch the television from the stove while cooking).

He opened his fridge and retrieved an energy drink. Before closing the door again, he took a careful inventory of how many drinks he had remaining and decided that three should be an ample amount for a night of research. As he made his way back to his office, he cracked the can and sipped the liquid that spilled out onto the rim. He wiped his hand onto his pants to clean the tiny bit of liquid that sprayed up when he opened the top. He sat down in his office chair again, more slowly this time, taking care not to spill his beverage. He placed it gently on a ceramic coaster to the left of his laptop.

He pulled out a ballpoint pen and a lined notepad from the top right drawer of his desk. He scrawled 'what I learned about asshole monsters trying to eat my future wife' across the top. This made him chuckle out loud to himself before he made a small dot in the margin of the first line and retrained his focus on his laptop.

II

At two a.m., he finally decided he couldn't read any more myths, legends, or folklore. He shut down his laptop and rubbed his eyes with his thumb and forefingers. He was certain he would now be permanently cross-eyed from the long hours staring at the screen. He lowered his hand from his eyes and gave them a quick blink. The hours of research compiled three pages of what he thought would be pertinent information.

He flipped back to the first page of notes and studied his findings. Nearly every group of people who had settled in North America for an extended period of time had (or still do have) some sort of myth or legend surrounding secluded rain forests of the Pacific Northwest. Although the origin of the creatures that live in the forests varies slightly, their characteristics are largely the same.

Most of the legends talk about creatures that are largely nocturnal but also have the ability to move around in heavily shaded areas and under thick cloud cover (which explains why they love the Pacific Northwest so much). Another shared characteristic is the ability to enter the minds of unsuspecting prey. This ranges from simple mind reading, to actually gaining control of the victim's body (similar to possession). The vast majority of the material he read claims the beasts are invisible because nobody has ever reported to have physically seen one. Due to this, it is believed they are celestial beings and some even believed they were some sort of Gods or divine beings.

Okay. So how do you kill an invisible celestial?

Kai sighed and continued reading through his notes. Some legends pointed out that the creatures were not particularly fond of water, especially salt water.

I should have told them there was no access to the forest and they needed to camp on the beach.

He finally came upon the notes about the specific forest Jeanie and Alan happened to be camping in. That side of the island used to be more populated and was a popular settlement for fishermen. The fishing village wasn't settled long before people started disappearing in the forest. They would go in to forage or take a walk and simply never come back out again. Search parties sent in to look for the lost villagers also began to disappear. The small group of people who served as village leaders quickly put a ban on entering the dangerous forest. Only a few short weeks after the ban went into effect, there was a mass murder suicide that wiped out the entire village.

Kai paused a moment and thought to himself, idly tapping his capped pen against his lips. All they had to do was get close enough to take control of one person, and they were able to take out everyone. It was that simple.

He slid the notepad away from him and sat back in his chair. If these legends were true (and something deep down in his gut was telling him they were), Jeanie and Alan didn't stand a fucking chance. Kai's stomach knotted viciously at the thought.

But how can I save Jeanie and her dad if I have no clue how to kill these fucking things?

Figuring that out would be a task for tomorrow. He would be useless if he was running on no sleep. He picked up the empty cans that littered the surface of his desk and chucked them into the trash can under the sink in the kitchen. Before heading back to his bedroom, he double checked the front door was locked and shut off the lights.

He didn't bother finding any pajamas. He stripped his shirt and pants off, tossed them into his laundry basket, and climbed into bed wearing only his boxer briefs. Normally he would watch a bit of TV before falling asleep but once his head hit the cool fabric of the pillow, he was asleep almost instantly.

DAY 2

3

I

Kai's sleep was fitful and restless. He woke up in a confused daze. He had to sit up and look around to realize he was home, in his bedroom. Cold sweat made the caramel-colored skin of his chest break out in goosebumps and as he looked around his room, reality began to settle in again. He breathed a sigh of relief and allowed himself to settle back down into bed.

He dreamt of a woman who had the answers to his questions about what lives in the forest. She knew exactly what they are; how they move, think, hunt. She knew how to kill them. If only it hadn't been a dream, he would have everything he needed to go find Jeanie and Alan and get rid of those parasitic bastards in the forest once and for all.

He propped himself up on one elbow and grabbed his phone from the bedside table. Though he didn't get to sleep until after two in the morning, his internal clock still woke him early. It was only five minutes to six and though you could tell dawn was fast approaching, the sun hadn't yet gotten close enough to the horizon to bring the dewy blue hues of morning twilight. Kai's work as an independently contracted fisherman allowed him to create his own work schedule and he was disappointed when his body wouldn't allow him to sleep in, even when he intended to do so.

He scrolled idly through his social media apps for a moment.

He returned his phone to the bedside table, stretched, and made his way to the bathroom. Just as he was flushing the toilet, he thought he heard a knock on this front door. He paused to listen for a moment. When nothing but silence was returned, he started his morning routine. Halfway through his shave, the knocking came again. With the razor still touching his skin, he paused a moment.

Boom! Boom! Boom!

Kai jumped at the sound of the pounding on his front door. He dropped his razor in the sink.

"Oh, shit!" His voice cracked with surprise.

He grabbed the hand towel from the ring by the sink and frantically wiped his face free of shaving cream. The knocking commenced once again, sounding more urgent.

"Hang on a second! I'm coming!"

He jogged to his closet, yanked the closest hoodie from a hanger and struggled his way into the sweater while he walked to his dresser. He couldn't see where he was going and stubbed his toe on the corner of his bed frame. He winced sharply from the pain and hobbled the rest of the way to the dresser. When he finally made it there, he retrieved a pair of basketball shorts from the top drawer. He hopped one leg at a time into his shorts as he made his way down the hallway toward the front door.

Boom! Boom! Boom!

Holy shit. This better be the police or someone dying or some kind of emergency. Who knocks like this on someone's door?

Kai was annoyed by the early morning interruption, but his intrigue outweighed his irritation. Before opening the door, he smoothed his hands over his hair a few times attempting to rid himself of bed head. He slid the deadbolt back and opened the door slowly. He opened the door just wide enough to pop his head through the crack, hiding his body behind the door.

It took him a moment to register the person who was standing on his porch, staring at him intently. He returned her gaze blankly. The woman staring at him was in her mid-thirties. She had platinum blonde hair, cut into a short, bouncy bob that fell just below her jawline. Her ice blue eyes had flecks of green scattered throughout them. She smiled at him sweetly, revealing a perfect row of sparkling white teeth. The more he looked at her, the more stunning she became.

"Are you Kai Rhodes? I'm sure you are. And I believe you remember me? Don't you?" Her words came quickly and seemed to simply tumble from her mouth, one after the other.

She stepped forward so Kai had to back his face away. He opened the door the rest of the way, still rendered speechless. He couldn't believe what he was seeing. He must be having one of those weird dreams that you wake up inside and you're still dreaming. A dream within a dream. The woman standing before him is the woman who had all the answers. The woman from his dream.

"Well, are you going to let me in or not?" she asked.

Her face now reflected a subtle annoyance. Without replying Kai stepped to the side and gestured for her to enter his home. She moved through the doorway and stood in front of him. Her proximity finally broke his trance. He shook his head slightly and smiled.

"I'm so sorry. You caught me just getting out of bed. Please." He stood aside and gestured toward his couch with his hands. "Have a seat. Would you like something to drink? Water? Coffee? Tea?" He stood in between the kitchen and the living room, waiting for her answer.

"If you have an Earl Grey tea, I'll have a cup of that. If not, coffee will be fine." Her reply was blunt but still polite.

Kai entered the kitchen and began digging through the cabinet near the refrigerator. He ducked down so he could see her through the opening to the living room.

"It looks like you're in luck, I've got the tea you want." He projected his words into the living room, toward the couch where she had settled.

From the same cabinet that housed his assortment of teas, he pulled his tea kettle, filled it with water, and placed it on the stove top. He turned the appropriate burner on high and joined the woman in the living room. He took a seat in a tattered recliner opposite his guest. For a moment they just sat together in silence. Kai cleared his throat gently.

"I remember you from my dream last night. How is that possible? Is this real?" He tried not to sound too desperate or panicked, but he wasn't so sure he pulled it off.

The woman smirked and nodded slowly.

"It is very real. I have the ability to project when I'm sleeping. It's similar to astral projection but I'm not always fully aware or conscious when it happens. The subject matter you were concentrating on before you fell asleep helped draw me to you. For years I've been studying the same creatures you spent your whole night studying last night. We were drawn together because we share a common enemy – a common purpose." She spoke in a straightforward, polite tone. It reminded Kai a bit of a teacher he once had in high school.

Kai took a moment and digested the information he had just received. Most people would probably write this woman off as a crazy person – an absolute lunatic. But he didn't have another explanation. Not to mention, he had just spent his entire night extensively researching how to kill an invisible monster. He believed her. His concentration was broken by the scream of the tea kettle. Kai held up his pointer finger to signal he would just be one moment.

"Let me go grab that," he said.

He did a light jog into the kitchen and killed the flame lit under the kettle. He grabbed two mugs, the box of tea, a spoon, small plate, and the kettle and headed back to the living room. He placed the tea materials on the coffee table and resumed his seat.

"I believe you. Does this mean you can help me?" This time he hoped she had picked up on his pleading tone. He needed all the help he could get.

"That depends on exactly what you need help with." She picked up the tea kettle and poured the steaming liquid into one of the mugs. She plopped a tea bag in and watched as it sank slowly to the bottom.

"My friend and her father went into the forest on the other side of the island. They went to the place those things live. I'm afraid for them. They won't make it out alive without help and *I* won't make it out alive if I go in to help. Not unless I know what I'm up against. Do you know how to kill them?"

"First off, let me start by introducing myself. My name is Misty."

She held out her hand for a shake. Kai's cheeks burned brightly with embarrassment. He grimaced and grabbed her hand to return her offer for a shake. His hand swallowed hers. He couldn't help but notice her skin felt like butter. Her nails were void of any polish but still looked well cared for and clean.

"I am *so* sorry. I promise I'm not normally a rude asshole. You just caught me off guard today. And you already know my name."

Misty held up her hands to stop his rambling.

"It's all right, really. I showed up unannounced and the situation is odd. Any normal person would be flustered."

She chuckled, removed the tea bag from her mug with the spoon, and placed it on the small plate. She took a sip and locked eyes with Kai. Her dark, smoky eye makeup made her eyes even more piercing. They sent a small shiver down Kai's spine. He hoped she didn't notice him gently shake it off.

"To answer your previous question – I *do* think I can help. I have extensive research and have even developed defensive weapons and tools to use against them. But…" She took another sip from her mug. "You will need to come to my place so we can go over all of it. I came here because my dream called me to do so. I didn't bring the materials we need."

Kai nodded firmly.

"I can follow you over there right now," he said. His tone was now excited and determined.

Misty raised an eyebrow and cocked her head slightly, then shook it.

"Pump the breaks, Captain America. I'm not ready right now. I know you're a bit frantic, but I need time to prepare my home. And maybe a nap. I'm not sure if you've noticed or not, but it is the ass crack of dawn."

Kai laughed coolly. He looked down at himself and remembered he wasn't even dressed yet.

"Okay, you have a point. I should probably finish getting myself put together too."

They both stood and he led her to the front door. He opened it for her, and she made her way onto the creaky wooden porch. She turned to face him as he stood in the doorway.

"Be at my place at noon. Here's my card, it has my address and my cell number."

Kai grabbed the card from her and placed it into the pocket of his gray basketball shorts. Misty turned to walk away and then paused and turned to look over her shoulder.

"Oh, one more thing."

Kai gave her an expectant look and waited patiently for her to finish her thought. She smiled her radiant smile.

"You've got a bit of shaving cream on your face. Just under your nose." She pointed a delicate finger at his face. "See you at noon."

Misty pranced down the porch steps and toward the curb where her practical sedan was parked. Too embarrassed to speak, Kai slowly closed the door behind her and latched the deadbolt. For a moment he just stood, frozen in place, too dazzled by Misty's presence to move.

She was the most beautiful woman he had ever seen. But that wasn't even the most attractive aspect of her. She was the most interesting person he had ever met, and intelligent. She held herself with poise but also knew her way around sarcasm. She was captivating.

You're getting way off track here, man. Focus on the task at hand. But hey, maybe Jeanie isn't your future wife after all.

He shook his head attempting to quell his inner dialogue. Finally able to find his legs, he cleared the coffee table and took care of the dishes. He wandered back into his bedroom, stripped down to his underwear, and started the shower. He closed the bathroom door and brushed his teeth while he waited for the water to get hot. After he spit the toothpaste in the sink, he glanced up in the mirror. Sure as shit, under his right nostril, there was a huge glob of shaving cream.

Kai studied himself in the mirror and began to laugh. He just sat with the most beautiful human being he had ever met with shaving cream under his nose, and only half of his face shaved. And she said he was the normal one?

I wonder what secrets she must be hiding.

II

Kai took his time in the shower. He finished his shave, making sure to not miss any spots or nick himself. He got dressed slowly, trying on multiple outfits before deciding on one and sticking to it. He hoped it would kill a significant chunk of time. He even decided to style his hair in lieu of wearing his signature ball cap. He always had the barber cut it into a long fade but rarely went anywhere without a hat. Kai chose to work a busy schedule (sometimes seven days a week) and the fish he pulled in on his nets never cared what he looked like.

On the way out of his bedroom he grabbed his cell phone from his bedside table. As he made his way down the hallway, he pressed the button on the side to reveal the time. He let out a heavy sigh and a small groan. It was only eight thirty. He still had three and a half hours until he was supposed to meet with Misty. He plopped onto the couch and turned the TV on. It was a rarity that he had idle time to watch a show, so he had an extensive list built up on Netflix.

He found a true crime documentary and pressed play. He was anxious and his attention span couldn't be held for very long. He picked up his phone and scrolled social media, not paying much attention to what was happening on the television. The mindless activity was interrupted by the loud growling coming from his stomach.

Thankful for something to do to pass the time, Kai made his way into the kitchen and opened the fridge. He was pleased to find eggs as well as bacon. He pulled out two pans and fried his eggs and bacon at the same time. While they cooked, he brewed a pot of coffee and threw two pieces of bread into the toaster. He ate his breakfast as slowly as he could, desperately wishing time would increase its speed.

He retrieved the card Misty had given him from his bedroom and returned to the couch. He plugged the address into his navigation. She only lived ten minutes away. This whole time she was so close, and he never had any idea.

Kai had lived in his current house for a good portion of his life. He lived there with his grandmother and when she passed away a few years ago, she had left it to him. The rest of his family lived on the mainland, in the United States, just outside Seattle, Washington. He enjoyed the solitude of the island, but most people did not. It wasn't easy selling a house here, let alone an older one with little to no upgrades in it. So, Kai decided it was easier to just stay put.

I wonder when she moved here.

Had she been under his nose this whole time?

4

I

At 11:45, Kai was backing his truck out of his cracked concrete driveway. If he was five minutes early surely, she wouldn't mind. At least he hoped she wouldn't. He couldn't stand to sit and stare at the clock any longer. He hated that she made him wait all day just to get the answers he needed.

His old truck bumped and rumbled down the road. He didn't need to follow his navigation to get to where he was going. Kai attended the high school in Misty's neighborhood. All the days skipping classes were spent wandering the streets with his friends. It was a small town, and he knew it well. There were also many summer days where boredom pushed them all outside and they would wander around, not doing much of anything, laughing and talking until the streetlights came on.

Kai's truck pulled up in front of Misty's home eight minutes after it left his driveway. Trying not to move too quickly (in case she was watching, he didn't want to seem desperate), he climbed out of the driver's seat and made his way up to the front door. He took a deep breath and knocked firmly.

The door opened quickly.

"Come on in, Kai. You're early," she spoke in the same quick, clipped tone she had earlier. She always sounded like she was in a hurry.

"I'm sorry. I hope that's okay?" Kai replied sheepishly.

"No worry at all. I had a feeling you would be. In all honesty, I wanted to call and tell you to come sooner, but I never got your number. Please take your shoes off by the door." The way she spoke reminded him a bit of the head mistress at a boarding school who was showing a new student the ropes. He kept waiting to hear her say *chop, chop now. Move along.*

Kai slipped his shoes off without untying them. Misty motioned him to follow her, and they made their way into the kitchen. Her house was larger than Kai's but was also on one level. It was far cozier than Kai's bachelor pad and the smell of warm sugar cookies and cinnamon apples filled the air. The kitchen, dining area, and living room were all connected and open to one another, making it feel larger than it was. The furnishings were minimal but very stylish. In the living room a large flat screen television hung over a fireplace surrounded by white quartz stone. A coffee table and sectional sofa sat facing the fireplace.

The surface of her high-top kitchen table was entirely covered with books, bottles, crystals, and other miscellaneous papers (it all looked to Kai like various knick-knacks – though he was sure they served some importance).

"Have a seat. Would you like something to drink?"

Kai pulled a chair out and sat at the table. He looked at everything she had laid out and tried to take it all in. She wasn't lying about having an extensive amount of information.

"I'll take some water. Bottle, cup, or glass. Filtered or from the tap. Doesn't matter to me," Kai replied without looking away from the table full of treasures.

Misty opened her refrigerator and pulled out two bottles of water. She took a seat next to Kai at the kitchen table and handed him one of the bottles.

"Thank you. Is this all of your research? Or do you have more?"

Misty chuckled.

"This is just a pile of the information I found to be most relevant at this moment. I've been researching these creatures for almost ten years now." Her tone and body language were relaxing, and the speed of her speech slowed from insanely fast, to almost normal.

"Is that when you moved here? Ten years ago?"

Misty nodded. She began sorting through some of the loose papers that were laid out on the table. She pulled a map out and laid it flat on the table in front of Kai and herself. There were red circles drawn in a few sections. Kai leaned in for a closer look.

"This is a map of the island," Kai said as he gently ran his hand over the surface of the paper to flatten it further. "What do these red circles mean?"

He pointed to the one closest to him. There were only circles drawn in heavily forested areas, and only on the abandoned side of the island. Misty looked up at him. Her eyes were lit up, but not in excitement. It was clear that she was very serious about her research.

"These circles represent the areas of the forest where it is known they reside. That doesn't mean they can't travel into the other areas of the forest, because they can, and they do. The circles just represent the most concentrated activity. I'm almost positive these are the areas they call 'home.'" Misty used her fingers to make air quotes as she said home. "They seem to be nomadic and don't stay in one area permanently but travel between a select number of favored locations."

Kai studied the map more closely. His stomach dropped. The area on the farthest side of the island had three large, red circles. They overlapped each other making Kai think of the Venn Diagrams from school. The other circles on the map were spread out and small. Jeanie and Alan went into the forest where the large, overlapped circles were drawn.

They were in the most dangerous spot on this map. Before he knew what was happening, tears began to well up in his eyes. He quickly picked up his bottle of water and drank it with his eyes closed. It gave him enough time to push the emotions back down into the pit of his stomach. He hoped like hell Misty hadn't noticed. It wasn't easy for Kai to be vulnerable, especially with someone he didn't know.

"Okay, so this confirms my suspicions that my friends went into the most dangerous place possible on the island. Now how do I go in and save them without becoming another snack for these things? And what *are* they?" Kai's words tumbled out one after the other. His fear and panic were beginning to show.

"One thing at a time, bud." Misty's tone was starting to warm up and become less professional and more friendly. "I'm not one hundred percent positive exactly what they are, but I do know they aren't natural to our planet, or our dimension. Personally, my vote is for extra-terrestrial or paranormal origin."

"What other options were there?" Kai gave her a curious expression.

"I also read about them being Gods or vampires. But I don't believe a God would stick around in the same forest for such a long time and vampires don't exist."

Kai chuckled and turned the information over in his mind. He couldn't believe he was having this conversation and that it wasn't about a movie or fiction novel. This was his current reality. The seriousness and fear of the situation was starting to set in. His heartrate climbed slightly. He took a deep breath to settle himself and wiped the palms of his hands on his jeans.

"When you say paranormal, do you mean ghosts?"

"Nope. More like demons."

Kai's eyebrows shot upward, and his eyes widened.

"Oh, that's just fucking great," he replied.

Kai let his head drop into his hands. He took slow, deep

breaths. Misty reached out and laid her hand gently on his shoulder. She let it rest there for a moment.

"Hey. I know it's a lot to try to comprehend at once. And I know you're worried about your friends. But I brought you here – the *universe* brought you here – for a reason. We can save your friends. We can get rid of these things, once and for all."

Misty wanted to add the words *I promise* to the end of her statement, but she couldn't be sure she was telling the truth. She wanted to believe they could rescue his friends and defeat the enemy, but there was no absolute way of knowing how it would all turn out.

Kai slowly raised his head and took one more deep breath. Misty let her hand fall away. Kai's eyes met hers. The same shiver he had encountered earlier went down his spine. It felt as if she could see straight through him. He swore her eyes were nearly glowing. Misty abruptly broke eye contact, stood up, and turned her attention back toward the table.

"It's obvious why I want to know about these creatures but what got you so interested in researching how to put an end to them?" Kai was genuinely curious. Most people didn't walk around hunting mystical creatures. Most people don't believe anything supernatural even exists.

Misty froze at the question. Kai wondered if he had crossed a line – if he had pushed too far into personal space. She sat down slowly and looked at Kai. Her eyes were duller now. She appeared to be somewhere far off, remembering something. Her expression was grim and sad. She opened her mouth and Kai thought she was about to speak but she stopped herself and took a steadying breath instead. She exhaled sharply.

"Ten years ago, my father came here to study the local wildlife. The abundance of bird species in the area drew him here. He went into that forest. He never came back out. The search party that came over from the mainland never returned either."

"Oh my God." Kai lifted his hand to cover his mouth. "I didn't mean to bring up such painful memories."

"It's okay. I relive it every day. I moved here after the search party disappeared. I've always believed in the strange and unusual. I've personally experienced the paranormal. Everyone said it was just a dangerous, remote forest – that it was easy to get turned around and lost." Her brow furrowed deeply, and an angry grimace crossed her face. She shook her head slowly. "I knew something more sinister had happened to them."

They sat together in silence. Emotionally charged situations made Kai anxious. He never knew the right thing to say. And no matter how much he wanted to provide comfort he didn't know how. He opted to look over the contents of the table, instead of looking directly at Misty. Most people would have thought he was being rude or insensitive, but he thought she would understand. He had a feeling she had the ability to know more about a person without them telling her. Kai cleared his throat to break the uncomfortable silence.

"So, what's the game plan then? How do I kill them?"

"We need to trap them first," Misty said in a very matter-of-fact tone.

Kai made a *wait a minute* face and held his hand up to stop her.

"What do you mean *we*? Are you planning on going in there *with* me?"

Misty gave Kai a devilish grin. Her eyes lit up brightly. Kai could have sworn he nearly saw fireworks go off behind them. The fire in her eyes was lit by a need for revenge. No, for vengeance.

"You *need* me. Trust me on this, bud." Her playful tone had returned.

"When I said I have experience with the paranormal…" she trailed off, a look of uncertainty on her face. "Look, just trust that

I know what the fuck I'm doing. I've been preparing for this for a long time. You thought you were the hero, but really, you're the sidekick I've been searching for."

She saw a brief flash of hurt and disappointment cross Kai's face. Her small heartstrings tugged, and she put both hands up toward Kai.

"Oh, shit. I am *so* sorry. That came out wrong. That was mean. I'm sorry. I've just been alone. For a long time. I suck with people and I'm sarcastic a lot. I really didn't mean it to be hurtful." Misty's playful tone was now replaced by a sincerely apologetic one. Her words came out awkwardly, in clipped sentences.

Kai could see in her eyes that what she said was genuine. He studied her face for a moment. She was truly beautiful. Like no woman he had ever laid eyes on. It was almost as if she wasn't fully human. He was starting to wonder. Her bright, mysterious eyes focused on him, and there was no way he could be upset with her. Kai shook his head gently and gave her a boyish smirk. A slight pink color rose into his cheeks.

"It's fine. I don't know anything about this stuff. Consider yourself my sensei. Now, tell me everything you know and let's go get these fuckers."

5

I

Kai let out an exhausted sigh. After three hours of information overload, he was feeling thoroughly drained.

"Let me make sure I've got this straight," he said.

He turned to face Misty. She waited patiently for her star pupil (well, her only pupil) to recite his recently acquired knowledge back to her.

"They don't do well in direct, prolonged sunlight. They can move in the daylight but are mostly active in nighttime hours. Water, especially salt water, is not their friend. Special abilities include, but may not be limited to, silent movement, telepathy, mind control, and full bodily possession."

For each attribute he listed, Kai held up a finger.

"Most importantly, the only way to kill them is by chopping off their head. And then burning the body. But the head and the body have to be burned in separate fires." Kai gave Misty an exasperated look. "Do have all of that right?"

Misty chuckled and nodded with a smile.

"Yep. A plus work, bud."

Even though Kai truly enjoyed spending time with Misty, and that she was being playful (dare he venture to say flirtatious?), he couldn't ignore the fact that she didn't seem to be taking the situation as seriously as he was.

"This is going to be impossible. We are going on a fucking

suicide mission, Misty."

Kai paced around the kitchen. He put his hands on top of his head with his fingers interlaced. His face was slightly pale, his honey brown eyes wide. He stopped and looked at Misty. She didn't respond, only sat there contently, and smiled back at him like she had won the lottery and hadn't told anyone yet. Kai let his hands fall to his sides.

"Why are you not more concerned about this?" Kai's voice broke on the last word. His voice was raised to a volume he wasn't accustomed to using. He stared at Misty in pure disbelief. He stood in front of her, hands on his hips, waiting for her reply.

Misty slowly stood up from her seat. A smile still graced her perfectly shaped lips. She walked past Kai without looking at him. She passed by him so closely; he could feel the heat of her body on his arm. He turned his body to follow the direction she was walking. With the most nonchalance Kai had ever seen, Misty opened the fridge and extracted two bottles of beer. She twisted both tops off and threw them in the trash can. She handed him one of the bottles before taking a long pull from her own.

"Hope you don't mind cheap, domestic shit. I don't mind the fancy stuff, but you can't beat a nice cold Bud Light after a long day."

Misty took another drink and wiped her mouth with the back of her hand. The bottle was already more than half empty. She sat back down at the table. Kai looked at the bottle in his hand as if it were something completely foreign to him.

"You're drinking *beer* right now? How is that the appropriate response to our current situation?" He moved a stack of papers to make space and set his open bottle on the kitchen table. He sat and faced Misty.

"You need to relax, Kai. I'm drinking beer because we deserve a beer." She drank the rest of her bottle in one long gulp and placed the empty bottle on the table. "I told you, I'm very experienced with this sort of thing."

She raised her eyebrows, reached across him, and grabbed his beer. She took a drink of it and placed his back down on the table next to her empty. Kai gave her a stern look.

"You're being cryptic and vague and honestly, it's really fucking annoying." He quickly grabbed the mostly full beer from her side of the table and took a drink. He reminded her of a child who was pouting because they weren't getting their way. "I never said I didn't want the damn beer. I just want to know exactly why, or *how*, you're so God damn calm right now."

Misty raised her brows again and looked up at him through her mascara-laden eyelashes. She pointed at his beer. "Chug that bad boy. Trust me when I say this; you're going to need it."

Kai let out an annoyed sigh. He closed his eyes, shook his head and then followed her instructions. It took him two attempts at chugging, but he eventually emptied his bottle and set it back on the table. By the time he had finished, Misty was standing in front of him with her hand out, waiting for the empty bottle. When Kai supplied it, she threw both bottles in the trash, opened the fridge and produced two more. She gave Kai a sideways smile and extended the fresh beer to him. Kai took the beer and twisted the top off, dropping it into the trashcan. Misty followed suit, took a drink, and then motioned him to follow her.

"Come on, kid. Time for me to blow your fucking mind."

II

Misty opened the door at the foot of the basement stairs. The door was thick metal that reminded Kai of a bank vault or a safe room. He followed close behind Misty as she entered the darkness that lay behind it. She closed the door behind them. The sound of an automatic locking system made Kai jump. He was overwhelmed by the pure darkness. It blinded him. His anxiety reared its ugly head. His heart pounded in his chest. Beads of sweat broke out across his forehead and his palms became slick. He gripped his bottle of beer tightly. He turned in a circle, looking wildly around himself, in hopes of being able to see anything at all.

"Will you please turn a fucking light on?" His voice snapped like the crack of whip, with more anger behind it than he had intended.

Just as his anxiety was morphing into panic, he heard the clack of a flipped light switch on the far side of the room. He froze as large, florescent bulbs began to light across the ceiling. They sprang to life, starting at the back wall, and making their way toward him.

Whoomp.

Whoomp.

Whoomp.

Kai looked around the room in utter disbelief. He spun in a slow circle, trying to soak everything in. The basement had been converted into one, large, open room. The concrete floor had been finished with a glossy resin that sent the industrial fluorescent lighting reflecting back up toward the ceiling. Misty slowly made her way toward Kai. The smile on her face could only be described as a shit-eating-grin.

"Told you I was about to blow your mind." She stood next to him and placed a finger under his chin. She pressed up to close his mouth, which must have fallen open in his utter amazement.

"You look like Charlie when he first walks into the fucking Chocolate Factory." Misty laughed hard at her own joke. It was the first time Kai had ever heard her laugh and the beautiful music of it broke his trance. She took a swig of her beer and gave him a smile that made her perfect nose scrunch. She held her arms out to her sides and spun in a small circle, a laugh still in her voice. "Go ahead. Take a look around. Explore."

The wall to the right was lined with miscellaneous weaponry, stored behind metal cages, and secured with padlocks. The cages were separated into three sections. Kai walked toward them with caution. As he moved past them, he ran his fingers across the cold, black metal. He thought of the fences from his childhood, and how he used to let his fingers idly thrum against their cold linked metal as he walked home from school.

"Want me to open them up for you?" Misty's voice drew his attention.

He snapped his head up to see her leaning against the wall near the first cage, arms folded across her chest. He thought she was standing behind him and seeing her standing there startled him slightly. The quick silence she moved with always caught him off guard. It made him feel foggy and off balance, like he was never fully paying attention. He looked at her and nodded slowly, the faintest hint of a smile at the corner of his mouth.

"I trust you're not going to attempt to murder me, seeing as I'm the only person who can help you," she said.

Misty punched several buttons on the pin-pad of a safe that shared the same wall as her arsenal. At her command, the door popped open with a slight squeak. She grabbed a ring of keys hanging inside. She unlocked the cages, and swung the doors open one by one, placing the padlocks on a high-top table that sat adjacent to the weapons wall. When she was finished, she stood in front of the wall and held her arms out to the sides.

"Behold! My babies! My bringers of death and vengeance!"

She stood silently for a few seconds, and then unable to hold back any longer, broke into an uncontrollable laughing fit. She bent over and braced herself with her hands just above her knees.

She took a breath in and slapped her thigh. Kai stood and stared in wonder, eyes wide. He took a sip of his beer, which was slowly being warmed by the grip of his hand.

"I'm sorry." She stood up and grabbed her own beer from the table.

She inhaled deeply and made a *woo* noise on exhale. Her heavy laughter had caused tears to form in the corners of her eyes, and when she stood upright, they began running down her cheeks. She wiped them away with the back of her free hand. "I told you, I'm alone a lot. Starts to make you a little weird." She made a twirling motion next to her ear with her index finger and shook her head. She finished her beer and placed the empty bottle on the table with the padlocks.

Kai smiled at her sweetly and shrugged. He had to admit, she was very weird. This room was fucking *weird*. And if he didn't have a trusting feeling in his gut, he would likely be very scared right now. But the more time they spent together, the more he developed warm feelings toward her. He couldn't help but imagine them both being magnets that the universe finally placed close enough to one another, that they were finally drawn together in an instant.

He made his way toward the wall to take a closer look at her collection. She was clearly very proud of it, and he very much doubted she had ever been able to show it to another person before. The first case held three handguns, hung neatly in a row. Below the handguns was a rather intimidating looking shotgun. When his eyes got to the bottom of the cage, he found empty pegs where a weapon once hung. Kai looked over his shoulder at Misty. He raised his brows and pointed at the empty space.

She smiled and waved her bottle of beer at him. "There was a slight… incident, a while ago. Don't worry about it."

Kai did a double take. The beer in Misty's hand was more than half full, but he had just watched her finish the one she carried down from the kitchen.

Where the hell did she get another beer?

He looked around the room for any kind of mini-fridge or cooler but found none. He rubbed the back of his neck idly. After a moment he pulled his hand away and looked at it, shocked. He sucked in a sharp breath.

Where the hell did my *beer go?*

He gave Misty a suspicious look. She sipped the beer and when he didn't break his stare, she pushed her chin forward slightly and widened her eyes. She looked around and then faced him again.

"Is there some sort of problem, bud?" She looked deep into his eyes, drinking from the bottle without looking away. It made him uncomfortable, so Kai broke his gaze. He looked at the ground and shook his head.

"No. No. I think I'm just a bit foggy from that first beer." He looked around the room, searching. "I must have put my second one down somewhere, and then you picked it up."

She held one finger up in a 'one minute' gesture while she guzzled the last of the beer in her hand.

"Oh, was this *yours*? My bad." She shot him a wink and chuckled. "You want another? I'll go grab a few from upstairs."

"Yeah, fuck it. I have a feeling shit is just going to keep getting weirder. I might need it."

Misty nodded and moved toward the stairs. Kai couldn't help but watch her walking away. She stopped at the door, looked over her shoulder at him, and pointed toward the guns.

"You better keep moving, or you're going to be looking at the same damn gun rack until midnight."

Kai held up his hands, brought his shoulders to his ears, and widened his eyes.

"All right, all right. Still a lot more to see. Got it."

He turned to face the wall. The second case was far more curious than the first. Much like the first, the weapons were arranged by size, moving smallest to largest from top to bottom. The top row contained five daggers of varying shapes, sizes, and design. Below the daggers, rested a sheathed Samurai sword. The bottom row contained a large sword that reminded Kai of the knights of the round table. The grip was braided metal and a strange, bright stone adorned the pommel. He leaned in for a closer look. It was captivating. He knelt down and rested his butt on his heels, making the sword eye level. He reached up to touch the stone.

"Uh, definitely wouldn't do that, champ."

Kai fell backwards, landing flat on the cool concrete. Misty appeared above him, beer in hand.

"I didn't mean to scare you." She extended her free hand. He grabbed it and was surprised at the amount of strength behind the arm that pulled him up. "I should have mentioned that most of the stuff in here is super dangerous. And some of it, is dangerous in a supernatural-will-try-to-ruin-your-whole-life kind of way. Just keep your paws to themselves unless otherwise instructed, padawan."

Misty pointed toward the cooler near the basement door.

"More refreshments in there, if you want."

Kai nodded, pointed toward the wall, and found his way toward the third, and final case. Row one was filled with sharp, wooden stakes. Kai let his shoulders drop and turned around.

"I thought you said vampires weren't real." He squinted his eyes with suspicion. When he didn't receive a response, he raised his hand, and pointed a thumb over his shoulder. "So, what's with the stakes?"

Misty was leaning against the table, propped up by her elbows. She gave him a bored look and cocked her head to the side.

"I've said a lot of things in life, some of it's true, some of it isn't."

Kai turned back toward the case and observed that the middle section of the case housed several hand grenades.

"Is that your way of telling me vampires are real? Cause at this point, I wouldn't…" Kai cut his sentence off abruptly, looked over his shoulder at Misty with a grin, and pointed toward the weapon in the third row. "A fucking crossbow?"

Misty gave him a smile, showing off her brilliant row of teeth.

"No arsenal is complete without a crossbow. Will you please quit fanboying and get another drink. I'm finally starting to feel a buzz and drinking alone is so boring." Misty widened her eyes and pushed her bottom lip out, making an exaggerated pouting face at him.

"First off, I still have to drive back home. Second, I still want to see the rest of this stuff. Third, you have a lot of explaining to do."

"First off." Misty held up her pointer finger, mocking Kai. "You're going to stay here tonight. Second, you can drink and look at the same time. Or is that too hard for you? Because if so, you're right, we are fucked." Kai narrowed his eyes at her, and Misty returned his look with a playful laugh. "Third, I can drink *and* explain. In fact, I'm better at explaining when I'm drinking."

Kai opened his mouth to speak. Before he could protest, Misty held up her finger again. This time she placed it to her lips, motioning him to be quiet.

"All the clothing and equipment you will need for our little rescue mission is in this house. And that explanation you want, well, it's long. So quit bitching, get a beer, and buckle up, bud."

Kai threw his hands up in a defensive gesture. He walked to the large cooler (still completely unsure how she got it down here) and opened the top. It was packed full with beer bottles and ice.

She must be able to really drink. I'm going to be so screwed.

Kai reached his hand into the cooler and pulled a beer out. He twisted the top off and placed it in the pocket of his jeans. It was the easiest way to keep track of how many he consumed throughout the night. He took a long drink and made eye contact with Misty.

"Happy now, princess?" Kai asked with a smirk.

"Ooo, the shy guy finally breaks out the sarcasm and nick names." She gave him a tiny golf clap. "I like it. Come on, come over here and do a shot with me."

Kai looked at the table. She had two shot glasses, already filled with translucent, brown liquid. As he approached the table, he noticed the bottle of whiskey.

"I've never seen a grown man look so scared of a shot of whiskey."

His face had betrayed him. He remembered what she had said earlier 'I'm alone a lot.' When was the last time she had fun? He picked up one of the shot glasses and held it out in front of him, waiting for her to cheers with him. The excitement and joy that crossed her face filled his stomach with warm butterflies. They downed the shots, and while he shivered and made a face, she drank the liquid like water. She noticed the look he gave her and shrugged.

"Runs in the family," she said.

III

One more round of shots, and a beer later, Kai finally began exploring the rest of the basement. On the wall opposite the weapons, there were several high-top tables adorned with assortments of vials, bottles, and equipment that reminded him of high school chemistry class. He weaved between the tables, examining the many different liquids. The smells that filled his nose were abundant and foreign. He didn't recognize a single one. He looked toward Misty, who was watching him intently.

"I can tell you're about to ask a question, but I'm going to request you hold the rest of them until after I give my explanation." Misty had abandoned her shot glass and was now taking small sips directly from the bottle.

Kai moved his way toward the back of the room. A large punching bag with duct tape wrapped around it several times hung from a sturdy chain in the ceiling. A short distance away, hung a speed bag. A pair of well-worn boxing gloves hung from a hook in the corner. On the wall next to them, hung a large stick.

She must be into sparring. Maybe I should be more afraid of her than I am. What if she can kick my ass?

He turned to make his way to the final corner of the room. This section was separated with a large, sliding curtain (like those found in the ER at a hospital to separate patients). Before he could search for Misty's eyes and ask for approval, he heard her voice call out from behind him.

"You can open it."

Kai stopped his hand short of the curtain, noticing that it was shaking quite badly. He took a deep breath and took hold of the curtain, sliding it slowly to the side. Behind the curtain, in the corner of the room, was a cage. As he studied it further, he decided it wasn't a cage, but more like a prison cell. Two of the square cell's walls comprised of thick metal bars, spaced only about one inch apart. The back two walls of the cell were created by the concrete foundation of the basement. There was a stiff, uncomfortable looking cot against the back wall. Next to it, a pair of chains with cuffs on the end were anchored into the concrete.

Kai's body began to shake. Fear flooded his chest and he turned around slowly. Misty was leaning on her elbows, face propped in her hands at the table near her armory.

"I'm not going to hurt you." Her voice was even and calm, even a bit condescending (as if to say he was very stupid for even letting the thought enter his mind). "I know you're probably thinking of all the true crime docs you've seen, but I'm not a weird serial killer. Come back over here." She took another small nip from the whiskey bottle. "It's explanation time."

6

I

"My mom died from cancer when I was eight. I remember her, but not as vividly as I used to. I remember her smile and her eyes. They were warm, kind, and bright. I was never sad or upset when she was around me. I know why, now, but we will get to that part later."

Misty had replaced the bottle of whiskey with a bottle of water. She chugged the entire bottle with surprising speed and ease. When it was gone, she smashed it like an accordion, replaced the lid, and chucked the now compact piece of plastic toward the cooler (obviously not caring about littering in her own home). Her hair was no longer neatly styled and had lost much of its volume. She tucked it tightly behind each ear. Her makeup had begun to run in places. Her speech wasn't slurred but her alcohol intake was becoming more obvious. Kai sat across the table from her, listening intently.

"My dad wasn't around a lot when I was growing up. He wasn't a bad father, but his job required him to travel for extended periods of time. Being an only child, I learned quickly to grow fond of my own company."

Without pausing, she got up and wandered over to the cooler. Her movement was dreamlike and a bit wobbly. She plunged her hand into the depths of the cooler and pulled it back out with a beer in tow. The *pffftt* sound of her beer opening sounded too loud to Kai as it echoed around the large, empty room. No other sound belonged in the air while she was speaking. As she continued her story, she moved back to her place at the table, wiping water and ice from the side of her bottle as she went.

"After mom died, dad started leaving me with our neighbor, my mom's best friend, when he would go on his business trips. Her name was Holly. *Is* Holly. As my dad started spending more and more time away from home, I grew closer to Holly. I never thought she felt like my mother. More like a cool aunt. I ended up moving in with her until I finished high school."

Misty took a long pull from her beer. Kai thought the water meant she was done drinking, but it seemed to be just a brief intermission. Her eyes were still focused and aware, but he could tell she was somewhere far away.

"Despite losing my mom, I had a pretty normal childhood. I went to a public school. I had friends and sleepovers. The older I got, the more I started to realize I wasn't like other people."

She chugged the rest of the beer. She burped, but not loudly. She just let the air from her stomach fill her mouth and blew it toward the ceiling.

"Once I hit puberty, the problems began. Every teenage girl has mood swings, but mine were off the charts. I mean, I was a *crazy* bitch. Holly started having a hard time controlling me because I was just so pissed off at everything and everyone, all the time. She owned a bar and we lived in a small town, so she was also the bar tender on most nights. She was out late just trying to keep her business afloat."

She finished her beer, setting the empty bottle down a bit too hard on the tabletop. It clinked loudly and she cringed.

"I started hanging out with older dudes and partying a lot. I mean *a lot*. At fifteen I was doing blow and drinking. I was out all night, doing whatever the hell I wanted. When my habit got bad enough, I would have my boyfriend drive me to the next town over so I could strip for money. The owner of the club took my fake ID for employment verification and never questioned it, but I always knew he *knew* my real age." She squinted her eyes as if straining to see something far away. "It's a goddamn miracle I lived to see twenty."

She picked up the beer bottle, swished it around, and realized it was empty. Her eyes came back to the here and now and locked onto Kai's. She gave him an exaggerated frown.

"Do you mind grabbing a few more of these out of the cooler, bud? You're closer." She picked up Kai's still half full beer and held it up to examine it. She looked at him with disapproval. The exaggerated frown returned in full force. "I thought you said you were going to drink with me. You need to catch up!"

"I know, I know. Your story was just really pulling me in."

Kai jogged over to the cooler and returned with an armful of beers. Misty helped him set them safely onto the table.

"There – three for you and three for me. Does that count as me catching up?" Kai gave her a *please forgive me* look, including full-blown puppy dog eyes.

"Nope! I'm leagues in front of you!" She spun the top off the whiskey, filled his shot glass, and slid it across the table. It came to a stop just before the edge of the table. Misty's eyes widened and she made an 'O' with her mouth. A small, relieved laugh escaped her chest. "Oh shit, that was fucking *close* to being a party foul. You have to do two shots, back-to-back. And keep up with me on the beers. Comprende?"

Kai picked up the shot and put it to his lips. With one quick motion he titled his head back and emptied the glass. He made a face and motioned with his hand for Misty to pour the second. As soon as it was full, he shot it back. As soon as the liquid hit the back of his throat, his jaw quivered, and his mouth flooded with spit. He had to close his eyes and focus hard not to lose the contents of his stomach. After a few moments of a clenched jaw and closed eyes, he successfully held it down.

"Are you happy now? Can you please continue? I really want to know what happened." Kai's voice gave away that he was still fighting a battle with nausea.

Misty rolled her eyes, capped the bottle, and took a drink of her beer.

"Holly thought I started partying for the same reasons any teenager does. Because it's fun and there isn't shit else to do, especially in a Podunk Mountain town. I was the only one who knew the real reason. When I got really upset, weird shit would happen around me. It started off small, like a pencil flying off my desk onto the floor. But then, it got *scary*. The pencil would fly off the desk, but instead of hitting the floor, it would stick into the wall. And not just the lead tip. It would be buried two inches deep into the drywall."

Kai raised his eyebrows in shock. Misty nodded.

"Yeah. Anyways, it kept getting more intense. I started hearing voices. My brain would get flooded with all these different conversations. I finally figured out it didn't happen when I was with other people or if I wasn't sober. That's why I started getting fucked up. It made it all stop.

"It's part of the reason I still drink so much. It controls all of it." She tapped an index finger to her temple and squinted an eye. "Fast forward to when I graduated and moved back into my parents' house, *my* house. I lived there from the time I turned eighteen to when I was twenty. Now, I'm going to cut a whole bunch of the bullshit out and summarize this part, because honestly, I'm getting tired of hearing myself talk."

She slammed the rest of her beer and opened another. She pointed lazily at Kai and then down to his beer. He followed her lead so she would continue. He was so intrigued but still hadn't gotten any answers about who she really was.

"Basically, around my twentieth birthday, I started seeing some really scary shit in the house. I didn't know if they were really there or if I was losing my mind, fully, finally. Not long after I started seeing them, they started attacking me. *Physically fucking attacking me.* I finally packed up a bag and went over to Holly's one night. I told her all about what had been happening to me, not just the recent stuff, *everything.* Here's the real kicker; she fucking *knew* about it, the whole time. And that's the night I found out who my parents really were. Who I really am."

She drew in a deep breath and closed her eyes.

"You're going to think I'm fucking crazy, but I'm drunk so, here it goes."

She opened her eyes and locked gazes with Kai. He reached across the table and placed his hands on top of hers, attempting to comfort her.

"I won't think you're crazy. I promise."

She let out a shaky laugh, and he thought she might break down and cry. But she took another breath and settled herself.

"My mom was a witch. A damn powerful and skilled one. I guess it's a genetic thing and Dad told Holly to keep an eye out for the signs. A lot of the time a witch will also have a special skill or ability. *One.*" She raised her eyebrows slightly and held up an index finger. "In my case, I've got multiple. Telepathy, a mild ability to control the emotions of those around me, psychic ability, and, as you already know, dream traveling." She took another swig.

"And the freak show doesn't stop there." She laughed and shook her head, clearly becoming more emotionally affected the deeper into her past she delved. "As it turned out, mommy dearest wasn't the only one who had a secret. Dad wasn't a businessman. He was a fucking demon slayer. Literally. He hunted down evil shit and killed it. That was also genetic. It came with the ability to see the other side. It also came with a flashing red beacon that draws the evil to me. Mine was activated when my dad died."

She took a moment to collect herself again. Her speech was becoming more disorganized.

"He didn't go into that forest because he loved birds, Kai. He was hunting the same creatures we're going after. After Holly told me everything, I found everything you see here in the cellar of my childhood home. I read his journals and notes and started training, and voila, I'm as bad ass as Buffy the fucking Vampire Slayer." Her voice had a hint of something Kai couldn't quite identify. Sarcasm? Annoyance?

Misty stood up and stretched, letting a large yawn overwhelm her perfect face. She let her arms fall to her sides and looked over the table, now filled with empty bottles. She made a get up motion with her hand.

"We better get to bed. I'll clean all this crap up in the morning. There's a guest bedroom upstairs, to the right of the front door. Bathroom over there too. All your clothes for tomorrow are on the bed."

Without another word, Misty moved toward the back of the room and shut off the lights.

DAY 3

7

I

"Rise and shine, bud!"

Kai's eyes snapped open, and he shot upright. Misty was standing at the foot of the bed with her hands on her hips. She was wearing black yoga pants and a black sport jacket.

"I don't remember requesting a wake-up call. Especially such a loud one," Kai's voice was gravelly as he replied.

His head was throbbing. He rubbed his eyes with the palms of his hands. He slowly turned and placed his feet on the floor. A wave of nausea flowed over him, and he groaned at the discomfort. Misty chuckled and plopped herself onto the bed next to him.

"Oh, please don't shake the bed," he pleaded.

Kai put his hand over his mouth and shut one eye. Misty smirked and pulled a small vial filled with a translucent, gold liquid from her jacket pocket.

"Drink this, lightweight. It looks like piss, but that hangover will be gone in less than a minute."

Kai gently took the glass container from his new friend. He turned it in the light as he examined it. He removed the small cork and sniffed. The foul smell he expected didn't come. Instead, the faint smell of honey filled his nose. He put the vial to his lips and gently tilted his head back. The liquid had little to no taste. As he swallowed, a warm tingle followed the liquid into his stomach. The feeling was intensely pleasant, and a slow smile spread across Kai's face.

"I don't know what that stuff is, but it is amazing. I feel better than I would have if I hadn't had a single drop to drink."

"It's just a little potion I concocted," Misty replied, clearly proud of her creation and pleased with his reaction to it.

Kai smiled and gave her an admiring look. Misty blushed briefly and shrugged her shoulders. She stood slowly from where she sat on the bed.

"Alchemy has proved to be one of the most helpful skills I've picked up over the years. It's one of my favorite pieces of being a witch. Anyway, get dressed and meet me in the kitchen. I made breakfast and we have a few more important things to go over." Misty paused in the doorway and looked over her shoulder. "And then we need to go, quickly."

II

Kai entered the kitchen, now wearing a similar outfit to Misty's. The papers, books, and crystals that covered the table the night before had been cleaned up. The table was set with two plates filled with steaming food (bacon, hashbrowns, and scrambled eggs) and two tall glasses of orange juice. Kai took a seat in front of one of the place settings. He inhaled deeply and his stomach greeted the smell with a loud growl.

"Dig in before it gets cold," Misty encouraged.

Misty placed a few bottles of assorted hot sauces on the table and took her seat in front of the other plate. She picked up the green Tabasco and shook it over her eggs and half of her hashbrowns. Kai watched as she shoveled her food into her mouth with remarkable speed. Even more remarkable, he still thought she was the most beautiful woman he'd laid eyes on. He'd never seen someone put food into their mouth that quickly and still somehow be elegant.

Kai also doused his food with a light sprinkle of hot sauce before digging in. The scrambled eggs were perfectly light and fluffy. The hashbrowns were golden brown and had wonderful crunch to them. Every bite was more delicious than the last and soon, Kai was eating just as quickly as his counterpart.

"So, you're a witch, a badass demon hunter, and a chef," he said with a joking smile in his voice.

Kai managed to speak through a full mouth of food. He would typically not practice such rude behavior, but he couldn't stop eating long enough to speak before putting another forkful into his mouth. His statement hit Misty and she almost spit her food out and choked on it all at once. She finished chewing and swallowed her nearly lost mouthful. She rinsed it down with a large drink of orange juice.

"I'm not sure about the validity of your statement, sir," she replied. Misty smiled and shook her head, the subtle blush from earlier returning to her cheeks briefly. Kai nodded and pointed at her with a finger from the hand that held his fork.

"I'm serious. I haven't had a breakfast this delicious in as long as I can remember. Maybe not ever." He stabbed the last few pieces of egg and potatoes on his plate and deposited them into his mouth. "Thank you for making that."

"I'm glad you enjoyed it. It was no problem. We need our strength for today; for what we are about to go up against." Misty let her voice drop slightly as she finished her sentence.

The chill of reality sent a shiver creeping up Kai's spine. He tossed his napkin onto the center of his empty plate and slid it gently away from him. Misty let him have a moment of silence to reflect on their situation. She collected his plate and stacked it on top of her own and took them to the sink. When she finished rinsing them (they both cleaned their plates, so it didn't take much) she made her way into the living room.

She returned a minute later with a large wooden box. She placed the box on the table and opened it, revealing bottles of various shapes and sizes, filled with liquids of different colors and textures. Some were opaque, some translucent. Kai thought he saw a few of them emitting a subtle glow.

"It's time to get down to business. There are a few potions in this box that are going to be key to our success."

Misty removed two bottles and one smaller vial from the case. She picked up the first bottle and held it up to the light. The liquid contained inside was a bright, opaque purple. Swirls of gold swam through it. Kai looked on in amazement, like a small child watching a magic trick.

"This potion is what we're going to use to set our traps. There's no way we will be able to catch them or get close enough to chop their heads off. So, trapping them is our only shot."

Misty looked at Kai. He nodded, signaling that he was listening and encouraging her to continue.

"The potion itself is already charged with a barrier spell, all you or I have to do, is pour it in a circle. If the creature steps within the circle, it will be trapped inside. That's when we make our move."

Misty slid her thumb across her throat.

"Or it will at least keep it in one place if we need more time to attend to another matter. I have an idea of what we are going up against and what we are going into, but I can't be positive about any of it," she continued.

Kai nodded slowly and squinted his eyes.

"That sounds way too easy. What's the catch?"

Misty laughed and shook a finger at Kai.

"It *sounds* easy. The likelihood of one, or both of us, being overcome by these creatures before we're able to lure them into our traps, is very high. We have a better chance of setting traps randomly and hoping one of them stumbles into one, honestly."

The color drained slightly from Kai's face. Misty picked up the second bottle. The liquid reminded Kai of ink. It was jet black and as thick as maple syrup.

"But that's why we have this helpful little drink."

"*Drink?*" Kai made a face that reminded Misty of a kid looking at broccoli.

Misty laughed and nodded.

"Yes. I brewed this to help fight involuntary compulsion. If one of your friends is possessed when we find them, we can force this down their gullet and it should kick the creature out of their mind with haste."

"Or if one of us ends up compelled," Kai added.

Kai's voice was low and serious. Misty's expression reflected his voice's solemn tone as she nodded in agreement. She picked the small vial up. It appeared to be empty. Kai tilted his head and looked at Misty with a confused expression.

"It isn't empty," she said. "This potion is one I'm particularly proud of. After it's brewed, it's boiled at a high temperature and evaporates into a gas, which is then trapped inside a small vial. Instead of drinking it, you inhale it."

"That…" Kai paused briefly, a wide smile on his face. He pointed at the vial Misty held in her hand. "Is so cool. What is it used for?"

"This one I created when I realized I was going to need a second pair of hands. I also realized that second pair of hands was likely not going to be quite as sturdy as my own. Inhaling this will give you a bit more strength and stamina than you would normally have. It'll also make your focus sharper and reaction times faster." She paused a moment and squinted her eyes slightly. "At least I hope that's what it will do."

Kai snatched the vial from Misty's hand and held it in front of his face, so close he almost went cross-eyed. Misty laughed.

"Easy, tiger, it won't make you a superhero or anything. But it should help lower our level of danger."

"How long does it last?"

"If my calculations are correct, you should feel the effects of the gas for anywhere between twelve to eighteen hours. But you're my first real test subject, so don't quote me on it."

Misty stood up and made her way toward the basement. Any sign of the playful sarcasm she had exhibited yesterday was completely gone. Her tone and body language were both very serious, even grave.

"Get your boots on," she said. "I'm grabbing the weapons bag from the basement, and then we're hauling ass to that little boat of yours. It's go time, Kai." She didn't bother stopping or even turning her head over her shoulder as she said her final words before descending into the basement.

8

I

Kai gazed out the passenger window as Misty pulled her worn Camry to a stop at the marina. On the drive over, his anxiety had kicked into high gear. His heart pounded; every beat could be heard in his ears. His palms had become slick with sweat. Misty looked over at him and tapped his shoulder. He was yanked from his daydream and turned to address her. He blinked a few times to bring her face into focus.

"You have to lead the way now. I don't even know what your boat looks like."

Kai nodded and got out of the car. When Misty grabbed the bags containing their miscellaneous arsenal of potions and weapons from the trunk, he offered to take it from her. Misty laughed and shook her head with assertion.

"I'm a lot stronger than you, kiddo. Plus, you look pretty green around the gills. You don't need any extra weight to carry right now." Misty's voice was beginning to take on an apologetic tone.

She slung the pack over her shoulder and stood in front of Kai. She grabbed him by the tops of both of his arms firmly (she was too short to reach his shoulders) and looked up at him to make direct eye contact.

"Take a deep breath. I know this shit is scary, but we are going to come out the other side all right. We have everything we need to succeed."

He didn't break eye contact with her and nodded. He took a deep, slow breath through his nose, and exhaled through his mouth. He swallowed hard but his mouth was dry, and his throat just seemed to stick together.

"All right, let's go," Misty said in a matter-of-fact tone.

Misty patted him on the shoulder before following him to the docks.

II

"This rig isn't as bad as you made it sound," Misty said. She nodded her head gently with approval.

Misty looked around as Kai finished preparing the boat to take off.

"Thanks. It's my most prized possession," Kai's voice had a hint of pride as he replied.

As he double checked the last few items on his safety checklist and untied the boat from the dock, Misty gently dropped the pack from her shoulder. She unzipped the front pocket and retrieved the small, seemingly empty vial.

"I think you need to take this now. I'm not positive how long it takes to start working. It's an inhalant, so it should be nearly instant, but…" She shrugged before continuing, "Better safe than sorry."

Kai took the vial and his excitement suddenly overwhelmed his fear and anxiety. He smiled broadly and made his way to the wheel of the boat, where he was protected from the wind. He motioned for Misty to follow him. He held the vial up in front of his face, so close it almost touched the tip of his nose. He held it there as he exhaled fully and removed the cork. He placed the vial under his nose and inhaled as deeply as he could.

Misty stared at him with anticipation. Kai turned around, started the engine of the boat, and began navigating from the dock to the open water. Misty opened her eyes wide and pushed her chin forward. When Kai didn't turn back around, Misty's annoyance boiled over. She shoved his shoulder hard enough to make him jerk the wheel of the boat, which he corrected without delay (and flawlessly, she noticed).

"What the hell, Misty? You could have made me wreck my boat!" Misty had never heard or seen Kai so irritated before and she felt a bit bad for being so rough with him.

"No. What the hell to you! Are you really not going to tell me if it worked or not? Or say anything at all?"

"I was going to wait until I was sure it was working. I might have just psyched myself up, but I feel great. I mean *really* great."

Kai finally turned to briefly make eye contact with Misty. When he did, Misty tried to keep her facial expression neutral, but her heart leapt into her throat. His pupils were dilated to the size of pennies, his smile was wild.

Oh God, did I just drug my partner?

Misty gave him an uncomfortable smile and took a seat in the tattered, worn seat to the rear of Kai. He seemed to be piloting the boat with ease and she hoped the insane visual appearance of her captain was just a mild side effect, and he wasn't actually tripping on some magical gas.

Once they hit open water, Kai increased his speed significantly. He was either feeling extremely confident because the potion worked as intended, or because he was extremely intoxicated. Misty hoped it was the first option and did her best to remain focused in case he began losing control of the craft. Within fifteen minutes, the withered dock and deserted beach were coming into view. Misty stood up and readied herself for battle.

9

I

Kai guided the boat gently up to the rickety wooden dock he had left Jeanie and her father on three days ago. He wasn't scheduled to return here for another day. He cut the engine and tied the boat up. He dropped the small anchor he had for extra security. The dock had seen better days and was likely ready to go any day now. He heard Misty unzip the weapons pack and moved to join her. As he approached, she held out a utility belt to him without looking up from what she was doing.

"So you can carry everything you need and still have your hands free. How are you feeling?" Her voice was flat.

Misty was afraid to look up at him, but when she finally found the courage, she was more than thankful her new friend was back to looking normal. The terrifying grin had diminished, and his eyes were his own again. Kai nodded, took the belt from her outstretched hand, and snapped it around his waist.

"I feel good, great actually. Confident. Sharp." He made solid, unwavering eye contact with Misty. "I feel ready."

Apparently, enhanced Kai wasn't as talkative as regular Kai. Misty guessed it wasn't fully the fault of the potion he had inhaled, but possibly also had to do with the severity of the situation he was currently facing. She guessed that was to be expected in anyone's first monster fighting situation. The possibility of death hits everyone differently. She was much more terrified on her first venture, but she didn't have any help. She took a deep breath, closed her eyes, and focused for a moment.

She opened her eyes on the exhale and began pulling weapons from the unzipped bag that lay in front of her.

Misty distributed two large, long bottles of trapping potion, a bottle of the anti-possession potion, a large hunting knife, and a handgun to Kai. As he strapped the materials into his utility belt, his hands shook. He took a calming breath to attempt to calm his nerves.

"I guess that potion can't completely take the anxiety out of the situation." Kai's voice also shook slightly with fear and embarrassment.

Misty laughed.

"If the worst of your symptoms are some shaking hands, I'd say you're in good shape," she said.

Misty finished attaching her equipment to her own belt and turned to Kai.

"Are you ready to do this shit?"

Kai nodded. He did not make eye contact. Instead, he looked out over the beach. It was now mid-morning, but the sun struggled to pierce the thick cloud cover. A thick fog was beginning to roll in off the water. The breeze that accompanied the fog was unseasonably cold and bit the bare skin on the back of Kai's neck sharply. The scene laid out in front of them was nothing less than ominous. Kai locked eyes with Misty and nodded sharply. Misty picked up her cross bow and loaded it. She tried to speak, and her voice caught in her throat for a moment. She coughed gently to clear it.

Finally, she said, "Let's go then, bud."

II

Kai led the way from the dock to the entry point of the forest. As he walked along the beach, he watched his shoes sink slightly into the wet sand, each step leaving a slightly darker imprint. His cheeks stung from the salty, cold air blowing in from the water. Kai walked from the dock straight to the forest line. He turned and looked at Misty.

"I'm not one hundred percent in the know on how these potions work, but…" He paused and looked down the tree line. He pointed at the ground where the beach met the forest. "If we poured this potion in a line along where the forest meets the beach, would it trap them inside the forest? At least along this beach."

Misty's face broke out into a wide smile. She wagged a finger at Kai and shook her head.

"You know, kid. You might end up being vital to this mission after all. That's not a bad idea."

"Do we have enough to do the entire tree line against this beach?" Kai asked.

"We should. The potion should work, even in a very small quantity. If even a drop is present in the ground, it should stop them from being able to get through."

Without hesitation Misty removed a bottle of the purple, sparkling potion from her belt. She removed the stopper and began walking in a squat down the tree line, pouring the liquid with slow precision.

Kai stood and watched the white caps of the ocean break before colliding with the sandy shore. He inhaled the cold, salty air through his nose and closed his eyes. When he opened them, he turned and watched Misty making her way toward the trail head, pouring the magical liquid as she went. He couldn't help but smile. The speed and accuracy of her movement, not to mention the immense amount of stamina she possessed, was unparalleled. He couldn't hold a squat for thirty seconds without a struggle. She was walking in a squat and showed no signs of fatigue.

Kai shook his head and freed himself of his daydream (he had started to think of it as the 'Misty daze'). He felt a surge of confidence as he started making his way toward her. He had to walk quickly to catch up to her. She was moving surprisingly fast, and he found himself feeling amazed, once again. He had a feeling this was going to be a common occurrence in her company.

He was still catching up to her when she stopped at the place where the trail met the beach. Kai jogged lightly to quickly close the gap between them.

"I'm going to run down the beach a bit further, and then make my way back to you with the potion. Stay here and act as a marker, so I can keep my bearings," Misty ordered.

Before Kai could respond, she was off again. He'd never witnessed her at an open sprint. Her movement was quick and fluid. It reminded him more of an animal than a human.

I guess she isn't all the way human though, is she?

He shook his head at the thought and let his mind wander as he watched Misty disappear around the bend and out of sight. The forest was alive with the sound of many birds and their songs combined with the ocean waves invoked a peacefulness. For a moment, Kai almost forgot about the danger lurking within the dark cover of the trees. Only a few minutes had passed when Misty's petite form came back into view and inched its way toward him. He was perfectly content to stand and watch her move (and would gladly spend all day doing so, if the opportunity ever rose).

He greeted her with a warm smile. She flashed her thousand-kilowatt teeth in return and nodded her head to the left once, gesturing him to follow her. When he went to move, he found his legs locked in place. His feet felt cemented to the ground. She stopped just inside the mouth of the forest and turned around to look at him.

"You won't make me do this alone." Misty spoke to Kai in a firm, yet comforting tone. "Just breathe. You're afraid and that's okay. But you're ready, I know you are."

The sound of her reassuring voice slid over him and melted his fear like butter in a hot pan. He moved forward slowly and in three short steps, he crossed the barrier into the forest.

III

The fog within the forest was so thick that it seemed to cling to everything the air touched. It was as if they were transported to a different world all together when they entered the forest. The peacefulness that was present on the beach was replaced by an oppressive anxiety and fear that pressed into Kai from every angle, threatening suffocation.

Tiny droplets formed on the waterproof surface of Kai's jacket. The material of his pants was not water resistant, and the lower part of his body was soaked to the bone. Thankfully, his focus was set on the task at hand, and that kept him distracted from the discomfort his pants normally would have caused him.

He pressed on, following closely behind Misty. He used her as a beacon, guiding him through the fog-laden trees. As they walked, he watched her blonde ponytail swing from side to side. Tiny droplets of water slid down the back of her jacket. The trail was clear and although they had plenty of room to move comfortably through the forest, the deeper they went, the greater the feeling of claustrophobia set in.

Kai was grateful for the spell currently operating inside him that was keeping him alert, focused, and mostly confident, but he couldn't help but notice the sense of fear lingering at the back of his mind. There was an anxiety hiding deep down in his chest that no deep breath could quite cure. Every step he took, he imagined the trees taking their own steps inward, closer to him and Misty. There was an ever-present feeling of the forest closing in on them.

After about thirty minutes of hiking, his mind drifted to his friend and her father. How far in were they? Were they getting closer to them? Without notice, Misty stopped short. Kai nearly ran into her backside but looked up just in time to miss her.

When his eyes met hers, her expression was concerned and concentrated. Her brow furrowed and a small droplet of water rolled from her hairline, and into her eyebrow. She wiped her forehead with the back of her hand.

"Can you feel them?" she asked.

Kai looked at her with an intense concentration and nodded tersely.

"I'm assuming that feeling of intense dread that's trying to work its way into my chest is them. Are they trying to plant negative emotions in my mind?"

"Basically. Bastards don't seem to know we're here for them. If they did, I don't think they would be so subtle. I think they're distracted. They're focused on your friends."

Misty placed her hands on her hips. The furrow in her brow deepened as she let out a heavy sigh.

"Unless…" she trailed off.

Her eyes were distant. Kai waited patiently for her to complete whatever thought she was formulating, never taking his eyes from her face.

Finally, she drew in a deep breath and spoke.

"Unless they *do* know."

She paused briefly before pointing a finger at Kai. She snatched the largest potion bottle from her belt.

"We need to start setting traps while we move along, starting right now," Misty said.

Kai acknowledged her and grabbed the bottle from his belt, too.

"How big do we need to make the circles for the traps to work?" he asked.

"About six feet in diameter. We don't want them too small because then there is a chance they will completely miss them. But we want to be careful not to make them too big either. We don't want them to have too much wiggle room once they're trapped. That creates extra danger for us." She let out a chuff. "Like we need that."

As she gave Kai instructions, she moved to the right of the trail a way and began slowly pouring her potion in a circle. When the circle was completed, the ground inside the circle emitted a faint glow. After about ten seconds the glow dissipated. Kai smiled. He couldn't stop the intruding thought that Misty greatly resembled an angel, the way the glow lit her body gently from the feet up in those short moments.

Misty noticed him staring and her glow now came from within. A smile lit up her face. She was wondering how she never noticed how naturally handsome he was. She locked eyes with him, trying not to blush.

"Pretty cool, huh?" she said with a grin. "I wanted a quick, easy confirmation that the trap is set correctly. It's hard not to get an accidental gap when you're in a hurry. So, I built the little glow into the spell."

She continued to move throughout the forest, carefully moving without a specified pattern. She moved quickly and gracefully and was soon out of view. Kai waited on the trail patiently for her return. It didn't take him long to realize she wasn't going to need his help with the area they were currently in. His patience quickly started to fade. He snapped his potion bottle back into his belt, feeling a bit disappointed. He let out a deep sigh, a hint of annoyance rising in his heart.

Why did she even bring me with her? I'm obviously just holding her up.

He didn't like the way the tone of his own inner dialogue sounded. It reminded him of a bratty teenager who isn't getting their way. Misty popped back into view and met Kai on the trail. She didn't seem to notice his slightly sour mood.

"All right, we need to keep moving. If you feel your intuition telling you to lay a trap down at any point, listen to it. Make sure it's random. Don't leave a pattern."

Before Kai could respond, she was moving forward again. He shrugged and followed her.

IV

They followed the trail, both of them taking small detours to lay traps, as their spirit moved them. They continued for about twenty minutes when they heard it. The shrill scream of a woman slammed into their ear drums and froze them where they stood.

Kai's heart immediately began to thunder in his chest. Misty turned around to make eye contact. They stared at each other. Their eyes were wide, nostrils flared with heavy breathing. They remained frozen.

Waiting.

Listening.

Kai inched forward slightly. Misty quickly shot her hand up, palm facing him, motioning him to stop. She pressed a finger from her other hand to her lips. Kai followed her instructions and froze again, mid-step. He reminded her of a child playing a game of red light, green light.

Misty's gaze remained unfocused as she stared into the forest. She listened intently. They waited there in the still silence for what felt like an eternity.

Thirty seconds.

Forty seconds.

And then it began.

V

From that moment forward, everything progressed with intense speed. In the not so far off distance, the sound of an argument rose through the dense fog and trees.

Misty moved quickly toward Kai. She made deliberate, piercing eye contact and grabbed him firmly by the shoulders. Her tone was serious. It was a tone Kai hadn't heard in her voice before, and it made him feel uneasy and nervous.

"Look at me. Are you listening?" she asked.

Kai nodded but could not seem to speak. Misty, on the other hand, spoke with elegance and speed.

"You need to go ahead alone, without me. From the sound of it, they're not far from here at all. Your friends and, I'm guessing, at least one of them."

Kai opened his mouth but before he could protest, Misty shook her head and clamped a hand tightly over his mouth.

"Don't freak out. Don't be upset with me. I am *not* abandoning you. But I need to lay *a lot* of traps, in a very small amount of time. And I need them to keep their focus on your friends. Go make sure that happens. Please." Her tone changed from stern to pleading on the last word.

To Kai's great (and pleasant) surprise, Misty grabbed his head firmly, pulled him close, and planted a gentle kiss on his cheek. Too shocked to move or speak, he watched her disappear into the forest. Kai took a deep breath to steady himself and began walking up the trail. Directly into grave danger.

VI

Misty ran through the forest as fast as her legs would take her. She bobbed and weaved between trees and ducked beneath branches. Her precision was damn good, but the occasional stray branch would whip her face and tear at her clothing. Blood speckled her face where pine needles and small branches graced her soft flesh with their sharp presence. Her pants were torn in a few places. Luckily her jacket was made from a sturdier material and remained (mostly) unscathed so far.

She could not slow down.

Another scream rose into the atmosphere. Only this time, it wasn't human. Not by a long shot. She had sensed someone following her and she knew Kai wouldn't be dumb enough to completely disregard her instructions. As soon as she felt the presence, she doubled back into an area she knew was overrun with traps she had set.

Her plan worked. She had one trapped.

Without slowing, Misty looked over her shoulder, a victorious smile beaming from her face.

"I got you. Not so scary now, are you?" Her voice had a slight hint of cockiness and she let it rise into the air around her.

If her calculations and supernatural intuition were correct, there were only three of them in total. One was in her trap. That meant there were two still free. She also had a feeling the other two were both occupied with Kai's camper friend and her dad (and now, hopefully, Kai as well).

If what she had studied about these beings was true, they would mostly stick together as a pack. Which meant, it was possible they sensed something and the creature she had trapped was sent out as a scout. The other two would surely be together, somewhere near where she had left Kai.

It was time to find them.

VII

Kai could hear muffled conversation. It seemed heated but he could tell there was also a great deal of sadness and fear present. He picked up his speed and was surprised at his ability to run without becoming tired or winded. He was fast too. He let a strong, victorious smile spread across his handsome face for a moment before becoming serious again.

It didn't take long before the voices became clearer and more distinct. They were coming from over the crest of the hill towering in front of him. Kai moved off the trail and made his way toward the top. A few feet before reaching the summit, he stopped and laid flat on his stomach, pulling himself the rest of the way with his arms.

As he army crawled his way to his destination, his heart pounded so hard it made it difficult to breathe. He was worried for a moment he might actually start coughing. His mind raced with every horrible scenario it could come up with.

What was he going to see down there?

Were they injured?

Why were they fighting?

Were they alone?

Where the hell was Misty?

Before peeking his head over the top of the crest, he closed his eyes and inhaled deeply through his nose. He hoped it would help calm his nerves. Dirt, pine needles, and stray clumps of dead moss clung to his sweat-soaked palms. He closed the final gap between himself and the crest of the hill, and slowly raised his head to see what was below.

His breath immediately caught in his chest. Bile rose slowly from his stomach and stung the back of his throat. He swallowed it back down with a wince. He shook his head in disbelief. He felt tears begin to well in the corners of his eyes.

Holy shit.

VIII

Misty stopped to catch her breath. She stood with her hands braced on her thighs for a moment before straightening again. She'd been searching for the two remaining beings for what seemed like hours, laying traps as she went. Her potion bottles were empty now, and she was no closer to knowing where the two free creatures were hiding out.

The scream ripped through the air.

It was unlike anything Misty had ever heard in her life. It was both human and not. She had come close to hearing something similar during an exorcism once. The scream did not come from one single location. It came from multiple points throughout the forest. As if she was surrounded by them.

Now there was one thing she could be one hundred percent certain of. They had a hive mind. She couldn't be sure if any of them were actively injured, but by the sound of the screams, they were frustrated at minimum.

And they were scared.

Now you know how it feels.

Misty took another moment to wait in silence. Then another scream came. The yell of a very human man. It was dripping with anger and hate but the fear they all felt was in it too.

Kai.

She ran toward his voice with a ferocity and feeling she did not know she possessed.

IX

It took Kai a moment to fully process what he was seeing (and to get his panic induced nausea under control).

Down below he saw Jeanie and Alan. But Alan didn't quite look like himself. His skin was sallow, and his eyes were sunken and jet black. He was smiling, but it was a sick smile, full of bad intentions. He was making his way toward Jeanie slowly.

Kai could hear them speaking to each other but couldn't quite make out the words clearly. Jeanie shook her head slowly, her damp, blonde ponytail moved back and forth slightly. She raised her hands in front of her body defensively. She began backing away from him inch by inch. Kai could tell she was full of fear and uncertainty. Alan began raising the hatchet he held in his hands.

You have to do something, Kai. You can't just sit and watch this happen.

Alan now had the hatchet raised fully overhead, both hands gripping the handle so hard his knuckles had turned white. Menace dripped from his body language. He continued his

236

advance toward Jeanie.

Kai could hear her crying now. Begging.

Without fully realizing what he was doing, Kai shot to his feet. He let out a long, guttural yell as he began running down the side of the hill to the pair below.

Alan's head snapped up in the direction of Kai's screams. Jeanie looked over her shoulder to view the new, oncoming threat, but she did not move her body away from the direction of her father.

Once she registered what was happening, her jaw fell slightly slack.

"Kai?" Her voice was shaking with fear and disbelief. And then panic. "Wait! Stop! That's not my dad. It'll kill you!"

"Not if I kill *it* first!" Kai growled.

He let out another furious yell as he closed the final gap between Jeanie and himself. He skidded to a halt between Jeanie and Alan. A spray of damp dirt and pine needles flew from beneath his feet. He bent forward slightly and placed his arms out at his sides in a protective stance. He looked at Alan with a savage look on his face, his lips curled up over his perfect teeth in a snarl.

"Stay behind me, Jeanie."

Jeanie continued to slowly back away but took his advice and stayed comfortably behind the protection of his body.

Alan's demeanor quickly changed. The smile faded from his lips, and his face fell flat. A slight flush of pink returned to his cheeks. The black of his eyes slowly receded, starting first at the outside corners of his eyes, and seemingly pouring back into the center of his pupils. The blue color returned slowly but never fully recovered to the bright, icy color Kai remembered from before. He looked at Kai and furrowed his brow, a worried expression taking over his face.

"What's going on? Please. Just let us go." Alan's voice shook.

Kai eyed him with great wonder and suspicion. Jeanie approached Kai from behind. She placed a hand on his shoulder. Her touch made his entire body go rigid. She leaned into his back and dropped her forehead on the back of his shoulder. He could hear and feel her crying. The sound of her gentle sobs made his stomach tighten into knots. She slowly lifted her head and positioned her mouth behind his ear, standing on her tip toes slightly to do so. She reached for his hand and gave it a gentle squeeze.

"It's still not my dad. Those aren't his eyes. And right now, he doesn't know who you are." Jeanie paused briefly. "My dad met you, he would know you."

Her whispered breath tickled the back of his ear, making his entire body break out into goosebumps. He suppressed a shiver. Not only because he never imagined Jeanie Risley would be whispering in his ear, but because of the content of what she was saying as well. The sudden and intense realization that there was no possible way for them to beat whatever was inhabiting Alan's body flowed through him. He was overwhelmed by feelings of fear and defeat.

They were all going to die here.

X

Misty struggled to hear their voices. She knew if she didn't find them soon, serious trouble was a surety. And more likely than not, at least one, if not all of them, would die.

As she approached the steep hill, her stomach leapt from the sound of voices. She ran the rest of the way to the top and the sight of the people below filled her with a moment of slight relief. There were three of them. She knew one to be Kai (obviously). The woman must be Jeanie, and the older man Jeanie's father.

Ah, shit. They've taken the dad.

She took a step back out of view. And watched the interaction between the three of them. She was close enough to provide protection if it was immediately needed and felt it was a good idea to stand back and observe for a bit.

She wished more than anything she could make out the words being exchanged between them. She could see the man (who she thought was named Alan) speaking, but with Kai's back to her, she couldn't tell if, or when, he was responding.

The woman hiding behind Kai whispered something in his ear. His body went rigid. A small pang of anger and jealousy hit Misty in the chest.

Damn these slightly human ears.

She gritted her teeth and continued watching.

Then she saw it. Movement in the trees behind Alan. It was so fast, she nearly missed it. She wasn't sure exactly *what* it was. She couldn't quite make out the shape of it. One thing she was quite certain of, was that whatever it was, it was not of this world. Not human. Not an animal. Nothing natural on this Earth moved that way.

It moved with great skill, fluidity, and speed. It reminded her of liquid mercury. Its form of camouflage not blending in but reflecting its own surroundings back outward. It was brilliant and perfect in this thick forested environment, she had to admit.

The next moments happened so quickly Misty would never be able to fully recall them.

She bolted down the hill and aimed herself directly at the possessed body of Alan. Before he could register what was happening, Misty crashed into him at full force. Their bodies collided and they fell to the ground in a violent tangle of limbs.

Kai didn't hesitate to take the opportunity to act. He shoved Jeanie backward gently and sprung forward into the area behind where Misty and Alan were currently wrestling on the ground. In one fluid motion, he unsnapped the largest bottle of potion from his belt, ripped the cork out with his teeth, and began to pour as he ran in a circle.

The magical glow confirmed he'd done what he set out to do and he darted back to Jeanie. He resumed his defensive stance in front of her.

"Now, Misty! Do it! Go!" Kai's yell ripped through his throat, leaving it feeling sore and hoarse.

He held his breath and hoped she understood him and knew what he was asking her to do.

XI

Although the possessed man had more stamina than he usually would, there were still limitations to what his very human form could do. It was clear to Misty that this man was not in top performing shape and by the labored sound coming from his lungs, he was also a long-term smoker.

He probably smokes something manly, like Marlboro Reds. Oh my God, Misty. Seriously, focus.

She shook herself in an attempt to quiet her inner dialogue and focus on the task at hand. She would never admit it to anyone if they asked her (if they made it out alive) but she was actually having a bit of fun wrestling this middle-aged man on the forest floor. It had been a while since she'd seen any real action.

She let out a small chuckle and allowed him to take the

advantage. She rolled underneath him and let him pin her to the ground. Once she was underneath him, she tucked her knees to her chest, took a deep breath, and with all her force she kicked him over her head. He flew forward and did a somersault before coming to a hard stop on the ground. The air could be heard escaping from his lungs as his back collided firmly with the forest floor.

It became immediately clear that she had hit her mark. Inhuman screams flew from Alan's mouth.

The same screams echoed throughout the forest.

XII

At first, Kai wasn't sure if the trap would hold Alan. He was possessed by the creature the potion was created for, but his body was still human. Alan was still in there somewhere. A small sliver of Kai hoped it wouldn't work, because in his mind, that meant Alan was still hovering somewhere very near the surface.

The horrible scream that came from him when he was forced into the circle proved that wherever Alan was, it was very deep below; hidden in the deepest recesses of his mind. But it also meant that the creature was not just taking Alan's mind, it was taking over his flesh as well.

Misty, Kai, and Jeanie stood back and stared in wild amazement. Alan – or the creature within Alan, *becoming* Alan – writhed and screamed in pain. Jeanie covered her ears, tears streamed down her cheeks. Her knees began to shake and then buckled beneath her. Her knees hit the ground. Jeanie covered her face with her hands and deep, aching sobs shook her body.

Misty looked at her. Though she felt bad that the woman was experiencing so much pain, she also let other feelings taint what should have been a feeling of sympathy inside her. She couldn't forget how jealous the interaction between Jeanie and Kai had made her. Misty also couldn't let herself leave warrior mode to comfort Jeanie. She was annoyed by the fragility of the woman on the ground.

The sound of the screaming creatures was beginning to make Kai nauseous again. He clenched his jaw, and closed his eyes, taking care to breathe steadily in through his nose and out through his mouth. The sound of Misty's voice brought him back to the present. She was addressing Alan.

"Shut up. Quit your whining. I hope it hurts but I think you're just throwing a tantrum right now," Misty taunted the creature residing within Alan.

She folded her arms across her chest and walked to the edge of the circle. Kai thought the toes of her boots must be right on the line, dangerously close to crossing it. Her lack of fear was impressive. She continued her interrogation.

"I think what you were trying to do, was make this man another one of *you*. I think this is how you reproduce. And you needed his daughter's life to complete the transition." Misty's voice was full of rage, malice, and disgust.

Alan was now on all fours, crawling from the center of the circle toward where Misty stood. A low, deep growl emitted from his throat. His eyes were jet black. Looking into them felt like looking into deep space. It felt like looking through a window into a different dimension. His lips curled back over his teeth, revealing black rotting gums. He dug his fingers into the ground. Pus squeezed from underneath his fingernails. The nail on his left ring finger popped off, revealing the rotting nail bed underneath. Thick, white drool began to fall from the corners of his mouth.

Misty did not back down. She continued her speech. She was

angry, and she had a lot to say.

"I don't know exactly what you are. But I know enough to beat you," she said with an arrogant smile.

Alan was fully focused on Misty now, and with his attention on her. He rose to his feet and poised himself in a defensive stance. His muscles were tense, and he was wound tightly, like a snake ready to strike. And when he did finally spring forward to strike, he ran face first into the barrier created by the potion. He screamed in pain and fell to the ground, hands grabbing at his face. A faint sizzle, like fresh meat put onto a hot grill, came from the area of flesh that made contact with the barrier. Alan's breathing had turned ragged. A gargle escaped his throat.

He slowly pushed himself up into a sitting position. He removed his hands from his face. Where skin remained on the left side of his face, it hung in loose pieces. The muscle of the cheek bone under his eye had been completely burned away, revealing white sections of bone.

Jeanie screamed through her tears. Her voice was hoarse and the sound of it was painful to hear.

"No! Stop hurting him!" Jeanie yelled.

Misty turned to her and gave her a piercing, angry look. She locked eyes with Jeanie until the woman leaned back and let her eyes fall. Misty let out an exasperated sigh. She walked away from the circle and knelt in front of Jeanie.

"I'm not meaning to be such a bitch. Just sit back, shut up, and let me take care of this. You're giving it what it wants. It is feeding on your negative emotions, your fear and your sadness. Do you understand what I'm telling you?" Misty spoke down to Jeanie, her tone condescending.

Jeanie nodded slowly. Misty patted her shoulder, trying her hardest to be comforting. Misty stood up and looked at Kai. He looked unimpressed with her treatment of Jeanie and a small pang of guilt and shame ran through her. When she turned to walk back to where Alan was trapped, Kai grabbed her shoulder. She turned back around and saw the look on his face was serious and unafraid, and angry. She had never seen him look that way before.

"Misty, it's your turn to listen to me." He grabbed her face and held it between his hands. "I know what I have to do now. You need to stay here with her. I can't tell you my plan because what he hears…" – he pointed an angry finger at Alan – "they *all* hear."

Misty opened her mouth to protest but before she could, Kai pulled her head forward and gave her a rough kiss on the forehead.

"Just trust me. Don't try to cure him yet. Wait until I get back."

Kai looked into Misty's eyes one last time and jogged into the forest. Misty stood and watched him until he was no longer visible. She looked down at Jeanie, who was visibly shaking.

"It looks like it's just you and me now, honey. Sorry I've been such an asshole. You look like you've been through hell, and I'm sure you have. Let's get you as fixed up as we can. It's almost over now."

Misty's tone was truly comforting now, and Jeanie could tell she was sincerely feeling bad for the way she had been treating her. She allowed Misty to pick her up off the ground and lead her away from her father.

10

I

Kai sprinted through the forest. He moved as quickly as he could, while still avoiding trees. He was soon forced to slow to a quick walk. The trees were thick, and the fog had become so dense, he could barely see a few feet in front of him.

He stopped and laid a trap. He'd lost count of how many he'd put down since he parted ways with Misty, but when he lifted his bottle, he saw that it was nearly empty. He took a moment to rest and think.

What are you doing out here, Kai? Since when do you just run off and do reckless shit because you felt like it was what you should be doing right then?

He sighed and put the butt of his hand to the center of his forehead. He let out a small, frustrated sound that couldn't quite qualify as a grunt. He looked around him and realized, he wasn't one hundred percent certain which way he had come from. The fog had closed in on him and he was turned around.

He should have felt disoriented, but a strange calmness had settled into his chest. Something told him he was supposed to be here, doing this, at this exact moment. He thought of the potion he had inhaled before entering the forest. He nodded to himself. If he was going to die, he was going to die trying, fighting, and being as brave as he could be.

He turned in a slow circle and stopped in the direction he

thought led back to Misty, Jeanie, and Alan. He had never blindly followed his intuition in life, and he thought it would feel foolish, but it felt like he was finally doing something right. He took a long, deep breath in through his nose. He held it for a few seconds, let it out in a big huff, and started walking forward.

Within seconds he heard something dart through the woods to the right of him. He stopped. The fog blinded him. He closed his eyes, trying to listen. The only thing he could hear now was the *buh-whoomp*, *buh-whoomp*, *buh-whoomp* of his own heartbeat.

Suddenly, he flew forward and hit the ground hard. The wind flew out of his chest, his forehead bounced off the damp forest floor. He found himself gasping for air, sucking hard. He rolled over, propping himself up on his elbow. He looked around himself wildly. Searing pain burned his forehead. Bright starbursts scattered throughout his vision. He blinked hard, trying to clear them away. His breath was slowly coming back to him, and he pushed himself into an upright sitting position.

He touched his forehead where it made contact with the ground. His fingers came away with blood, and he could feel a small trickle beginning to slide down the side of his face. He continued to look around him. He could sense another living being near him. His head was on a swivel.

And then he saw it. Something was moving in the fog. It was cloaked somehow but he could see the fog swirling around it where it stood. It moved toward him slowly. Kai's heart and lungs began working overtime. He clambered to his feet, grabbing for the gun in his belt. When he couldn't find it with his hands he looked down and noticed it wasn't there.

Damn, it must have gotten knocked free somehow when I fell.

He found the large hunting knife instead and ripped it free

from the belt. He gripped the handle with both hands, holding it out in front of him with shaking arms. He was bent over slightly, ready to pounce at any moment. He moved in a slow circle. He found that he wasn't scared at all. He was angry.

"Come on, you coward. It's just you and me here. Show yourself. Quit hiding."

Kai was surprised at the calm and steady way his voice flowed from his throat. He felt confident and completely in control. His eyes remained focused on the strange section of fog. He could see the creature take a few more steps toward him. He fixed his grip on the knife and planted his feet firmly, holding his ground.

He started noticing sections of the strange fog becoming darker. As it moved closer, the outline of a tall, slender, humanoid creature began to take shape. It bent forward, matching Kai's defensive stance. It was now phasing in and out of view. When it phased into view, Kai could see its smooth, extremely pale skin. It looked almost lavender in places. It had no nose, just vertical slits for nostrils. They flared open and closed as it breathed. Its large almond shaped eyes were black but didn't seem solid. They seemed to be filled with black liquid, with a strange iridescence. A strange, low clicking sound was coming from its throat. In the center of its forehead, an intricate symbol, almost resembling a Celtic knot, glowed faintly.

It didn't speak out loud, but it was projecting into Kai's mind. He knew it intended to end his life. Kai gave a mocking laugh and began swaying slowly back and forth, readying himself for the fight. The fog began to thin again, and Kai remembered passing through the area they were in now. He looked to his right and immediately recognized a large, moss-covered boulder. He knew just beyond was a trap. He knew he had to lure it over there.

He locked eyes with the creature and let out another mocking laugh.

"Let's go then, asshole. Bring it on. Come on!" He wagged the hunting knife back and forth, trying to antagonize the creature.

II

Kai had been gone for over two hours. Alan hadn't moved in one. Misty was on edge. Something didn't seem right. She wanted to go find Kai, but she couldn't leave Jeanie alone and defenseless. She was worried about him, but she was also mad at Kai.

How could he just leave her on babysitting duty?

She was the stronger one.

Misty paced back and forth with her arms crossed over her chest.

Jeanie sat on the ground near the fire Misty built when Kai left. She took a sip of water as she watched Misty.

"Will you please sit down? You're making me anxious."

The laugh Misty returned was dripping with venom. She stopped pacing and turned to Jeanie, pivoting on her heel before firmly planting her feet. Her arms were still folded over her chest, her left hip jutted to the side.

"*Excuse* me? I'm not looking for anything from the peanut gallery right now. *You* are the reason we are in this situation right now. The reason Kai is out there alone right now." Jeanie let her head hang in resign.

Misty moved close to Jeanie and knelt in front of her, making sure their eyes were level. She put her finger under her chin, forcing Jeanie to look at her.

"I want to make it perfectly clear – I do not care how I make you feel. I do not care about *you*. I care about Kai. And I care about killing these things. And that is *it*."

Misty shoved Jeanie's head to the side slightly before moving away. She resumed pacing. Misty could not figure out why she was acting toward Jeanie with such malice. She didn't hate her. In fact, she actually sort of liked her. Guilt flooded Misty's gut and she felt her chest tighten.

She stopped suddenly as Alan began to stir. She stared at him as he stood up and brushed the dirt and debris from his clothing. The wound on his face was red and inflamed. It had begun to ooze a clear liquid. He was now missing nearly all of his fingernails. He turned his head to the side and spit a thick putrid liquid onto the ground. It appeared to contain a few of Alan's teeth. A yellowish foam stood at the corners of his mouth.

Jeanie stood and now joined Misty near the circle. Alan looked at them with his black eyes and began to quietly laugh. And then, finally, he spoke.

"You won't win this fight. Once you are dead, and I promise that will happen soon, your little spell that keeps me here will be broken." He pointed a decaying finger at Jeanie. "And now I will not show her the mercy of death. I will gnaw the flesh from her body while she lives."

Jeanie's wounded facial expression drew another laugh from Alan. He began to pace at the edge of his prison.

"We are with your little boyfriend now. It won't take long for us to kill him. If you leave now, you might be able to save him. You were right, Misty; it *is* almost over."

Jeanie was crying again. But this time, Misty pulled her in and hugged her. She whispered in her ear.

"He's trying to get me to leave you because he's worried. I won't leave. They won't win. I won't let them."

Jeanie squeezed Misty a bit tighter.

III

Kai yelled out and slashed the hunting knife down hard, almost clipping the creature's shoulder. It kept phasing in and out of its solid form. Kai didn't think it was intentional. The forest had been deserted for so long and they had nobody to feed on. They were weak. And they were afraid. No human had ever dared to challenge them in this way before.

Kai moved backward, enticing it to follow. Its sole intent and purpose was to eliminate him. It wasn't paying attention to its surroundings. Fear elicits the same response in every creature. It makes them reckless. They were closing in on the trap Kai set. He stopped suddenly and swung the knife again, only this time he swung low, and it clipped the leg of the creature. The blade cut into the creature's flesh, leaving a gaping wound in its thigh. It turned its head toward the sky and screamed.

It lunged forward quickly and swung a hand at Kai. Razor sharp claws raked across his stomach before he could pull away. A look of scared shock fell over Kai's face, and he grabbed his stomach, still holding the knife with his free hand. He stumbled backwards. The creature closed in slowly. It raised its hand, preparing to administer the final blow. Kai's blood dripped from the sharp end of one of the fingers.

IV

A wicked scream filled the air. Alan's face grew angry and concerned. Misty froze as every muscle in her body went rigid.

Come on, Kai. You can do it. Please don't die.

Jeanie was nearly catatonic now. Staring into what remained of the fire Misty had built a few hours earlier.

A second scream.

"I'm going in after him," Misty said.

When Jeanie did not reply, Misty picked up a small rock and chucked it in her general direction.

"I don't have time for this damsel in distress shit!" Misty screamed.

Jeanie stood up and pointed behind Misty. Her face was ashen and her finger shook. Misty spun around to see Alan standing, shoulders hunched, breathing heavily. He began to yell, spit and foam flying from his lips. His yells transformed into wicked laughter as he unzipped his jacket. He discarded the jacket on the ground and raised his hand to his chest.

He curled his rotting fingers and began digging them into his chest. Misty could not comprehend what she was seeing until it was too late. His fingers ripped through the thin fabric of his shirt and began to sink into the flesh.

Jeanie let out a small yelp and covered her face with her hands. She shook her head violently.

"It's not real. It's not real, Misty. They're making me see things. It's not real." Jeanie's words came out in a string of rapid hysterics.

Misty looked on as Alan's fingers sunk deeper. Blood had soaked through the gray t-shirt he was wearing and began spreading down toward his stomach. He began to cough slightly, and foamy blood sputtered from his lips. He smiled, showing blood covered teeth. The sickening sound of breaking bone echoed through the night air. Then, with one final push, he forced his hand the rest of the way into his chest, up to the wrist.

Misty gasped and stepped back, grabbing at Jeanie with one hand. Alan wiggled his hand inside his chest cavity, stood still for a moment, and then he yanked his hand out of his chest. He hung suspended for a few seconds, knees slightly bent, before crumpling to a pile on the ground. A pool of warm blood spread quickly outward from his body.

Misty walked cautiously toward him. Jeanie trailed behind, grasping her with both hands. As Misty approached, she could see the bloody hand was clutching something. It was Alan's heart, still pumping slightly. Misty gasped and quickly turned to Jeanie. She grabbed her head and pulled it down and close to her chest.

"Don't look. Don't look at that. You don't need to see it," she told Jeanie.

Jeanie pushed Misty away with surprising force. The scream that escaped her was worse than anything Misty had ever heard in her life. Emotion flowed through her; anxiety gripped her chest. She reached out for Jeanie but didn't hold her back. Misty knew there was no danger there any more. Alan was dead and the creature was gone.

Jeanie ran to her father and collapsed to her knees on the ground next to him. She shook him, begging him to get up through violent sobs. Misty watched as realization settled in over Jeanie.

"No, Daddy. No. God please. No."

Jeanie lifted her lifeless father's body into her lap and hugged him. His head hung back. She cried loudly, letting an occasional scream escape her chest. She let her head fall to his chest as she rocked back and forth. Her rocking caused Alan's arm to fall to the ground, his heart rolled out of his hand.

Misty could no longer contain her emotion and, for the first time in years, she began to cry.

V

The creature took a final step toward Kai. It froze suddenly and let out a scream of intense pain. Kai rolled to the side just escaping before it fell to the ground. He sat up and pushed himself backward with his arms, doing a sort of crab walk. He turned around and tried to stand but the monster latched a hand around his ankle and used what little energy it had left to yank him back to the ground, digging sharp claws into his shin as it did.

Kai let out a small scream of pain and kicked at the creature, eventually making contact. It yelped and let go of him. With the help of Misty's potion and his own adrenaline, Kai was able to push himself to his feet and run, half limping away from the creature. Once he was sure he was a safe distance away, he allowed himself to collapse. He sat and stared at his opponent, now caught in the trap. It was standing now, unmoving, staring back at Kai. The flickering had stopped now, and its form was fully visible. It's long, thin arms hung at its sides. Its nostrils opened and closed rapidly with panicked breathing. Black eyes swam with rage and fear. Exhaustion overwhelmed the being and it collapsed to its knees.

When he was finally able to catch his breath, he stood up slowly. He dragged himself to where his knife had landed on the ground. It had been knocked out of his hand when he fell backwards. He picked up his weapon and made his way over to the creature, trapped in its prison.

He took a wide stance to steady himself as best as he possibly could. He raised the large knife over his head with both hands. He paused with the weapon held over his head, elbows bent. He stared at the creature with as much hate as he could create on his face.

"Fuck you," he said the words quietly, but he knew it heard him, because it looked up at him.

Their eyes connected. He took a deep breath and plunged the knife down with all of his remaining strength. The blade lodged squarely in the middle of the creature's forehead. It fell to the ground. He knew this wound was not fatal to the creature, but it would do for now. He walked over to it and spit on its unmoving body before he heard Jeanie's screams.

He turned toward the direction of the sound and began limping as fast as he could back to Misty and Jeanie.

11

I

Misty held Jeanie in her arms near the fire and rocked her, attempting to regulate her breathing.

She had already pulled a tarp from Alan's pack and wrapped him in it. She dragged him to the edge of the clearing. She felt he needed to be protected. Or maybe she thought Jeanie was the one who needed protecting. She wasn't sure what she was doing any more.

She gently pulled away from Jeanie and made eye contact with her. The front of Misty's jacket was soaked in the grieving woman's tears. Misty's heart broke for her.

"They killed my dad, too. A long time ago. That's the real reason I'm here."

Jeanie's face lit with the shock of the statement. But she could not think of the right words to say, so she just gave her a tight hug instead. Without lifting her head, she spoke.

"Then…" she trailed and sniffled slightly. "They all have to die, too."

Misty squeezed Jeanie more tightly in recognition. Then she pulled away and stood up, dusting the dirt from her pants.

"Stay here. Make that fire *big*." Misty pointed a finger toward the fire. "We're going to need it. I'm going to find Kai."

Jeanie nodded and immediately got to work gathering what wood she could find near them. It didn't matter if it was a bit wet, since the coals were hot now. The sun had begun to set and if they were going to make it out of this forest, they needed to move quickly.

Misty started to run into the forest but stopped near the edge. "Hey, Jeanie."

Jeanie looked up from her wood gathering.

"I promise, I'll be back."

Jeanie gave a short nod and got back to work gathering her wood. Misty ran as fast as her legs could take her.

II

Jeanie had piled wood onto the flames until it was large and bright. She stood next to it for a moment, and stared at her father's body, rolled in a blue tarp. She was no longer capable of crying. She wasn't sure if she was even capable of feeling anything any more.

For what seemed like hours, she swam alone in her numbness, gathering firewood as the world around her sunk into darkness. She wasn't sure if anyone else was alive – if they were coming back. She just gathered wood and put it in the fire.

She didn't stop.

III

Misty only needed to run a short way before something reached out of the forest, grabbed her leg, and sent her crashing to the ground. She landed with a thud. She made a small ugh sound as the air was forced from her lungs. She could feel something gripping her ankle, sharp pain digging into her flesh.

She kicked herself free without too much effort and quickly

scrambled to her feet. The pain in her ankle seared and made her stumble a bit. Once she was able to steady herself, she turned to see what had happened. She fully expected that she misjudged her surroundings and got hung up in the forgotten trap of a hunter or a large fallen tree branch.

When she saw what was on the ground she quickly backed up. She retrieved the crossbow from her back and shot without hesitation. The creature lay outstretched on its stomach, an arrow stuck in the center of its back. It crawled toward her, refusing to give up.

She reloaded her weapon.

She shot again.

This time, her arrow met the back of the creature's head, and exited through its forehead, pinning its head to the ground. Misty stood and stared at the incapacitated creature; her breathing was heavy. A feeling of victory began to nudge its way into her chest.

Her head snapped up when she finally heard something in the distance. She listened patiently. The groaning of a human man was coming from what she thought couldn't be more than twenty feet away. She scanned the forest frantically, moving as silently as she could. The glint of something sharp caught her eye.

Broken glass.

She ran to it, picked it up, and immediately recognized it as a piece of one of her potion bottles. She cupped her hands around her mouth and shouted into the growing darkness.

"Kai! Kai!"

A low moaning sound coming from directly behind her made her jump. She spun on one heel, ready to pull the crossbow from her back. Her eyes settled on Kai. He was sitting on the ground, propped up against a large pine tree. Even in the dim light, she could see he was bleeding heavily from his stomach. She ran to him and dropped to one knee.

"Kai, can you hear me? Kai?" Misty's voice was higher pitched than usual, bordering on frantic.

He tried to look up at her, but his head was too heavy. She gently laid him on the ground and made a quick assessment of his wounds. They were bad. Pieces of tattered cloth were shoved into the wounds on his stomach where the creature scratched him. His ankle was visibly swollen above his shoe, and she thought it was likely it was broken. She checked his belt for his potions, but every bottle was missing.

She gently touched his cheek and tried to rouse him. His eyes fluttered briefly but then went still again. She reached to her own belt and retrieved the small bottle containing the healing potion. She tilted his head back slightly, squeezed his cheeks, forcing his lips to part and opened his mouth, pouring the liquid inside. She thought she heard him swallow but she couldn't be sure.

Panic filled her entire body. Tears streamed uncontrollably from her eyes.

"I'm so sorry. I never should have brought you here. This is all my fault."

She sat next to him and ran her fingers through his hair. It was full of debris from the forest, and she tried her best to brush it out. She grabbed his hand and held it in her own. She closed her eyes and lifted her head to the sky; sobs now shook her whole body.

"Hey, I thought tough girls like you didn't cry," Kai's hoarse voice rose into the air.

Misty's eyes snapped open, and she leaned in and hovered above him.

"The potion worked! It worked!"

"It worked." He croaked and gave her a weak smile.

Misty hugged him from the side, taking care to not squeeze too hard or knock him over. The small smile that tugged at the corner of his mouth remained there, and he lifted both arms to return her hug. He winced and let them fall again.

"What happened to all your potions? The bottles; they're all gone."

"They all got smashed when that bastard attacked me. I ditched the sharp pieces that were left. You know, safety first." He gave a weak laugh and winced again. He lifted a hand and gingerly placed it over the wounds on his midriff.

"Agh. I think those things have some kind of poison or something. These weren't this bad when I first got them. I was running back to get you after I trapped it back there." He shoved a thumb over his shoulder.

Misty looked in the direction he suggested. Concern crossed her face.

"Wait, you trapped one back there? I shot one on my way to you."

He nodded his head weakly.

"I planted my knife into its forehead, too. It should be just on the other side of that boulder."

Misty sprung to her feet. Hope completely filled her chest. They had gotten all three of them. They only needed to decapitate them and burn them, and then they were out of here alive.

"Can you stand? Walk?" Misty asked.

"I don't know. I can try," Kai replied.

Misty extended her hand out to him, and he grabbed it firmly. She counted to three and helped pull him to his feet. She held onto him for a moment, making sure he wasn't going to fall back down. She stared at him intently, waiting for him to speak.

"I think I'm good," he croaked.

He held his hands out at his sides for balance. He took a couple steps. He had to limp on his injured ankle but seemed stable. Misty felt more hope starting to replace fear, anxiety, and worry. She gave him a quick, tight squeeze.

"Can you start going back to where we came from? Jeanie is there alone, tending the fire. I'm going to go make sure these two things are still down for the count and then I'll be right behind you."

Kai was about to protest, but then looked down at the state of himself. He nodded and began hobbling in the direction of what he now was calling 'camp' in his mind. The feeling of hope was in him too.

We're going to make it out of here, after all.

IV

Misty trotted in the direction Kai claimed he had trapped one of them. When she rounded the boulder he had pointed to, she stopped short. She put her hands on her hips and gave a long slow whistle while she shook her head. Sure enough, there it was, lying on the ground with his hunting knife stuck in between its eyes. A pool of silvery blood had formed around it.

Serves you right, asshole.

Misty grabbed a long stick from the ground and poked at its arm cautiously. It flopped about limply. Satisfied that it hadn't yet had the time to regenerate, she approached it. She planted one foot on the creature's face and grabbed the knife with both hands. As she bent over, she noticed a faint symbol on its forehead. She yanked the weapon free, making the whole process look effortless. She stood over the creature for a moment and then looked down at the knife in her hand.

Without hesitation, she knelt next to the limp body of the creature and pushed the blade hard into its throat and began sawing back and forth. After a few minutes of hard labor, the head finally detached from the body. It rolled to the side before coming to rest near its shoulder. Misty picked the head up and held it under her arm, like a child carrying a basketball.

She sprinted toward the other body, knife in one hand, head tucked under one arm. She secretly wished she could see how badass she looked in that moment.

V

Jeanie froze, her arms full of firewood. She gently plopped it onto the ground and turned slowly into the direction she heard the branches snapping. She strained her eyes against the dark, trying her hardest to see into the forest. She fumbled a hand into her coat pocket and retrieved her knife. She removed the sheath and threw it onto the ground.

She held the knife out in front of herself, hand shaking furiously. She stood, frozen in place, gripping the knife. Her knuckles were turning white. Her heart thundered in her chest. A dark figure stumbled out of the woods and fell onto the ground. It groaned in pain. She moved toward it slowly. Once she was in range of the fire, its light illuminated the battered face of Kai. She rushed toward him.

"Oh my God, Kai! Are you all right?"

His only reply was a faint groaning noise, accompanied by him rolling over onto his back. He lay there, breathing heavily. His wounds weren't deep, but they appeared to be extremely infected. A dark yellow fluid was oozing from the gashes in his abdomen. As she moved closer, she could smell the odor of rotting flesh coming from him.

How could they have gotten so bad in that amount of time?

"Can you sit up?" Jeanie asked.

Kai nodded and opened his eyes. Jeanie helped pull him upright and supported his back. He shooed her away with one hand.

"I'm fine now, the trip back just took it out of me," his voice crackled from his dry throat.

Jeanie gave him a questioning look.

"Trust me. I was mostly dead about an hour ago. Misty saved me with a potion. She shouldn't be too far behind me."

Hearing that Misty was also safe and would be back soon made Jeanie breathe a sigh of relief. She handed Kai a bottle of water and as he sipped, he looked around curiously.

"Where'd your dad go?" Kai questioned.

At the mention of Alan, Jeanie's heart skipped a beat and then sank. Her stomach knotted. She sat down next to Kai and planted her face in her hands. She sat still for a moment before she lifted her head and looked at Kai, eyes brimming with tears she didn't think she had left.

"He's dead. They…" She choked on her words for a moment and then continued, "They made him commit suicide." She looked behind them and Kai's eyes followed. "He's in that tarp over there."

Kai didn't know what to say. He embraced Jeanie in a tight hug, kissed the top of her head, and then just held her. They sat this way, in silence, for what felt like a very long time.

VI

Misty burst into the clearing where Jeanie and Kai were waiting. She gave an excited wail when she saw her friends waiting there for her, fire blazing. She held up the two heads she had carried back to camp.

Kai had hobbled his way to the edge of the clearing before her arrival and was now leaning against a large tree for support. Jeanie was placing more wood in the enormous fire. Misty now stood near the edge of the blaze. She looked first at Kai and then at Jeanie. The fire reflected in her eyes. Misty held up the first head and examined the marking on its forehead.

"Do you see this?" she asked Jeanie.

Jeanie leaned in to take a closer look at what Misty was pointing out. As soon as she saw the symbol, the memory flooded back and Jeanie gasped, putting one hand over her mouth. Misty widened her eyes in surprise.

"What is it? What's wrong?" Misty asked.

"I found that same symbol carved on a tree on the edge of our camp. When I touched it, it made me feel really strange." Jeanie shook her head slowly. "And as soon as I quit making contact with it, I started to forget it existed, like I had dreamt it."

"That sounds about right," Misty said. "They probably use this sigil as a source of extra power, like a boost. They were most likely using it to magnify their manipulative abilities while you guys were at camp."

Jeanie didn't respond. Tears began to stream down her cheeks again but Misty thought this time, they looked like rageful tears more than ones of sadness.

"Are you ready for this?" she asked as she held the first head in both hands, moving it toward the inferno of the fire.

Jeanie nodded.

Misty threw the first head in, followed quickly by the second. They quickly began to sizzle. Black ooze began to pour from the slitted nostrils. The smell was putrid, and Jeanie ran to the edge of the clearing, making it just in time for the contents of her stomach to empty onto the ground. Misty covered her face with one arm and squinted as she watched them burn with satisfaction.

"All right, one more left. Then we need to build a second fire and torch their bodies. We should probably do that…"

She trailed off midsentence and turned around when she heard Jeanie scream. Jeanie was standing near Kai, looking down at him. Misty quickly joined her, kneeling next to him. His eyes were open, cloudy and vacant of life. Misty touched his cheek. It was already going cold.

Misty stood up and punched the tree he was leaning against. She let out a scream, feeling it rise from the depth of her stomach. He was the first person she had let herself love since her father died. And now he was dead, too. And it was her fault.

She collapsed under the weight of her pain. Once on the ground, she curled her body into a ball and wrapped her arms across her chest in a tight hug. She felt if she let go, her whole body would fall apart, into tiny pieces on the ground. Her heart felt like it was pulling apart, not breaking, but tearing, into excruciating shreds.

"I healed him," she wailed. "It should have…" She sucked in ragged breaths. "Why didn't it work? Why did my leg heal and his wounds didn't?"

As soon as the words left her mouth, Misty remembered, she was supernatural, and Kai was not. Jeanie slowly laid next to her, holding her until her breathing normalized a bit. Then she whispered in her ear.

"We have to finish the job. We can be sad when we're free. We have to do it for them; for our dads and for Kai."

Misty took in one deep, uneven breath and pushed herself upright. Her head swam a bit from crying so hard. She wiped the remaining tears from her face with the sleeve of her jacket, creating a muddy mess on her cheeks. She slowly got to her feet, pushing herself upright by bracing her hands on her knees. She looked at Jeanie, holding her hand out. Jeanie took it and stood up.

"Do you want to take the last one's head off, or would you like me to do it?" Misty asked through broken breaths.

The corner of Jeanie's mouth rose slightly; it might have passed for a small smile. She walked over to the place where her father had dropped his hatchet, when Misty tackled him to the ground, and picked it up. She grabbed Misty's hand. And they walked hand in hand into the forest, toward the last of one of *them*.

12

I

Misty and Jeanie dragged the limp, headless body into the clearing. Two fires raged in front of them. The smaller of the two fires contained what was left of the head that once belonged to the body they dragged behind them.

When they made it close enough to the fire, Misty moved to the bottom and grabbed the feet, and Jeanie moved the top of the body, grabbing the arms. They swung the body back and forth, counting to three before letting it go. The body launched through the air and landed in the center of the flames. Stray coals and hot embers flew up around it.

The women stood in silence and stared as the body burned. Once they were sure it was fully aflame, they turned to each other and hugged tightly.

Misty pulled away first.

"You know, I really hated you when I first met you." She let out a little laugh, through the tears that flowed down her cheeks. "I guess you're okay now, since you helped me kill some – whatever these things are."

Jeanie let out a gargled laugh and wiped her own tears with the back of her hand.

"I'm glad you don't hate me any more," she said.

They both turned and looked at the bodies at the edge of the clearing. Each was wrapped in pieces of blue tarp. When Kai died, they removed Alan from the tarp, ripped it in half, and then rolled them each up. Jeanie looked at Misty with questioning eyes.

"How are we going to get them home? It's only about a thirty-minute hike to the beach, but they're not exactly light."

"I know, but we can't just leave them," Misty said, sadness in her voice.

Misty stood in silent thought for a moment and then turned to Jeanie, genuine concern on her face.

"If I unwrap Kai, and carry him over my shoulder, do you think you can drag your dad? We can put him on the tarp. The trail is pretty wide and clear, it shouldn't get hung up on anything."

Jeanie didn't speak but nodded in response.

They worked together to unwrap Kai. Jeanie found bungee cords in Alan's pack and used them to secure his wrapped body to the flat tarp she would drag him out of the forest on.

As the pair made their way into the forest toward the trail. It began to rain.

13

I

The rain was coming down in torrents. The wind was forcing it sideways in heavy sheets that made it difficult to see. Thunder rumbled in the distance. The waves crashed into land with gusto, covering the beach in white foam where the water met the sand.

Jeanie and Misty stumbled out of the thick forest and onto the beach. Jeanie gave the tarp she was pulling one more hard tug, making sure it was fully out of the trees before collapsing onto the sand. Misty, who was towing Kai over her shoulder, gently laid him on the sand and plopped down next to him in relief.

Even though they had vanquished their enemy, they didn't feel one hundred percent safe until they were clear of the trees. The beach meant true safety. It was a confirmation that they really did make it out alive, though, there would be times when they both wished they hadn't (Jeanie explained to Misty later in life that this is called survivor's guilt). They took their rest in silence. The wind began to calm, and the heavy rain turned into a steady drizzle. Misty watched as the ocean lost most of its anger and the waves began kissing the sand, instead of crashing into it.

Jeanie lay on her back, letting the rain fall on her face. Her ponytail was in disarray and long strands of blonde hair clung to her cheeks and neck.

II

Jeanie woke to a gentle pushing on her shoulder. She opened her eyes slowly, blinking in the light. Misty's face was hovering just above hers.

"We fell asleep. We are soaked to the bone. We've got to get to the boat so we can get dry and avoid getting hypothermia," Misty spoke in a gentle tone, just above a whisper.

Jeanie looked around, slightly confused. When her brain finally cleared, she remembered they were on the beach. Her dad was dead. So was Kai. She groaned and rolled onto her stomach, and then pushed herself up, first to her knees and then to a standing position. Her ankles, knees, and hips all popped loudly in protest. She wondered if she had moved at all while she was asleep. She guessed she probably hadn't. She stretched hard and let out another groan, followed by a tiny chuff of sarcastic laughter.

"Wouldn't that be something?" Jeanie asked.

"What?" Misty replied.

"If we made it out of this shit storm alive and then died because our dumb asses got hypothermia."

They both took a moment to laugh at the ironic thought.

Misty stood and brushed the sand from Jeanie's back and butt. She hoisted Kai's body up onto her shoulder. It was no longer limp. He was going to be very difficult to carry, and she was angry she had let them spend the night on the beach. But she wasn't sure how rough the water would be after last night's storm, and she was not skilled at driving a boat. Jeanie's human body was also completely exhausted, so it was a risk Misty decided was okay to take. She was glad it didn't turn out to be a mistake.

The morning was sunny. There was a very light fog settled on parts of the water, but the sun was working hard to burn it all off. There were very few clouds in the sky. If circumstances were different, Misty would have probably enjoyed waking up in a place like this, on a morning like this. She was pleasantly shocked to find Kai's boat still secured to the dock. If she was honest, she was surprised to see the old dock still in one piece, but she was relieved.

Jeanie started dragging her father's lifeless, tarp-clad body down the beach, toward the battered dock. Misty followed closely behind.

III

When they were all loaded on the boat, Misty did a quick check to make sure nothing had been damaged by the storm. She was happy to find that the boat hadn't sustained any injury. She took a quick look at Kai's lifeless body and let a tear escape. It was warm as it rolled down her cheek.

Sturdy old thing you have here, bud.

The thought of Kai, and how much he loved this beat-up, old piece of crap for a boat, brought a sharp pain to Misty's chest. She shook her head, trying to will it away. She started the engine of the boat.

Jeanie untied the rope from the dock. She joined Misty where she stood behind the wheel, and they both gazed out over the beach. They studied the forest for a while longer before Misty turned her gaze to Jeanie.

"Ready to get the hell out of here?" Misty asked.

Jeanie began crying and nodded fiercely. She let herself collapse into the torn seat behind her. Misty picked up the radio and pushed the button on the side. She was able to contact another human on the other end. She didn't know who they were or where they were, but the relief that swelled in her chest when she heard the sound of their voice was immeasurable. She informed whoever it was she had been speaking to, that they were in need of emergency aid at the dock on the other side of the island, two casualties were also in tow.

When she hung up the receiver, she placed the boat into gear. Before she began navigating them away from the place she hoped she could forget about for the rest of her life, she took one last look at the forest they had escaped, and in true Misty Bishop style, she held up a middle finger to wish it farewell.

As she sped away, she started to cry.

AFTER

ONE MONTH LATER

Jeanie sat on her deck, coffee in hand, watching the ebb and flow of the ocean. The way the morning sun glinted off the surface, and the powerful sound of the moving water, had always been a great comfort to her. She hoped it would be just as comforting to the new owners. She finished her coffee in one last gulp and rose from her chair.

She made her way through the large sliding glass doors and looked around her empty home. A few stray boxes littered the corner of the living room. The men from the company she hired to help transport her things moved freely about the house around her, focused only on the task at hand. Jeanie leaned against the granite countertop and smiled warmly as she remembered eating pizza with her dad in this room for the last time. It was a happy memory, and that's why it hurt so much.

Alan and Kai both had memorial services held just outside Seattle. They were only two days apart and Jeanie and Misty shared a hotel room, rather than travel back and forth from island to mainland. They had already bonded through tragedy but, in those few days spent together, they bonded even more through attempted healing. Their connection was one nobody would or could ever understand.

Fate brought them together, Misty was sure of it. Jeanie didn't even believe in fate but, since meeting Misty, the scope of what she believed in was growing immensely.

They decided it would be best if they both moved back home. Even more coincidently, 'back home', for both meant Colorado. They formulated a plan to pack up, find a place together, and take the time to heal in the beautiful Rocky Mountains.

Jeanie had saved up quite a lot over the years and was able to find a new home for them, quickly. She was able to sell her home just as fast (which also felt a bit like fate). Misty didn't want to sell her house on the island. As she put it, *I would have one hell of a time explaining the basement*, so she simply packed up and headed east.

"All packed and ready to go, Miss Risley."

The booming echo of the man's voice in the empty living room made Jeanie jump. She laid a hand flat on her chest and took a deep breath. The man looked as shocked as she had felt and held a hand out in front of himself.

"Oh man, I'm sorry, lady. I didn't mean to scare you," he said.

Jeanie shook her head and gave a small chuckle.

"No, no. I was just in my own world, and you caught me off guard. Thank you. I'll be out in just one moment."

She looked around her kitchen and living room one last time before she walked slowly to the front door. She crossed over the threshold and pulled the door behind her. Before fully shutting it, she took one last look inside. A single tear rolled down her cheek. She closed the door for the last time.

She pulled her cell phone from the pocket of her cardigan. She pulled up her conversation with Misty and typed a single text. It simply read *"See you on the other side, girl."* She slid into the passenger seat of the moving truck and started traveling toward the first day of the rest of her life.

She had no idea her biggest adventures were yet to come.

CPSIA information can be obtained
at www.ICGtesting.com
Printed in the USA
LVHW041406300623
751145LV00005B/216